# MISSION MULTIVERSE

## DOPPELGANGER DANGER

### REBECCA CAPRARA

AMULET BOOKS
NEW YORK

Cataloging-in-Publication Data has been applied for and may be obtained from the Library of Congress.

ISBN 978-1-4197-4825-7

Text copyright © 2022 Abrams
Book design by Jade Rector

Printed and bound in U.S.A.
10 9 8 7 6 5 4 3 2 1

Amulet Books are available at special discounts when purchased in quantity for premiums and promotions as well as fundraising or educational use. Special editions can also be created to specification. For details, contact specialsales@abramsbooks.com or the address below.

Amulet Books® is a registered trademark of Harry N. Abrams, Inc.

**ABRAMS** The Art of Books
195 Broadway, New York, NY 10007
abramsbooks.com

*For Mia, Isla, and Hunter—*
*neatest nieces and most cosmic cousins*

# CHAPTER 1

**DEV KHATRI'S RULES FOR SURVIVING THE MULTIVERSE WERE** pretty simple: Speak up. Act out. And kick some serious butt.

These were the exact opposite of his rules for surviving middle school back in Ohio, where most people knew him as a quiet and nerdy band geek who avoided confrontation at all costs. But that life felt a world—no, *worlds*—away.

He glanced around at the parched, crumbling landscape. It was drained of color, like an old sepia-toned photograph, without the nostalgia or charm. Behind him, a steel and glass building sagged sadly, most of its windows shattered, its halls and labs empty. The faded NASA sign above the front doors hung at a crooked angle.

Rusted cars littered the road, parked haphazardly and forgotten, as though people had been in a hurry to escape. Dev couldn't help but wonder, what had happened in this place before he and his friends arrived? Why did it look so . . . apocalyptic? What had the people been running from?

Far in the distance, yellow lights blinked and smoke-stacks coughed up noxious plumes. Ash floated through the air, stinging Dev's eyes. Blackened vines snaked through the cracked concrete at his feet. He exchanged a worried look with Maeve, who was putting on a brave face and leading them toward the eerie city in the valley below. Lewis, Tessa, and Isaiah followed, their gazes set on the horizon, each lost in their own thoughts.

The wind whispered and the vines at their feet writhed and twisted. A tendril wrapped itself around Dev's ankle. He kicked it away and quickened his pace, his heart beating hard. None of this was right. He and his friends weren't sup-posed to be here. They had tried to travel home, where their families were waiting for them, back on Earth in Dimension14. *Their* Earth. This parallel place was definitely not it. Dev exhaled, shaking off his fears and steeling himself for whatever lay ahead. There was no doubt about it: In the past few days, everything had changed. Himself included.

It all started when Dev and his fellow marching bandmates—the Conroy Cadets—accidentally activated a quantum collider during a class field trip to the Gwen Research Center, a NASA field station where Dev's father worked as a catastrophysicist. The collider transported them to Station Liminus, a central meeting place between dimensions governed by the Multiverse Allied Council. As if stumbling into a new dimension and meeting a dazzling array of sentient life-forms hadn't been mind-blowing enough, the cadets then learned that Earth was on the brink of collapse. Oh, and the MAC, mistaking the cadets for an envoy of Earth's best and brightest, expected the kids to fix everything. No pressure, right?

In the past, Dev had worried about normal middle school stuff like pop quizzes, body odor, and embarrassing himself in front of his crush. After arriving on Station Liminus, those past worries seemed silly by comparison. Especially when the cadets realized the fate of their home planet—and the entire multiverse—rested in their well-intentioned but rather clumsy hands.

Thrust into uncertainty and peril, the cadets rose to the occasion as best they could, using their musical talents to reestablish contact with Queen Eryna, a powerful and important ally. In addition, they'd thwarted duplicitous General Shro, unmasked Dr. Genevieve Scopes as a traitor, and revealed the Empyrean One's malevolent plans for destruction and domination. Not too shabby for a bunch of middle school misfits who'd previously been frequent victims of the school bully's supersonic-atomic-bubonic-wedgie attacks. Sure, the cadets had made some pretty epic mistakes along the way, disrupting interdimensional diplomacy, damaging critical gateways, and setting loose a seriously scary spacebeast, to name a few. But overall, Dev was proud of himself and his friends.

*GAHROOARR!*

Uh-oh. Speaking of spacebeasts . . .

Dev, Tessa, Isaiah, Maeve, and Lewis wheeled around and instinctively huddled together, each one facing outward, eyes wide and watching.

*KRRAAGHH!*

Something resembling the long-lost cousin of the colossadon crashed through the nearby forest, toppling the blackened trees like toothpicks. The cadets froze. The beast lurched forward, nostrils flaring.

"What. Is. That?" Tessa whimpered, moving closer to Dev, her arm brushing against his, which made him blush the slightest bit. The Hawthorne-Scott sisters had a way of doing that to him, even at the most inopportune times, like right now.

"Looks like a harbinger of doom," Isaiah croaked, his gray eyes unblinking, his feet rooted to the ground.

Lewis frowned. "Harbinger of doom, huh? That's catchy, but I think *dragomander* has a better ring to it."

Dev studied the creature with terrified fascination. Only a few days prior, his mother had told him that in order to be a knight, he'd need dragons to defeat. Of course, she'd been speaking metaphorically, and then somewhat literally about a revoltingly healthy breakfast smoothie, but that was beside the point. Now Dev was face-to-face with an actual dragon. Or, something vaguely dragon-esque, like one of the creatures they'd viewed (and accidentally released, oops!) from within the Station's Menagerie. This so-called dragomander was twice the size of his family's minivan, a mix between a mutant salamander and an armadillo, with the nose-numbing stench of a skunk.

"Shh! It hasn't spotted us yet," Maeve breathed. "Large reptiles often have poor eyesight. But they can see movement. Everyone stay still."

Lewis raised an eyebrow, like he'd much rather make a run for it. As a former member of the school's track team, he'd have the best shot at getting away. Yet he didn't try to escape. He stuck by his friends, lowering himself into a fighting stance, with his knees bent and his arms out. In each hand, he clutched a drumstick.

Before their departure from Station Liminus, Secretary Ignatia Leapkeene had kindly returned the musical instruments they'd unwittingly brought from Earth—a clarinet for Tessa (who'd been impersonating her identical twin sister, Zoey, on a dare), a trumpet for Isaiah, drumsticks for Lewis, an oboe for Maeve, and a shiny saxophone for Dev, which he now realized were the closest things to weapons they had.

"Let's hope this little fella doesn't actually breathe fire, like a real dragon," Lewis whispered.

"Oh, please," Maeve hissed. "There's no such thing as a *real* dragon."

"Maybe not in our dimension, but clearly we're not in Kansas anymore," he shot back, a little too loudly.

"Ohio," Maeve corrected. "Not Kansas."

Lewis huffed. "Would someone please tell Little Miss Know-It-All that now is not the time to—"

*GAHROOARR!*

The dragomander's head whipped around, its small ears pricked. It had spotted them. It shot out of the forest, its four clawed feet tearing up clods of dry earth, heading straight for the cadets. It roared as it approached, its pungent breath blowing their hair back from their faces and bringing tears to their eyes. Tessa shrieked and dropped her clarinet.

In the blink of an eye, the dragomander flicked its long, sticky tongue and snapped up the instrument, crunching it like a pretzel between its sharp, yellow teeth.

"Aww, no!" Tessa moaned. She'd promised her sister nothing would happen to that clarinet. How was she going to explain *this*? "Zoey is totally gonna kill me!"

Isaiah grimaced. "Assuming that thing doesn't kill us all first..."

Before they could escape, the dragomander began circling them, eyeing them like prey. It opened its jaws and roared again, hungry for more.

Anger welled up in Dev, more powerful than fear. He was no longer that shy, meek kid who bullies picked on without consequence. He was a Conroy Cadet, darn it, and he was prepared to kick some serious butt.

"Hey! You!" he shouted at the beast. "Leave me and my friends alone!" He looked straight into the dragomander's green eyes. He tightened his grip on his saxophone, lifted it in the air, and roared right back.

The others stared, dumbstruck for a moment, then they all followed suit. Maeve held her oboe poised like a javelin.

Lewis jabbed his drumsticks like little swords. Isaiah aimed his trumpet over his shoulder like a grenade launcher. Tessa, who'd already lost her clarinet, struck a karate-style pose.

The dragomander's pupils dilated. It reared up on its hind legs, towering over the cadets. Its limbs were thick and muscular, covered in brown and yellow scales. Dev's courage fizzled. With a queasy lurch of his stomach, he realized how ridiculous he and his friends looked. How unprepared and outmatched they truly were. What did he really expect to do with a measly saxophone? Whack the dragomander over the head? Annoy it to death with a medley of super cheesy show tunes? He suspected that even his best Kenny G impression wouldn't cut it.

The creature turned and swung its spiny tail, aiming directly for Dev. He held up his saxophone to block the strike, but the power of the impact sent him flying through the air. He landed hard on the asphalt several feet away.

"Dev! Are you okay?" Tessa shouted, rushing to his side.

Dev nodded and rubbed his knee, where a sharp pain blossomed. His saxophone landed nearby with a sad clang, denting badly. Within seconds, the dragomander snatched it up and gobbled the entire thing in a single bite.

"We've got to get out of here!" Isaiah called out as the creature turned its attention to the silver trumpet in his hand.

"It wants the instruments!" Maeve began backing away. "We need to create a diversion. On the count of three, throw the instruments as far as you can. Over there!" She pointed to a ditch on the other side of the road. "Then we run and look for cover!"

With Tessa's help, Dev slowly rose to his feet. He winced in pain. He wasn't sure he could run, not with his knee throbbing like this, but he'd do his best to keep up.

"One! Two! Three!" Right as Maeve hurled her oboe, a high-pitched noise pierced the air.

The dragomander recoiled.

"Talk about off-key!" Maeve frowned, tugging her ear. "What was that supposed to be? A C-sharp?"

"Where did it come from?" Tessa asked Dev, anxiously looking around. He shook his head, wondering the same.

The sound rang out again. Two distinct blasts.

"Reminds me of the dog whistle we used to train our retriever, Goldie," Lewis said. "Only much louder and more intense."

The dragomander flattened its ears atop its massive head, like the noise bothered it. It didn't even try to eat the broken oboe lying on the ground nearby.

The sound also pained Isaiah. It rang deeply in his ears, as though it were burrowing into his skull. He crouched and tucked his head between knees, but the noise burrowed deeper, finding a way into his mind. Something cold filled the space between his ears, as though he'd chugged a super-sized Slurpee too fast and was now suffering the worst brain freeze of his life.

In that cold, numb moment, he had the distinct and unsettling feeling that someone was trespassing on his thoughts, riffling through his memories and ideas, searching for something. The feeling was unbearable. He clenched his fists, gritted his teeth. Heat built behind his eyes, forcing back the icy, uninvited intruder. His palms opened, his fingers stretched, emitting a faint blue glow. When he couldn't take it any longer, Isaiah screamed, sending a shock wave of energy outward from his palms.

A sonic pulse rippled across the ground with a flash of light. And then, everything was quiet, the air still. The piercing, whistling noise stopped. Even the dragomander appeared stunned.

Isaiah's chest rose and fell as the pain subsided and the sensation faded, leaving only a faint tingling in his fingertips. The dragomander shook its head, howled, then bucked. As quickly as it had appeared from the woods, the creature loped away, whining and grunting.

"Wh-what just happened?" Tessa asked, blinking.

The others turned and stared at Isaiah, regarding him anew. "Did you get superpowers or something?" Lewis asked. "Because if you did, that's seriously cool. But I'm also super jealous."

"I . . . I don't know." Isaiah hadn't been completely truthful with the others about the changes he'd experienced on the Station. He was still trying to figure it out himself. He'd managed to hide his burgeoning telekinesis fairly well. Until now. He'd felt threatened and he'd lost control. The need to protect himself and his friends overtook him. It was exhilarating but also frightening.

"Are you all right?" Maeve asked, eyeing his hands, which had stopped glowing.

He didn't feel all right; he felt weird and wired and confused. But Isaiah didn't want them to worry. He nodded, rubbing his temples. The intense cold was gone, but a dull throb lingered. On Station Liminus, they'd learned that some life-forms tolerated Transfer—the trips between dimensions— better than others. His uncle, Ming, for example, and even that deceitful shape-shifter, Dr. Scopes, suffered cellular degradation with each journey. Isaiah struggled with nausea after Transfer, but once that pukey feeling waned, his other senses lit up and his newfound abilities amplified.

"Nice work scaring away the dragomander," Tessa said gratefully. "I just wish you could've flexed that power move before he devoured my sister's clarinet."

"Seriously. Way to keep us on our toes," Lewis said, giving Isaiah's shoulder a nudge. "I nearly peed my space-suit. I thought we were toast! For real this time."

A tremor moved through the ground, an aftershock perhaps, like the quivers—or mini earthquakes—that frequently shook their hometown of Conroy. The kids steadied themselves, trying to find their balance. A fierce gust of wind rattled the tree branches, kicking dust and leaves into the air.

Dev held up a hand, protecting his eyes. Something large and dark moved on the horizon. "I wouldn't get too comfortable just yet," he said warily. "I'm pretty sure the dragomander was running from *that*."

# CHAPTER 2

ISAIAH'S BLAST AWOKE SOMETHING ON THE DESOLATE PLANET. It arose from beneath the cracked earth and descended from the smog-choked sky, gathering into a powerful storm cloud, dense and charcoal gray, swirling and sparking with putrid greenish light. As soon as he saw it, Lewis declared it a *smogmonster.*

Around the cadets' feet, the wind stirred dirt and dust into little eddies, sweeping up litter and debris, gathering momentum. Thorny vines thrashed. Tessa's braids came loose from her bun and whipped across her face. Even the slip of paper with the note supposedly from the Empyrean One herself tore away from Maeve's hand. *If you think you can stop me so easily, you are gravely mistaken.* Their adversary's cryptic words disappeared into the sky, but the sense of foreboding lingered.

Lightning crackled. The wind began to wail. The cloud on the horizon grew larger and more dangerous, like a tornado feeding on everything in its path. A monster born of decay and ash and fear. And it was headed straight for them.

"Isaiah! Make it stop!" Tessa yelled as she stumbled toward a blackened tree trunk and held tight.

"I don't know how!" Isaiah called back, frantically opening and closing his palms, willing the power to return. But he felt nothing. No spark or surge of energy. What good were his abilities if he couldn't summon them on demand?

"We need to find cover!" Maeve cried, clutching an old telephone pole so she wouldn't be swept away by the increasingly strong wind. "Maybe the NASA building has a basement. A secure place we can hunker down until this thing passes."

"That building is already in shambles," Dev said, reaching for the telephone pole, wrapping his arms around it, too. "It'll be a death trap in a storm like this."

The wind howled louder in response, ripping a chunk of the NASA building roof straight off. Time was running out. The smogmonster would be upon them in minutes.

Just then, Lewis shouted, "The hot dog! We need to get to the hot dog!"

"Honestly, Wynner? This is absolutely not the time to be thinking about food!" Maeve called back angrily.

Lewis shook his head. "No, look! Over there! Behind the lab!"

The kids took their eyes off the angry funnel cloud for a brief moment, just long enough to realize that Lewis was telling the truth. Now that part of the NASA roof was gone, they could see a very large, hot dog–shaped vehicle parked in a back lot a hundred yards or so from where the cadets stood, clinging to telephone poles and tree trunks.

"What the heck is a gigantic wiener doing here?" Maeve asked in disbelief, brushing her red hair from her eyes.

"Actually, it's a *Teeny* wiener," Tessa pointed out. "Not a gigantic one. It says so right on the side." Maeve shot her a look, but Tessa was correct. Teeny's was a fast-food chain in Ohio that served hot dogs and bratwurst with all kinds of toppings, ranging from basic ketchup and mustard to gourmet caviar with wasabi crème, and even peanut butter with Froot Loops. Somehow one of their signature food trucks had ended up in this parallel dimension.

The air spun with cyclonic force, yanking a nearby street sign from the ground.

"The hot dog is our only hope!" Lewis declared dramatically, ducking as the uprooted sign shot overhead with the speed of a missile.

"Lewis is right," Isaiah agreed. "It might be our only way out of here." All the other cars and trucks on the side of the road had flattened tires and corroded axels, but the wiener-mobile appeared to be in decent shape.

"Honestly? This is no time for a joy ride!" Maeve scolded.

"Not a joy ride, an escape plan!" Lewis called over the wind. "Let's make a beeline for the hot dog and try to get it started. I'm sure Dev can figure it out. And then we ride off into the sunset . . . or at least outrun that nasty-looking smogmonster headed our way."

Dev's eyes grew wide. He was good with electronics, but he wouldn't get his license for another four years, and he wasn't sure how to jump-start an engine. "Even if we can't get it started, it might be a good place to hide out. It looks pretty sturdy and heavy. Plus, its cylindrical shape should resist damage from flying debris," Dev added.

Maeve thought the entire idea was absurd, but she also knew they couldn't waste another minute arguing. She was their leader and she needed to make a decision, no matter how ridiculous it might seem. "Everyone, to the hot dog!" she hollered, cringing as she said the words. "And stick together! We can't have anyone blowing away in this wind."

Leaning against gale-force gusts, the cadets made their way around the dilapidated NASA building and toward the back parking lot. Dev's knee was still giving him trouble, and he stumbled a few times.

"Here, let me give you a hand," Isaiah said, helping Dev along.

"Thanks," Dev replied, trying to shake off the pain in his knee and keep up with the others. "Hey, that was pretty cool what you did back there."

Isaiah gave him a side-eye. "What? Awakening a smog-monster and unleashing a killer tornado?"

"No." Dev shook his head. "The other part. The sonic boom bit. How did you do that?"

"I don't know," Isaiah said, which was the truth. "I started feeling some changes on the Station. But this was different. More intense."

They were nearly to the parking lot, and just in time. The funnel cloud loomed darker and fiercer, racing toward them.

"Why didn't you say anything?" Dev asked Isaiah.

Before Isaiah could answer, the ground shook violently and the sky thundered.

"Hurry!" Tessa called, waving them toward the hot dog. She and Maeve had managed to pry open a door-like hatch on the side of the truck, right below the Teeny's logo.

"Get inside! Now!"

Isaiah and Dev moved as fast as they could, limping and half running, diving through the opening. A blast of wind slammed the hatch shut behind them.

Inside, the wiener-mobile was dark and smelled like stale bread and gasoline, with faint mustardy notes. Broken grills and empty cardboard boxes cluttered the floor, as though someone, or something, had ransacked it long ago, looking for food. The wind still howled outside, and the wiener-mobile rocked slightly with each powerful gust, but the cadets felt safe inside. At least for now.

"Do you think you can get it started?" Maeve asked Dev as they pushed the boxes aside and climbed toward the cab. There were no keys anywhere to be found.

"How hard could it be?" Lewis said, high-stepping over a busted cash register. "People hot-wire stolen vehicles all the time in movies."

"I'll try, but no guarantees." Dev's hands shook as he unscrewed a metal panel below the steering wheel. "I've never hot-wired a car before," he said, starting to sweat. His NASA-issued suit was supposed to have a thermodynamic management system, but it didn't seem to be working.

"You built an interstellar radio out of a potato. I have no doubt you can hot-wire a hot dog," Lewis said, leaning over to watch him work.

Dev paused and looked up at his friend, a smile tugging at his lips. "Do you have any idea how completely bonkers that sentence sounded?"

Lewis shrugged and smiled back, flashing his signature dimple. "Hey, man, it's the truth."

"Well, thanks for the vote of confidence," Dev replied, offering Lewis a weak fist bump.

"You can do this," Tessa said. She grabbed Dev's hand and gave it an encouraging squeeze. "I believe in you."

His heart nearly imploded. Forget the raging smogmonster outside. Dev just about died right then and there when Tessa squeezed his hand like that.

"Dev?" Maeve asked, snapping him back to life. "I don't mean to rush you, but I'd sorta like to survive, so hurry up, okay?"

"Right." He swallowed nervously, feeling the familiar flutter of stage fright. He hated that they were all watching him, waiting to see if he would succeed. And if he didn't? Ugh. He didn't even want to think about what might happen.

"I wish Virri were here," Tessa lamented, missing the friend they'd made during their time on Station Liminus.

"We could really use her electromagnetic shock touch right about now."

Isaiah wished he could harness his own abilities, but no matter how hard he tried, he couldn't summon the current of power he'd possessed only minutes earlier.

"When my parents sent me to electronics camp last summer, I don't think they ever imagined I'd be doing this," Dev said, biting his lip as he twisted a red wire and a green wire together.

The view outside the large windshield grew ominous and gray as the spinning storm approached. Hail and debris—rocks and rubble, an old tire, a lone sneaker—pummeled the vehicle's exterior. Maeve was grateful they were safely inside. She just hoped the wiener-mobile would hold up.

*Ding! Ding! Vrooom!*

The dashboard lit up and the engine growled to life.

"Woohoo! You did it!" Lewis jumped and high-fived Dev. The others cheered.

"Move over, boys," Maeve said, not wasting a minute. She slid behind the wheel. "I'm driving!"

She'd driven her grandfather's tractor countless times, back when they still had the family farm. This would be a piece of cake. "Hang on to your hats, cadets! We're outta here!" She shifted the wiener-mobile into gear and hit the gas.

The oversized hot dog lurched forward. Then it stopped, grinding to a halt with a sad squeak. "Oh, come on!" Maeve pounded her fist on the steering wheel. She shifted gears again, flipped a few switches on the dash, then jammed her foot against the gas pedal.

*Whoosh!*

"Whoa!" Tessa cried as she was thrown backward, falling with a crash into a pile of cardboard boxes and ketchup dispensers. The hot dog took off, screeching and burning rubber in a wide curve across the parking lot. Dev helped Tessa up, and they perched together on an overturned cooler, the closest thing to a seat they could find.

"Go! Go!" Isaiah yelled, peering out the window at the ravenous funnel cloud. He'd witnessed storms before— Conroy often experienced shivers, which were weather anomalies that struck without warning, sending temperatures soaring or plummeting in a matter of minutes. But this was different. Everything that the spinning, charred cloud touched withered and crumbled, reducing the already-damaged landscape to colorless, lifeless dust. "It's gaining on us!"

Maeve gritted her teeth, gripped the wheel, pressed her foot to the floor, and whizzed toward the highway.

"Hot diggity dog!" Lewis squealed, enjoying himself way too much from the front passenger seat.

"Running for your life is not meant to be this much fun," Maeve said, keeping her eyes focused on the road ahead of them. She turned the wheel sharply, dodging a fallen tree limb. The wiener-mobile tilted onto two wheels, then slammed back down again, gaining speed. The desolate landscape passed by them in a blur as she navigated toward the city in the valley below, putting more and more distance between them and the smogmonster.

As an aspiring actress, Maeve had often daydreamed about starring in blockbuster action films, the sorts with high-speed chases in a luxury automobile, like a Lamborghini or Ferrari. She envisioned flashy pyrotechnics, exciting explosions, and daring off-road maneuvers. Never in a million years had she pictured her getaway vehicle looking quite like . . . an enormous wiener. Or a Teeny wiener. Or whatever this ridiculous vehicle was.

Still, she couldn't help but admit that it was sort of fun to drive. She drove faster, getting the hang of the gears, steering and swerving more nimbly. She cast a quick look over at Lewis. He was grinning ear to ear. He shot back a double thumbs-up.

A faded sign indicated an upcoming exit. She steered the wiener-mobile onto the ramp, careful not to turn too sharply. They drove a little farther, riding up and over a crest. Brush fires burned along the side of the road. The city—if you could even call it that—rose up before them. Brutal concrete structures and jagged smokestacks dotted the skyline. Maeve checked her rearview mirror. The smogmonster was still visible, swirling and sparking with flashes of green lightning, but the funnel cloud looked smaller and less menacing from this distance.

Lewis pointed. "There are lights down there. Which means there are probably people, too."

"Living creatures, maybe," Isaiah said, moving to the front of the vehicle. "There's no guarantee they're human."

"Right. Think of all the life-forms we saw on Station Liminus. The multiverse is full of variety," Dev added as Maeve slowed the wiener-mobile to a less breakneck speed.

Tessa swallowed, remembering Shro and the snarling six-headed wolves he'd set loose to attack them. She could feel the hot stench of their breath. She could see the flash of their bared teeth. She could practically hear the dragomander and the colossadon roar.

"Whoever or *whatever* we meet, let's just hope the inhabitants of this Other-Earth are friendly," Tessa said, shivering a little.

"And helpful," Isaiah added. "We need to find a portal as quickly as possible, some way back to the Station." He wasn't even sure where to begin looking for something like that. He wished again that Uncle Ming were with them. Ming had known all the ins and outs of the multiverse. "If we get back to Gate Hall, Ignatia or Duna can help reroute us back to Earth—*our* Earth." He also secretly held out hope that they might find Ming there and finally be able to bring him back home with them.

"Just remember, if we do encounter other humans, we need to avoid our doppelgangers at all costs," Dev said seriously. "Ira told us the space-time continuum could get seriously messed up if we run into ourselves in a parallel dimension. And then we'll be in an even bigger pickle."

"Technically, we're in a hot dog. Not a pickle," Lewis said.

Maeve rolled her eyes. "I cannot deal with your jokes right now, Wynner."

Lewis elbowed Dev and waggled his eyebrows. "Hear that? Maeve says I've got jokes."

Even Dev shook his head. "No offense, Lew, but quit goofing around. We really need to focus." He glanced anxiously at the passenger-side mirror. It was cracked and hanging at an odd angle, but he could still make out the dark twister raging along the horizon. They weren't in the clear yet.

"Right, got it," Lewis said, a little dejected. "Avoid Lookalike Lewis at all costs." He started to wonder what his doppelganger's life might be like here. Was there a parallel dimension where he was a bigger jerk than his older brothers? Or a professional athlete? Or a total dweeb? Based on everything they'd learned so far about the multiverse, the possibilities were infinite.

Tessa gazed out the window as they got closer to the city center. The buildings appeared vacant, plazas and sidewalks empty, trains and buses abandoned. "Do you think the Cataclysmosis virus hit this place?"

Dev shrugged. "Who knows? But whatever happened wasn't good."

Isaiah nodded. "Maybe it has something to do with that smogmonster thing chasing us. Did you notice that the funnel cloud was leeching color from everything it touched? The vibrance, the life, everything just...gone. Not that there was much to begin with, but the landscape looked even worse."

"Yeah, this place gives me the creeps," Tessa said, tucking her knees up to her chest, feeling homesick. "I can't wait to get off this dimension."

Just then, a small animal with brown fur and a long pink tail darted out of a nearby storm drain, dashing in front of the wiener-mobile. "Watch out!"

Maeve reflexively swerved, avoiding the animal but hitting the curb hard. The wiener-mobile was so top-heavy that it tilted awkwardly. "No, no, no!" Maeve cried, feeling the vehicle lean. She wrenched the steering wheel and pumped the brakes, but it was too late.

The giant hot dog groaned and tipped off-balance, crashing onto its side. There was a loud *clang*, followed by the sound of metal scraping against concrete, then a muffled "Ouch!"

# CHAPTER 3

**THE CADETS TUMBLED AND CRASHED INTO EACH OTHER AS THE** oversized vehicle fell to its side. There was no way they'd be able to push it back upright.

"Everyone okay?" came Maeve's voice from beneath the rubble of cardboard and crinkled napkins.

"Yup," someone called back.

Dev winced as the pain in his knee grew worse, but he didn't dare mention anything to his bandmates. He would push past the discomfort. He didn't have a choice. They needed to find shelter, or help, and he did not want to be the weak link.

Lewis opened the driver's-side door, which was now the roof, and climbed up and out of the wiener-mobile. Standing atop the wreckage of their getaway vehicle, the cadets took in the view. The air was hot and hard to breathe, but the wind was less fierce. Maybe the tornado had died down, or retreated. Now that they were nestled among the towering city structures, they could no longer see the smog-monster on the horizon.

One by one, they slid down the curved side of the hot dog and began exploring the nearby plaza, searching for signs of life.

"Hello?" Lewis called out. Only his echo answered him, his voice bouncing off the barren concrete buildings.

Isaiah looked around nervously. He didn't like being out in the open like this. Their crash had made a lot of noise, and he didn't think they should draw more attention to themselves. He had the distinct, skin-tingling feeling that they were being watched.

"Hey, I recognize that building," Tessa said, her voice brightening. "It's a version of the city hall, where my mom works. And that—" She pointed. "That looks like the bank back home. Which means..." She started walking briskly down the sidewalk. She turned left at the next intersection and crossed the street. The others followed.

"Aha!" Tessa said triumphantly. "I knew it! Look, it's a school." She gestured toward the double doors. They were coated with a thick layer of dust, and some of the glass panes were webbed with cracks, but the entryway did resemble their middle school back home. The similarity sent a shiver down Isaiah's spine. This didn't feel right.

"In Real-Conroy, our school doubles as an emergency shelter," Tessa explained, noticing Isaiah's hesitation. "So maybe this one does, too."

"Waiting here while we get our bearings isn't a bad idea. Especially if that storm returns," Dev said as a breeze picked up and the sky overhead dimmed. He ignored the pain in his knee and pulled the front doors open. The hinges creaked and whined. The cadets stepped inside. It was cool and dry. The air smelled faintly of old gym socks, just like school back home.

Isaiah's heart galloped. There, painted on the wall, was the cartoonish Space Cadet mascot, floating in an outer space mural. Beside it was the hall of fame case, the principal's office, the front desk, and a large bulletin board. The interior lobby was nearly identical to the one in their school back home, but everything here was stripped of color, all muted browns and grays. It reminded him of the nightmares he used to have, or the way his vision used to play tricks on him, morphing from views of Conroy to a desolate wasteland in the blink of an eye. Had he been seeing this place all along? Had those visions been premonitions, hinting at something that would occur in the future? Is this what their home dimension would look like if they didn't stop the Empyrean One?

"Anyone want to visit the cafeteria to search for snacks? Maybe we can find some vending machines with stale chips and drinks," Lewis offered hopefully as his stomach rumbled.

"That actually sounds good. I'm so thirsty," Tessa said. If they were going to be stuck here for a while, they'd need to find food and water eventually.

On the way to the cafeteria, they passed a row of metal lockers. Maeve's heart dropped. Only a few days ago, back in Real-Conroy, her locker had been the victim of a spack-attack, a prank executed by the class bully, Gage Rawley. He had smeared the front of her locker with a nasty concoction of slime, tuna salad, paste, and who knew what else.

The word *FREAK* had also been written in thick marker. Maeve had put on a good face and changed the word *FREAK* to *BREAK*, adding the word *DANCER* below. She'd even used the unfortunate event as an opportunity to show off some of her break dancing moves to the other kids in the hallway. It hadn't gone as well as she had hoped, though she'd nearly forgotten about the embarrassing incident until now.

She stepped closer to the locker. Her breath caught in her throat. There, in handwriting nearly identical to her own, were the words *BREAK DANCER*. Except this time, someone had crossed out the word *BREAK* and turned the *C* to a *G* . . . spelling out a new message: *DANGER!*

Her chest tightened. Her pulse raced. "Umm, you guys? Something tells me we need to get out of here. Now!"

Just then, a window smashed and a plume of acrid gray smog forced its way inside the school, stretching out dark fingers made of smoke and shadows. It howled and reached for the cadets.

"Run!" Isaiah yelled. They took off, desperately searching for an escape route.

An exit light at the end of the hall flickered on. It began to blink frantically. Maeve stared at it. "That way!" she screamed, not even pausing to second-guess the strange and sudden signal.

The smogmonster grew larger and more powerful, rattling lockers, smashing linoleum tiles into pieces, sucking the last remaining color from the Space Cadet mural and anything else it touched.

The cadets raced down the hall. Dev hobbled behind, moving as fast as his injured leg allowed. "Hurry!" Tessa called back to him.

"I'm trying." He grimaced.

"We got you, buddy," Lewis said, swooping in and throwing Dev's arm over his shoulder. Isaiah took the other side, and the three of them maneuvered away from the roiling, ravenous smogmonster as fast as possible.

"In here!" Maeve called to them, flinging open the first unlocked door she could find and ducking inside. As soon as they were all safely hidden in the room with the door locked behind them, she flicked on a light switch. To her surprise, the electricity worked.

Music stands were strewn here and there, bent at odd angles. Reams of sheet music lay scattered across the floor. By some strange miracle, they'd found themselves in the band room. Maeve found something oddly comforting about that. But as she leaned over to pick up a page of music, her skin prickled.

"You've got to be kidding me," she breathed.

"What now?" Lewis asked, moving beside her and glancing over her shoulder.

"This is the piece we're supposed to play at Regional Marching Band Championships in two weeks," she said, unnerved by the similarities between their home dimension and this awful parallel. "Except there's a different riff, and a few key changes." She pointed to the notes.

"Do you think the kids here were practicing for the same competition?" Lewis asked.

Maeve's head spun. "It's possible."

Something across the room caught Dev's eye. He limped over to a folding table and picked up a saxophone. It wasn't as shiny as the one the dragomander had gobbled up, but it was intact. It was rusty and the mouthpiece was a little cracked, yet he had a hunch he could still get a decent sound out of it. Beside it lay several other instruments, including drumsticks, a trumpet, a clarinet, and an oboe.

Maeve walked over to the table with the sheet music still in her hands. Her eyes grew wide when she saw the instruments. This was too weird to be a coincidence; it felt eerily convenient. Maybe even intentional.

When she looked up, her eyes grew even wider. On the chalkboard mounted to the opposite wall was a message, scrawled in the same handwriting she'd seen on the locker earlier. It was unmistakably her own handwriting; however, she hadn't written it. She squinted, reading the single word: *PLAY!*

Her pulse thrummed as she reached over and grabbed the dusty oboe from the table. "I can't explain what's going on, but we need to play."

"Monopoly? Charades?" Lewis asked, always ready with a joke. But Maeve was dead serious.

"No, you wingnut! We need to play this piece of music." She waved the sheet in his face, then set it on the nearest music stand with shaking hands.

"We elected you drum major, not drill sergeant," Lewis muttered.

Outside, a terrible howling sound grew louder, followed by a loud crash. The smogmonster was getting closer.

"Please," Maeve pleaded with them. "I know none of this makes sense, but that thing is coming for us, and I just have a feeling that we need to do this. Music helped us before. Maybe it can help us again."

Isaiah lifted the trumpet off a table. It was covered with a thick layer of dust and ash. He swiped a finger across the grimy surface, then cleaned the mouthpiece with the edge of his shirt. "On your signal, Captain," he said, stepping closer to the music stand.

"Um, I can't play an instrument, remember?" Tessa said, turning the clarinet over in her hands, wondering if it would make an adequate replacement for the one she'd lost to the dragomander earlier.

"Your voice worked all sorts of magic on the Station," Dev said, tuning the saxophone he'd found. "Sing along with us, and we'll see what happens."

"Okay." She set the clarinet back on the table and cleared her throat.

Isaiah held the trumpet to his lips. The first few notes were screechy and tinny. Not as bad as the awful sounds just outside the door, but still not up to their marching band standards. "Ugh, this is seriously out of tune," he said.

"Don't blame the instrument. Blame the musician," Maeve replied. But then she tested out her scratched-up oboe—it sounded like a dying duck. "On second thought, maybe it *is* the instruments." She fiddled with the reed. "Let's try again. First time's never a charm. We always need a good warm-up before we find our groove."

The cadets began to play and sing, hesitantly at first, the dingy instruments feeling clunky and awkward in their hands. Beyond the door, the smogmonster blustered, wreaking havoc throughout the school, growing stronger and louder.

Maeve raised her voice above the howling storm. "Again! From the top! Focus, everyone." She counted them in.

The music swelled and the bandmates finally fell into the rhythm. It certainly helped that they were familiar with this particular piece—a catchy medley of Harry Perry's greatest hits. Tessa had never played the songs, but the pop anthems were near-constant fixtures on the radio. Plus, she'd heard Zoey practice the medley many times at home, so she knew the tune well enough to follow along.

The air around them began to shimmer.

*Blerk! Wroonk!*

"Oops, sorry," Isaiah said, lowering his trumpet and blinking his eyes. "It's just . . . did anyone else see that?"

"See what?" Tessa asked, catching her breath. She'd been giving the vocal section all she had.

Isaiah blinked again, wondering if his eyes were playing tricks on him. "The air, it shimmered. And sort of warped a little."

"Good. Keep playing," Maeve commanded. She couldn't see what Isaiah was talking about, but she could *feel* it. A tingling sensation rippled across her skin. Like goose bumps, but with a faint electrical charge. The music was working.

The bandmates played and Tessa sang, matching them note for note. As the music rose and swelled, the shimmering returned. This time they all saw it—a wide, oval patch of iridescence in front of them, like the soap bubbles they'd blown as little kids. Dev wanted to reach out and touch it, but he didn't dare take his hands off the saxophone. He knew better than to interrupt whatever was happening. Inexplicably, their music was forming a Rip—a dimensional tear, like a portal, linking one dimension of the multiverse to another.

Maeve paused for a split second, taking a deep breath. "As soon as the opening is big enough for us all to fit through, we move." She had no idea where the portal might lead, but it had to be better than where they were now. Sometimes, surviving in the multiverse meant taking a leap of faith. "Got it?"

The others nodded and readied their instruments.

Almost in response, a cavernous, teeth-chattering howl rumbled just outside the band room. Dark wisps of smoke crept beneath the door frame, clawing at the ground, desperate to devour the cadets and silence their music for good.

The five kids played like their lives depended on it. As the music surged, they could feel the power of it, the sound traveling invisibly through the air and shifting the membrane of the universe. The louder they played, the larger the shimmering opening became, stretching, swirling, and glowing with marbleized purples, yellows, and blues. The Rip's edges flashed with bursts of quantum lightning. Still, the cadets played without faltering.

The howling grew more intense, accompanied by the snap and crack of tile and wood, the shattering of glass, the whine and squeal of metal wrenching apart. The band room door began to splinter into pieces. In mere seconds, destruction would be upon them.

Not many people can play music and execute a perfectly synchronized forward march at the same time—especially with a snarling smogmonster threatening to consume them at any moment. But the Conroy Cadets were no ordinary musicians.

Adrenaline coursed through Maeve's veins. She gave the signal.

Together, the bandmates stepped (in flawless formation, no less) into the unknown.

# CHAPTER 4

THE GIRL NAMED EM TIGHTENED HER PIXELATOR, PULLING THE specially designed hoodie over her head and tugging at the dangling strings to make sure she was completely obscured from view. The garment wasn't an invisibility cloak; that was the stuff of fictional wizards, after all. This was a much cooler prototype crafted by the cross-dimensional team of inventors who worked out of Station Liminus. Em's pixelator was a fairly recent acquisition, pinched from a capsule bag–wielding trader she'd outsmarted on her way to this lousy dimension in the boonies.

If only she had been banished to a more picturesque dimension, like Mertanya with its orange skies, L'oress with its crashing turquoise ocean waves, or Klapproth with those priceless memory pearls. But her aunt was *teaching her a lesson* and said spending some time on this dump of a dim would be a *character-building experience.*

Then this ragtag group of Earthlings turned up. How and why the Earthling cadets ended up here was beyond her, but she hoped they might be her ticket out of this place. Even though she'd been taught to fear and avoid their kind, Em decided to stick close to them, fully invisible thanks to the pixelator. When she noticed a redheaded girl among them, she began to wonder if there was something else afoot. Had her aunt intentionally rerouted the Earthlings here?

The girl looked eerily like Em—medium height, wavy red hair, pale skin, steely blue eyes. The others called her Maeve and she seemed to be their leader. Em had watched the hapless cadets blunder their way around the deserted NASA complex. They were nothing like what she had imagined Earthlings to be, but studying Maeve was like looking in a mirror. Although Em, in her humble opinion, had considerably better style, superior smarts, and much more swagger than the Earthling girl.

A doppelganger certainly complicated things. As curious as she was, Em knew to stay a safe distance away from Maeve and absolutely not touch her, no matter what. She wasn't entirely sure what would happen if she did, but her tutor made it clear that no good ever came from confronting one of your doppels. The last thing Em needed was another mistake on her record. She was tired of being a disappointment.

The pixelator hummed faintly, its cells realigning, masking her presence. She had to admit, the technology was pretty impressive. She had never worn one before, so she was hesitant at first. But she had stood mere inches from the Earthlings and none of them—well, except for that gray-eyed boy—had suspected a thing. Only Isaiah, as the others called him, kept glancing her way. Not *seeing* her exactly, but perhaps sensing her.

Still, the pixelator had worked well enough. She had been able to lead the rather clueless cadets to safety, with a few small bumps along the way. When they tried to fend off the dragomander with those dinky instruments, she'd stepped in, calling the beast off with her training whistle. She'd smuggled it onto the dim, suspecting she'd need some sort of protection against the larger carnivores that roamed the multiverse. What she hadn't anticipated was how Isaiah would react to the sound.

She was so perplexed by his reaction that she'd attempted to sift his thoughts. Of course, that hadn't gone well. How could she have known that he would react so violently to the cerebral intrusion? And she certainly never imagined he might possess the ability to unleash such a powerful energy blast, awakening the broken soul of the lost dimension—a turbulent, destructive force that the Earthlings had called a smogmonster. Which, Em thought with a shudder, was a rather apt description.

While the smogmonster presented a fairly serious wrinkle in her plans, she had handled that rather well, too, helping rewire that nonsensical meat-shaped vehicle so the Earthlings could escape. (She'd let the boy named

Dev think he had fixed it, of course. He seemed like he needed a win.) Then she'd doctored the message on the school lockers, tampered with the EXIT signs, and guided the cadets to the band room, where everything had been arranged perfectly. She wasn't one to brag, but she thought she deserved a pat on the back. She hoped her aunt would feel the same.

"Trust in the plan, earn your way back home," her aunt had said coldly, before banishing Em to this wasteland, all alone. The memory still stung. Em had no idea when her aunt or tutor might make contact again, or how they would communicate with her, but she was sure they'd find a way. *Relentless*, that was her aunt in a nutshell.

Well, Em would be relentless, too. Unfortunately, even the pixelator couldn't save her from the voracious hunger of the smogmonster, so there was only one choice left: Escape.

She watched and waited for the right moment, hidden in the corner of the band room. Word had spread across the multiverse that Earthlings possessed strange sonic devices with unknown powers. Their so-called music had restored communication with Queen Eryna, for example, even though she was quarantined on Klapproth, where the silvox plague rendered the population incommunicado. And now Em was witnessing the Earthlings utilizing their instruments to rend open a new portal. It baffled and amazed her. It also made her feel more than a little jealous.

She had trained under her aunt's elite team of combat warriors since she was old enough to walk. She could wield a stunclub with impressive dexterity, hit spear targets with near-perfect accuracy, and execute a flawless back handspring. She was a novice mind-sifter, and with her special hoodie she could even become invisible. Em had many talents, but she had never been able to cleave open a dimensional membrane and slip between worlds. No one in her lineage could. Yet these clueless cadets were doing exactly that.

An idea blossomed . . .

Perhaps the Earthling music was more than just a ticket off this dimension. Perhaps it offered a chance to prove herself, to show her aunt and everyone else who doubted her that she could be trusted with important tasks. That she was clever and cunning. That she was valuable. That she was more than just a burden.

Em began to formulate a plan in her mind. She would follow the Earthlings and learn how to do what they did. She would steal their instruments, impersonating her doppelganger if need be, and master the musical magic they possessed. Then, finally, she would be welcomed home with fanfare, elevated to her rightful seat alongside her last living relative, her aunt . . . the Empyrean One herself.

Em narrowed her eyes. She pulled her hoodie tighter and got into position, like a cat preparing to pounce. As soon as the cadets entered the portal, she would be right behind them.

The red-haired girl gave a signal and the cadets stepped forward, doing some sort of strange dance move.

A second later, the invisible girl ran and leaped, diving through the Rip before it collapsed and closed, following her doppelganger across the Threshold.

# CHAPTER 5

**"AND NOW, FOR THE BEAUTY AND TALENT PORTION OF TODAY'S** event!" A gentleman in a pale blue suit spoke into a bedazzled microphone.

The audience clapped excitedly, filling the large auditorium with thunderous applause. A huge banner hung above the stage, announcing the 13th Annual Miz Soy Blossom Pageant. An arch of pink and yellow balloons stretched over the doorway. The air was humid, laden with the heady sweetness of flowers, candy, and far too much hairspray.

The man in the blue suit smiled, his teeth gleaming. "Let's welcome to the stage some of Central Ohio's finest—"

The audience murmured and rustled in their seats, breathless with anticipation. The velvet curtain parted. All of a sudden, five middle schoolers materialized out of thin air, landing in a sweaty, dusty heap on the floor. Tessa, whose eyes were closed, belted out the last notes of the song they'd been performing back on Other-Earth in a final, operatic crescendo.

The audience gasped. Tessa's eyes snapped open. The cadets instinctively reached for their instruments, not knowing what fresh threats they might face in this new dimension. But as they sat up and looked around, they realized they weren't in immediate danger, unless you counted rhinestone-induced blindness or excessive hair-spray inhalation.

One by one, the cadets pulled themselves onto their feet. Their legs felt like spaghetti and their ears rang, but they were alive. To their great relief, there were no signs of smogmonsters or dragomanders in this new world. Just a whole lot of glitter.

"Uh, does anyone know where we are?" Dev asked, coughing. He reached down to rub his injured knee, relieved yet surprised to find that the pain had almost completely disappeared. Instead of cellular degradation, the Transfer process had seemingly healed him.

Groggy and disoriented, the other cadets blinked into the bright stage lights. Girls and boys dressed in elaborate costumes waited in the wings with tap shoes, batons, Hula-Hoops, and decks of playing cards.

"Well, that was an unexpected entrance!" the man in the blue suit said, gliding over to the cadets, his voice extra chipper. "It appears we have a late entry into the competition!" He looked the motley crew up and down. "An ensemble, so it seems. Would you mind introducing yourselves?"

He held out the microphone to Isaiah, whose face turned a faint chartreuse color as a wave of nausea overtook him. Before he could answer the man's question, he ran offstage and vomited into an overturned top hat on the prop table.

The announcer grimaced but quickly forced a smile back onto his face. "It seems somebody has a case of stage fright, am I right?"

Someone in the audience snickered. Someone else huffed, clearly appalled.

"How about you, little lady?" the announcer asked. "Care to introduce yourself to the audience?"

Maeve did not appreciate the man calling her a little lady, but she was a performer to her core, and she never shied away from a shot at center stage. She ran a hand through her frizzy hair. She smoothed the front of her silvery space suit and lifted her chin, putting on her best game face.

"We are the Conroy Cadets, members of an elite Earth-ling task force." This was a bit of an exaggeration, but she liked the way it sounded, and she knew how important it was to make a good first impression. "We're also part of a middle school marching band," she said, lifting her oboe and speaking clearly. "We come in peace," she added, just in case. This place looked a whole lot like Earth, but judging from some of the mile-high hairdos she spotted in the front row of the auditorium and the announcer's unnaturally white teeth, Maeve couldn't be sure.

Questions hummed through the crowd. *What were a bunch of band geeks doing at the prestigious Miz Soy Blossom*

*Pageant? Why were they holding such dingy instruments? Where were their tuxes and gowns? Why were none of them wearing rhinestones of any kind?*

A reporter rushed down the aisle toward the stage. He began snapping photos of the disheveled tweens. "I can see the headline now: Local marching band members crash pageant!"

"Wait, what?" Lewis said, scrunching up his forehead. "We're not crashing anything. We ended up here by accident! We took a portal from another—"

Maeve shot him a look. Until they knew what was really going on here, they shouldn't give too much away.

"How dare you!" A women with a stiff brunette bob appeared from the wings, gripping her daughter's hand tightly. "You ruined my puddin's chances at this year's title! The crown was hers! Until you wrecked her act!"

"Wrecked her act?" Maeve shook her head.

The woman pointed with disgust at the black satin top hat, which Isaiah had unfortunately used as a barf bucket. "Trying to steal her thunder, aren't you? This is sabotage!" the woman wailed. "You better believe the mayor is going to hear about this!"

Tessa stepped forward, her heart hammering her ribs. "Wait, who's the mayor?"

The woman's face reddened. "Valerie Hawthorne, of course! Just wait until she finds out about this! I plan to file a formal complaint."

Tessa turned to Dev, tears welling up in her eyes. "We're home," she croaked. "We're really home!" She hugged him tightly, and he nearly melted into a puddle on the stage, both of his knees suddenly weak.

Just then, a burly security guard approached and began escorting the cadets off the stage. "If you're not going to perform and compete, I'm going to need you kids to stay off the premises until the pageant is finished," he said apologetically.

Normally, Maeve would have jumped at the chance to perform in front of an audience of this size, but judging from the heckling sounds coming from the crowd, she didn't think their musical act would go over too well. Besides, she and her friends had been through a lot these past few days. She was ready to give her oboe, and herself, a well-deserved rest.

"We didn't mean to cause a scene," Isaiah said to the security guard, fighting off another wave of nausea. "We need to get home anyway."

"Home!" Tessa echoed, relief and happiness fizzing through her.

The security guard nodded, leading them to the auditorium's front steps. "You kids stay out of trouble, you hear?" he said, before turning to leave.

"Our bad! Sorry! It won't happen again." Lewis gave a friendly wave and flashed his signature dimple, which usually worked when he needed to get out of trouble. Then he flopped down onto the steps, breathing in fresh Earth air and gazing up at the clear sky, letting the early-autumn sun warm his skin. "Man, it feels good to be back."

"Hey, how do you suppose we actually get home?" Isaiah asked, sitting beside Lewis. "Like, to our houses. We don't have phones, and Tessa's eChron watch is busted."

"Maybe we can ask to borrow someone's phone?" Dev pointed across the street where a lady pushed a baby in a stroller. "She looks nice. Maybe she'll help us." He knew his dad would be worried sick, probably pacing the floor at NASA, fretting over why the kids hadn't traveled through the quantum collider like they had planned.

"Or, we could hop aboard that," Lewis said as an electric bus pulled up to the curb.

*Honk honk!*

A cheerful, heavyset man leaned out of the front window. "You kids need a ride?" he asked, eyeing them inquisitively. Tessa realized they were dressed pretty oddly, in torn and dirty silver space suits, holding a bunch of rusty instruments in their hands. Their hair was a mess, and their faces were smudged with grime and dust. They didn't smell so hot either.

"Benni?" Maeve's eyes widened as she jumped up and trotted over to the bus. "What are you doing here?" It felt so nice to see a familiar face, she almost cried.

"I drive the school routes on weekdays, but on weekends, I drive the city bus routes," he told her.

"So, it's the weekend?" Isaiah asked hesitantly. He wasn't sure if time on other dimensions worked the same as time on Earth.

"Sure is. Sunday afternoon. October second." Benni checked the clock on the dash. "Three thirty-seven, to be exact." He glanced back at the kids, somewhat concerned. "Why? What's got you all so confused?"

"Nothing. Never mind." Isaiah gave a weak laugh. "Just a momentary brain fart, you know?"

Benni nodded but still seemed skeptical.

Tessa studied the large blue bus and scratched her head. "I've lived in Conroy my whole life and I've never seen a blue metro bus." Vehicles in the municipal fleets were painted a vibrant green hue. Tessa knew this because it was part of her mother's sustainable transportation initiative. Originally, the new highly efficient trains, buses, and ride share vans were supposed to be boring tan. But Tessa, being the most fashion forward of her family, convinced her mom that rebranding with a pop of color would help spread the word and get some good buzz going. Her mother had agreed, even letting Tessa help select the exact shade of green paint.

"Oh, they made an exception for Ol' Blue," Benni said, patting the octagonal steering wheel. "She's top of the line, retrofitted with solar panels, a clean energy converter, and a few extra special modifications." He winked. "She's the best thing on wheels, if you ask me. You'll never drive anything better."

Maeve pursed her lips, silently disagreeing with him. Clearly, he'd never driven a Teeny's wiener-mobile while running for his life. Now *that* was something special.

"Where are you all headed?" Benni asked, then paused. "Wait a minute... weren't you five supposed to be doing some sort of sleep study at NASA? How'd you end up all the way downtown?" A curious look danced across his brows.

"Ah, um, we did the sleep study. And it was... a total snooze, if you know what I mean." Lewis laughed nervously.

"But we finished early," Maeve interjected. "And we came downtown to play a gig."

Benni raised an eyebrow. "You performed at the beauty pageant?"

Maeve improvised. "Sure. We were invited to play some music during intermission," she fibbed, hoping it sounded like a solid excuse. "A gig is a gig, right? Plus, we have regionals coming up in a few weeks and we need all the practice we can get." She held up her grimy oboe.

Benni nodded. "Well, I hope the experience was everything you hoped for... and more."

"Oh, it was!" Lewis chuckled. "It was out of this world."

"Literally," Isaiah said under his breath.

Maeve stepped closer to the bus. She noticed there were no other passengers on board. "Benni, listen, we actually need to get back to the Gwen Research Center now because we, um, left some of our belongings there."

"You're in luck. I was just heading east. I'll be passing by that area on my way out of town."

"You're leaving town?" Maeve asked.

"Just for a little while," Benni replied. "I haven't taken a vacation in quite some time."

"A vacation sounds amazing," Dev said, his eyelids growing heavy.

Benni smiled. "Indeed. I'm overdue for a visit with my granddaughter."

"That's nice," Maeve replied. "I'm close with my gramps, too. Where does your granddaughter live?"

Benni tapped a finger to his chin, like he was trying to decide how to respond. "Far away from here. And yet, not so far away either."

"Umm, what's that supposed to mean?" Tessa whispered to Lewis, who was standing beside her.

He shrugged. "Benni often talks in riddles, so your guess is as good as mine."

Benni pressed a button and the bus's folding door creaked open. "Hop on."

They climbed aboard and came face-to-face with a ticketing machine.

"Aw, shoot." Maeve sucked in a breath. "We don't have any money right now, Benni. Could we pay you back at school someday after your vacation?"

He shook his head. "I don't think that will be necessary. Something tells me you possess adequate fare."

"No, we don't. I'm really sorry. But I'm sure I could get my mom to reimburse you for all five rides," Tessa offered.

Benni got a funny look in his eyes, then said, "That which you seek is already yours." This only confused the cadets more. Then Benni sighed. "Check your pockets."

They searched their NASA-issued suits, which had an array of hidden pockets and buttons. Lewis found an old snack wrapper and a wad of space lint, but nothing that looked like a bus ticket or money.

Then he reached into one of his back pockets. He pulled out a palm-sized magenta square. Tessa found one in her pocket, too, as did the others. With all the near-death excitement of their recent dimensional jaunt, they'd completely forgotten about the strange souvenirs Kor had given them. She had told them to guard the squares carefully, even though she refused to tell them what exactly they were.

Kor was a smuggler, a trickster, and a bit of an enigma, but she'd proven her loyalty to Ignatia and the MAC by helping Virri reunite with Queen Eryna. Before that, in a rather shady deal, Kor had agreed to return the cadets' missing instruments (which she had stolen in the first place) so long as they promised to transport the squares safely back to Earth. They had assumed the items were far more valuable than . . . bus tickets. Then again, the multiverse was full of mysteries, big and small.

Isaiah studied his square, holding it up to the light. It glowed faintly, humming with some sort of compressed energy. It felt powerful, maybe even dangerous.

Maeve eyed the ticketing machine at the front of the bus. The slot on the top was the exact size and shape of the magenta square. "Would this work?" she asked Benni, perplexed and a little doubtful.

He stared at the square in her hands, unblinking for a long moment, like his mind was somewhere else entirely.

"Benni?" she said gently.

He snapped out of whatever trance he'd been in. The poor guy definitely seemed like he needed a vacation. "Er, yes," he said, clearing his throat. "Those will work just fine. Better than expected, in fact."

One by one, the kids slipped their squares into the slot. The machine made a satisfied beep after each deposit. Isaiah was last, but as he reached out to slide his square into the machine, Benni held up his hand. He shook his head. "You keep that one. Something tells me you might need it more than I do. At least for now."

This unsettled Isaiah. "Are you sure?"

Benni bobbed his head. "I insist."

Isaiah thanked the bus driver and tucked the square away. He wished he still had his Journal of Strange Occurrences, because this certainly felt strange. Actually, everything lately fell into the seriously strange category.

Benni shifted the bus into gear. "Take a seat, please," he called over his shoulder.

The cadets sat down and whispered, keeping their voices low so Benni wouldn't hear.

"Do you think Kor would be mad?" Maeve asked.

Tessa shook her head. "No. We did what she said. We brought the squares back to Earth. That was the deal. It's done."

Over in his seat, Dev fought to keep his eyes open. The cadets had been running on pure adrenaline for the past few days, and the sheer exhaustion of interdimensional travel coupled with multiple near-death encounters was finally catching up to them.

Dev yawned and stretched his arms over his head, curling up in his seat as the bus rumbled along. Tessa yawned next, and soon the contagious yawn traveled from cadet to cadet. Maeve rested her head on the window. In a matter of minutes, Lewis was snoring.

The only one who didn't instantly conk out was Isaiah. He was still energized from the Transfer, something stirring in his blood. He pulled the magenta square from his pocket and studied it. Back on the Station, he hadn't had time to really examine it. It was paper thin now, yet it had started out blocky—the size and shape of a Rubik's Cube—until Kor had flattened it between her palms for easier transport. He tried crumpling it up, like a scrap of paper, but as soon as he opened his palm, the creases disappeared. He tried to tear it in half, but it was too strong.

He pictured Kor pressing it between her palms. How had she done that? Could he return it to its original shape or transform it into something else entirely? He laid the square on one open palm, then smushed his other hand over the top of it. Slowly, he lifted his hand. The flat square began to glow and expand, from 2D to 3D. He twirled his fingers above it and the cube slowly rotated, pulsing with an indescribable energy.

He gasped loudly. Benni hit the brakes, startled, jolting the others awake. Isaiah clasped his hand over the cube, instantly smashing it back into a flat slip of pinkish paper.

"Everything okay back there?" Benni called over his shoulder.

Lewis grumbled groggily, extending his long legs into the aisle, the power nap far too short for his liking.

Isaiah swallowed and called back, "Yup. All good." He stashed the square carefully in his pocket, his heart racing. He still didn't know what it was, but he'd have to investigate later, because out the bus window, the Gwen Research Center—Conroy's own world-famous NASA field station—came into view.

# CHAPTER 6

HIDDEN BY HER PIXELATOR HOODIE, EM SLIPPED BETWEEN THE heavy velvet curtains in the auditorium, watching the pageant with odd fascination. The Earthling cadets had been escorted outside moments earlier, and Em had every intention of following them, but then she'd caught sight of a girl in a frilly lavender tutu clutching what appeared to be a lethal weapon. The scene was too deliciously perplexing to ignore. She decided to stay and watch, just for a few minutes, to see what might transpire.

The girl began to twirl her weapon—a long, thin, stick-like apparatus with sparkly tassels that the announcer called a *baton*. Em was certain the baton would transform at any moment into a shock-spire—a popular form of weaponry from her home dimension. But alas, the only thing the baton did was . . . twirl. And sparkle. And twirl some more. It didn't even explode when the girl accidentally dropped it on the stage floor. What fun was that?

Em huffed and brushed her hair from her eyes. The next competitor was equally confounding, shuffling onto the stage in a black-and-white sequined tuxedo and shiny shoes that clacked awkwardly. Music began to play. Had the cadets returned? Em's ears pricked as she searched for the music's source. It was not instruments, like she'd expected, but a pair of box-shaped sonic blasters positioned at the edge of the stage. Peculiar indeed. The boy in the tuxedo proceeded to dance, if you could call it that. Mostly, he just smacked his noisy feet around and waved his hands, fingers stretched wide, as though he had touched something either very hot or unpleasantly sticky.

Again, there was no fighting. No sparring, no self-defense, nothing remotely deadly about the competitors' so-called talents. Aside from some hair-pulling and sassy name-calling backstage, none of the boys or girls even attempted to assassinate each other. How could they ever expect to prove their worth and loyalty to the panel of leaders judging their performances from the front row? Odder still was the fact that the audience never once called for the contestants to be thrown to the bile pits. No matter how cringeworthy the performances were, the people continued to clap. Sure, they'd been angered by the cadets' earlier disruption, but Maeve and the others had merely been escorted outside, with no mention of the kids being fed to a pack of hungry cracks, as Em had anticipated.

Em shook her head. Nothing about this dimension was adding up. For as long as she could remember, her aunt had told her how dangerous and cruel the inhabitants of other worlds could be, especially the Earthlings of Dim14. When the Empyrean One called for an expansion of the Cataclysmosis and defense forces, recruiting even the youngest Empyrii children, the citizens of Dim8 had not protested; they understood that this was for their own good, for their protection and survival. Eons earlier, when the multiverse was a very different place, the Empyrii had been ousted, their fragile dimension Untethered over a gross misunderstanding. The burgeoning Multiverse Allied Council had shown Em's ancestors no mercy. And thus, the Empyrean One vowed that her people would show no mercy in return.

The Earthlings and the Empyrii may have resembled each other in physical form, but that was where the similarities supposedly ended. Earthlings were greedy, destructive, bloodthirsty creatures to be feared and avoided. In fact, when Em had first spotted the cadets on that desolate Other-Earth, her first inclination had been to attack them. *Offense beats defense*, her aunt often advised. But the cadets seemed so hapless and helpless that Em had reconsidered her whole strategy. Looking back now, she wondered if her aunt would view that decision as yet another weakness.

The music ended. Em watched as the dancing boy shuffled offstage to deafening applause. His mother met him backstage and planted an enormous red lipstick kiss on his cheek. He beamed up at her, pride shining in his eyes. Pain, sharp and distinct, pierced Em's chest with the force of a well-aimed spear. She tried to shake the feeling away, to steel her heart, as she'd been taught. But the heart is a stubborn muscle. Em watched the boy and his mother, longing for her own mother, or at least some semblance of the bond a parent and child were supposed to share. It was something she'd never experienced herself. Her father had perished in combat before she was born, her mother died in childbirth, and her aunt tolerated her, at best.

A wave of emotion overtook her. In her short time on this version of Earth, Em hadn't seen anything even close to the stories her aunt used to tell. Earthlings were supposed to be the enemy. Yet most people here seemed... nice. Caring. Loving, even.

Em's skin grew hot, her pulse irregular. She needed some fresh air. She slipped out of the auditorium and exited the building. To her great disappointment, the cadets were gone. She walked a loop around the entire block, but they were nowhere to be found.

She wanted to scream, but she couldn't afford to bring attention to herself. The hoodie rendered her invisible, but not silent. She paced back and forth, regaining her composure, formulating a plan. Too much was riding on this quest. She couldn't let these Earthlings, or the feelings they stirred deep in her chest, get the best of her. She needed to focus.

# CHAPTER 7

DR. KHATRI SQUINTED INTO THE LATE AFTERNOON SUN, LOOKING to the sky for answers. He removed his glasses and polished them on the hem of his button-down shirt, which was untucked and wrinkled. He hadn't slept or showered for two days; he'd been too busy trying to locate and then guide his son and his fellow bandmates back to Earth.

Thinking about the missing kids made his head swim. In the wee hours of the morning, Zoey had made contact with her twin sister, Tessa, and they'd coordinated an exit strategy. But the portal that the kids were supposed to travel through had glitched, and the five middle schoolers hadn't returned. Dr. Khatri didn't know where they might be or if they were safe. He was used to contemplating the infinite unknowns of the universe, but this particular uncertainty was too much to bear. He replayed the weekend's events over and over in his head, searching for something he might have missed, some clue that might help him find his son.

He and Professor McGillum had managed to refuel the Syntropitron—a reverse dynamite contraption capable of instantaneous regeneration—which they'd successfully used to repair the damaged quantum collider. The collider had been constructed in secret by a rogue colleague, Dr. Genevieve Scopes, within an abandoned NASA lab. During the middle schoolers' field trip to the Gwen Research Center on Friday, the kids had accidentally activated the collider, which transported them unwittingly to another dimension.

As a catastrophysicist, Dr. Khatri was accustomed to big thinking. He'd researched multiple world theories in the past, intrigued by the premise and possibility that parallel dimensions might exist. He'd just never imagined that his own son might somehow journey to one of those unknown places, let alone become trapped there.

Dr. Khatri sat down on the curb and rubbed his temples, where a headache pounded like a hammer. He breathed deeply. Mayor Hawthorne had insisted he take a break, and Professor McGillum promised to keep watch in case anything changed with the collider. Dr. Khatri resisted at first, his nerves far too raw and jumpy, but the mayor was a powerful and persuasive woman, and she wouldn't take no for an answer. Now that he was outside, he was grateful for the crisp autumn air.

The center's front doors opened and Zoey appeared with her mother. The mayor clutched a steaming cup of coffee, and Zoey nibbled on AstroCrisps, freeze-dried potato chips sold in the cafeteria's vending machines.

"Mind if we join you?" Valerie Hawthorne asked.

Dr. Khatri smiled. He was tired but glad for the company. "Not at all."

They sat beside him on the curb and gazed up at the clouds, each lost in their own thoughts. Several minutes passed, and then an unexpected sound interrupted the quiet.

*Honk! Honk!*

Dr. Khatri jolted to his feet, trying to get a better view of the access road leading to the center. There was rarely any traffic or deliveries on Sunday afternoons, and the city bus route didn't connect this far into the outskirts of town. He hoped whatever had honked wasn't a press vehicle. If the media got wind of what had transpired at NASA over the weekend, it would be disastrous.

"Look!" Zoey said, rising to her feet.

A large blue bus came into view, chugging up and over the hill. *Honk! Honk!*

Dr. Khatri polished his glasses once more and blinked. He shook his head. Could it be?

"Dad!" a boy shouted, waving from the open bus window.

"Dev!" Dr. Khatri cried out, his throat hoarse, tears springing to his eyes.

"Mom!" a girl with warm brown skin called, peering out a different window, her long braids swaying in the breeze.

Three more faces appeared in three more windows. They were soot-covered but smiling.

Mayor Hawthorne let out a relieved wail.

Zoey jumped up and down. "They're back!"

After much hugging, crying, and breathless, mile-a-minute snippets of conversation, the five cadets attempted to fill Dr. Khatri, Mayor Hawthorne, and Zoey in on their recent escapades. Their story was sweeping and at times unbelievable. Each cadet took turns adding little details and anecdotes, trying to paint a picture of their mind-boggling adventure, but they still only managed to scratch the surface.

"This is a lot to process," Dr. Khatri said, dazed but incredibly grateful. "I'm so relieved you're here now, safe and sound!" He hugged Dev for the tenth time. Normally, Dev would have been mortified by his father's display of affection, especially in front of both Hawthorne-Scott sisters. But he was so happy to be home that he hugged his dad back.

"I'm extremely proud of you," Tessa's mom said tenderly, her voice somewhere in between mom-mode and mayor-mode. "You all displayed remarkable poise, intelligence, and teamwork. Aside from a few minor hiccups, it sounds like you were exceptional ambassadors for the city of Conroy and all of planet Earth. No small feat, I must say!"

Tessa couldn't remember the last time her mother had spoken about her like that. Usually, Zoey was the one who received all the praise for impeccable grades and overachiever extracurriculars. For a fleeting moment, Tessa wondered if the woman standing in front of her might not actually be her real mother but some doppelganger version instead. "You really mean that?" Tessa asked.

"Of course!" her mother replied.

"Cross your heart?" Tessa prodded.

"Cross my heart, hope to fly, stick a paintbrush in my eye!" Mayor Hawthorne declared, using their family's unusual riff on the promissory expression. Tessa sighed with relief; no one else—not even a doppelganger—would know that silly phrase. Her mother smiled at her. "You did great, sweetie."

Tessa beamed. Her mother's praise felt like sunshine. She wanted to bask in it, let it warm her all the way through. Then she caught Zoey's frowning face out of the corner of her eye, and her own smile drooped. Was her sister still mad at her? Was she jealous?

She followed her sister's gaze. Zoey eyed the rusty saxophone in Dev's hand, then the scratched-up oboe in Maeve's hand, Lewis's scuffed drumsticks, Isaiah's slightly dented trumpet, and then . . .

Zoey's hazel eyes grew wide. "Tessa! Where is my clarinet?"

Tessa cringed, empty-handed. "Riiight. About that . . . It may or may not have been eaten by a dragomander."

"A what?" Zoey gawked.

"Long story. I'll make it up to you. Promise!"

"You'd better!"

"Ahem, you two," Mayor Hawthorne said, placing a hand on each of her daughter's shoulders. "A clarinet we can replace. A person, not so much. Let's keep everything in perspective, shall we?" Then she pulled the girls into a tight hug and kissed them both on the tops of their heads. "Oh, my baby girls! What would I do without you?"

Zoey wriggled out of the bone-crushing hug and faced her identical twin sister. "Mom's right. I'm sorry." She sighed. "I really missed you, goober."

Tessa bopped her sister on the nose. "Same, booger."

Zoey reached out and held her sister's face in her hands, squishing her cheeks like their grandma Martha always did. She knew it drove her sister nuts, which made it that much more fun. "I've missed bugging you most of all!"

"Ack! Get off!" Tessa laughed and swatted her away.

Zoey cackled. "Only if you promise to tell me everything! I wanna know all about this drago-whats-it that ate my clarinet, and everything else."

"Promise." Tessa looped her pinky through her sister's and gave a squeeze. It was something they used to do as little girls, back when they still shared secrets. Tessa hoped they could be close like that again. They'd drifted so much since starting middle school, but maybe the field trip fiasco was the fresh start they needed.

The corners of Zoey's eyes softened. She squeezed Tessa's pinky back.

Mayor Hawthorne smiled, pleased to see her daughters reconciling. "Dr. Khatri and I would like to hear more from each of you over the coming days, but for now, I think it's best if we got all of you home to your families."

"What should we tell our folks?" Lewis asked.

Mayor Hawthorne and Dr. Khatri exchanged concerned looks. "I'm glad you asked," Dr. Khatri said. "It's important that you tell your families you've been participating in a NASA-led sleep study this weekend. This is the story we communicated to them when you first went missing, so we should all be consistent."

"Right." Mayor Hawthorne nodded. "We don't want to cause undue alarm. We'll need to do some additional investigating, hold a classified briefing session, and conduct individual interviews with all of you. Until we figure out precisely what happened with the collider, we think it's best if we exercise discretion."

Lewis raised an eyebrow. "So, you want us to lie?"

Mayor Hawthorne grimaced. "Normally, we would never encourage you to lie, but these are clearly not normal circumstances, by any stretch of the imagination."

"You can say that again," Isaiah mumbled under his breath.

The other cadets nodded, all except for Lewis. Part of him wanted to tell his parents and his brutish brothers the truth. He'd outrun spacebeasts, played alien video games, eaten extraterrestrial snacks, and performed some sweet tunes in front of an interdimensional audience. Heck, he'd even helped thwart a super evil villain's attempt to destroy the whole freaking multiverse! That was infinitely cooler than scoring a few goals during a lacrosse game, or running a speedy hundred-meter dash. But his family would never know about any of it. And even if he *could* tell them, he knew they'd never believe him. His shoulders slumped.

"You okay, dude?" Dev asked, giving Lewis a nudge.

Lewis sighed. "Yeah, just a little bummed."

"I get it," Maeve said. "Coming home after everything we've experienced is . . . a lot. If you ever need to talk, we're here, okay?"

Lewis looked up. Maeve could be bossy and annoying at times, but she'd proved to be a good leader and a loyal friend. He smiled, and she smiled back.

Mayor Hawthorne glanced at her watch. The day was quickly slipping away. "Dr. Khatri and I will drive you all home. Isaiah, you can come with us. Your apartment's not far from our house," Mayor Hawthorne said.

"Okay, thanks," Isaiah replied, hoping the whole sleep-study excuse hadn't worried his mom too much.

"Maeve and Lewis, why don't you come with us?" Dr. Khatri suggested.

Maeve bit her lip. "Um, thanks, but totally not necessary. I'll just give my grandfather a call. I'm sure he'd love an excuse to get out."

Dr. Khatri cleared his throat. "Speaking of Gil Greene, your grandfather actually helped us locate the portal that Dr. Scopes jumped through."

"He did?" Maeve blanched. "How?"

Dr. Khatri described the scene behind the silo, out in the fields beyond Miss Mary's Dairy.

"Ah," Maeve said, putting the pieces together. The Rip at the farm explained the missing cows, including the one she'd spotted in the Menagerie on Station Liminus.

"Best to let your grandfather believe it was a sinkhole after all," Mayor Hawthorne advised.

"Will do," she responded, then described their encounter with Dr. Scopes on the Station.

Dr. Khatri looked especially distressed by the extent of his former colleague's deception. "At least you're all safe now. She can't hurt you here," he said, giving Dev's shoulder a reassuring pat.

Dev nodded at his father, then turned back to Maeve. "You're sure you don't want a ride? It's really not a problem."

Maeve shook her head. "Thanks, but I'm sure. Besides, your dad probably needs to close up the lab and do some other important tasks around here." She gestured to the NASA building.

In truth, Maeve couldn't bear to think about her fellow bandmates seeing the worn-out trailer where she lived. She'd opened up a lot over the past few days, but now that they were back on Earth, things felt different. Plus, she couldn't be sure whether or not her mom would be home. It was hard to guess what sort of mood she might be in or how explosive her temper could be.

Mayor Hawthorne handed Maeve a cell phone. She dialed her home number. Thankfully, her grandfather picked up the call on the third ring.

"Hullo?" he said.

Maeve took a breath. "Hi, Gramps. It's me, Maeve. I'm ready to come home," she said, surprised by how shaky the words came out. Perhaps because deep down, she didn't really want to go home. She wanted to see her grandfather, of course. And her mother, too. Sort of. She wanted to see a certain version of her mother. The loving, lucid version. Not the unpredictable, angry version. Or the glassy-eyed, empty version. It was complicated. Maeve felt almost seasick with emotion.

"How'd the sleep study go?" he asked.

"Fine. Great, actually." Maeve played along, just as she'd been coached to do. She was a skilled actress, after all.

"While you were snoozing away, I had a little adventure of my own," he said. "I'll tell you all about it tonight over dinner. I was thinking we could grab some hot dogs at Teeny's. What do you think?"

She chuckled. "That sounds perfect." After she hung up and handed the phone back to the mayor, Isaiah came over to her side.

"Hey. Is everything all right?"

Maeve quickly rearranged her face, masking her real feelings. "Sure, why?"

Isaiah studied her eyes. "You just looked a little . . . sad. And anxious."

She shook her head. "I'm fine," she lied. "Just a little tired and dizzy. Must be the residual effects of Transfer. You know how it is."

A few minutes later, an old red truck pulled up to the

curb. Gil Green leaned out the driver's side window and waved.

"Heya, buttercup!"

Maeve waved back. "Hi, Gramps!" She turned to Isaiah and the others, this time with a more genuine smile. "See you tomorrow!" she called out, climbing into the truck with her oboe in hand. It felt weird saying goodbye to her friends after all this time together, even though she knew she'd see them again soon. The thought of going back to school was weird, too. Could they just suddenly return to normal? What did normal even mean? She was a star performer, but could she really pretend like none of this had ever happened?

As her grandfather's pickup truck drove away, she caught Isaiah's eye out the window, and then Lewis's, too, sensing that they both understood.

Zoey turned to her sister. "Listen, I'm stoked that you're alive."

Tessa wrinkled her nose. "I sense a *but* coming . . ."

"But," Zoey said, raising a finger, "if you dare leave me behind the next time you jet off to some new world, I will seriously kill you."

"Don't worry," Tessa said, giving one of her sister's braids a playful tug. "I don't think we'll be doing *that* again anytime soon."

The sisters looped their elbows together and took off toward their mother's sedan, their steps perfectly in sync.

"Coming?" Tessa called over her shoulder.

"Coming," Isaiah replied, taking a breath. As eager as he was to see his mother, a restlessness thrummed beneath his skin. Questions crowded his mind. He'd just come home, but he felt the allure and pull of the multiverse imploring him to come back.

He shook out his shoulders, releasing the tension he was holding there. He followed the twins to the car. Surely he'd feel better, more grounded and settled, when he saw his mother. One bowl of her homemade noodles would settle his stomach and his mind. At least he hoped so.

# CHAPTER 8

EM WAS LOST. SHE HATED TO ADMIT THIS, BUT IT WAS TRUE.
She'd been wandering up and down the streets of Conroy for what felt like hours, and she still hadn't spotted the cadets anywhere. Worse, she'd become disoriented and lost sight of familiar landmarks—the auditorium, a bank, a large municipal building, a statue of a man on a horse. She was somewhere on the city's periphery now, cold and alone.

A strange weather pattern had blustered in with no warning, sending the temperature plummeting from crisp to brisk to downright blizzardish in mere minutes. Em wrapped her hoodie tighter around herself, grateful for its powers of invisibility but wishing it were a little warmer. She had been determined to track down her doppelganger, but she'd have to resume her search tomorrow. If she didn't find shelter soon, she'd surely freeze.

An older woman turned the corner, heading in Em's direction. She walked slowly, with arthritic steps, pushing a grocery cart down the street. Em's stomach growled; she couldn't remember the last time she'd eaten anything. A full day, at least. Maybe longer. She eyed the woman's cart, imagining the food that was likely inside. Perhaps darberries, a wedge of sheerhorn cheese, or whatever else people ate on this dim. The woman was old and weak. Em, on the other hand, was a trained fighter, agile and strong, with invisibility on her side. She would steal some food and run. If the woman fought back, which Em doubted she would do, Em could easily strike her down with a single blow.

Em snuck closer. When she was only a few feet from the woman's cart, a strong gust of bitter wind tore the hoodie from Em's head, disrupting the pixilation effect and exposing her. Em gasped. The woman did, too.

"My! Where did you come from?" The woman looked incredulous but not angry. "What on Earth are you doing out here in the cold?"

Em didn't answer. Her teeth chattered as she tried to zip the hoodie back up. The zipper snagged and refused to budge.

"You poor thing," the woman said. "Haven't you ever experienced a shiver before?"

Em looked up. "A what?"

"An unfortunate side effect of climate change, I'm afraid. Frequent in Conroy, and other cities, too." She pushed her cart closer and Em noticed that it was not full of groceries, as she'd suspected, but empty plastic and glass bottles, an umbrella, some books, and a few tattered blankets.

"You're not from around here," the woman said, less as a question and more as an observation.

Em nodded. "Just arrived today. Lost my whereabouts when the weather changed."

The woman clucked knowingly. She reached into her cart and removed one of the blankets, offering it to Em.

Em backed away, unsure what to do.

"Take it, dear," the woman, who was heavily bundled herself, said.

"How much?" Em asked, eyeing the warm fabric, hoping she could trade something for the blanket.

"Oh, I'm not selling it. I'm giving it to you. It's a gift." The woman smiled, displaying several gaps where teeth were missing. "Go on. I can't let you freeze out here, now, can I?"

Em bit her lip. She wasn't accustomed to generosity or charity of any kind. On Dim8, those attributes were equated with weakness. She eyed the blanket, then looked up at the woman. This felt like a test. It unsettled her. But not as much as the cold chilled her. Finally, she reached out and accepted the blanket, wrapping it around her frigid shoulders.

"Good girl. Now come with me." The woman turned the cart and began walking through the snow toward an underpass that would hopefully shield them from the weather for the night.

Em hesitated, but then her feet seemed to move on their own, her body desperate for warmth. The woman parked her cart under the bridge, where a collection of people lived in makeshift tents and huts. She unloaded her belongings into a small shelter built of cardboard, corrugated metal, and plastic tarps.

Em followed her inside. "What is this place?" she asked.

"My home, of course. It's not much, but we're traveling people. We like to keep a light footprint, moving from town to town, city to city, never tied to one place too long." She gestured to a pallet on the floor with a thick woven mat. "You're welcome to stay until the shiver breaks. We'll be moving on from Conroy soon, though. This place is too unpredictable, even for my tastes." She leaned over and rummaged around in a burlap satchel, retrieving a can of soup. "Sit, child. I'll fix us something to eat."

Em sat on the pallet, her bones thawing, her eyes adjusting to the dim light. All of the woman's worldly possessions were contained within the small hut. And yet she chose to share what little she had with a total stranger.

"Why are you helping me?" Em asked, guarded.

The woman set a dented pot atop a small portable hot plate. She stirred its contents. "Why shouldn't I?"

"You don't know me. You have no reason to trust me."

"Don't I?" the woman replied, her wrinkled face calm, unafraid.

Em lowered her eyes. She had intended to steal from the woman earlier, to fight her if need be. The memory made Em cringe, regret and guilt needling her.

The woman spoke quietly. "I was once a girl like you, lost and on my own. I know how far an act of kindness can reach. I may not have a lot, but I still have much to give." She ladled warm broth into a mug and handed it to Em. She was starving, but she waited, her stomach growling in protest. She knew better than to accept food from a stranger. She'd been taught to distrust others, after all—especially Earthlings.

Em watched the woman fill her own mug and slurp loudly. Only then did Em sip the soup, part of her still expecting the cloying taste of vimsar or some other poison. Instead, it was rich, savory, and delicious. Within seconds, she had downed the entire mug. She wiped her mouth with the back of her hand and burped. "Oh!" Em blushed. "Excuse me."

The old woman chuckled and refilled her mug. Em accepted it gratefully. "Thank you," she said quietly. The words were awkward and unpracticed, but they felt oddly nice to say out loud.

Later, the woman took the empty mug from Em's hands. "Rest, child. Tomorrow is a new day."

Em, warm and content, leaned back on the pallet. She pulled the blanket up under her chin. Her eyelids fluttered and closed. As she drifted off to sleep, she thought perhaps she'd been wrong about this place and these people. Perhaps the Empyrean One had been, too.

# CHAPTER 9

**"I'M HOME!" LEWIS CALLED OUT, KICKING OFF HIS SHOES IN THE** front hall. He waited for the eager click of Goldie's paws on the marble floor. She was always happy to see him. But the house was quiet. "Hello?" he said, his voice echoing throughout the palatial home.

"In here!" his mother hollered back.

Lewis followed the sound and found her riding on her stationary bike in their home gym. Upbeat dance music pumped while some virtual instructor yelled inspirational quotes from a screen mounted to the bike's handlebars.

"Hi, honey," his mother said, barely lifting her eyes from the screen. "How was track practice?"

"Um, I was at NASA," he reminded her. He hadn't told his parents that he planned to quit the track team, but now didn't feel like the right moment. "I was doing that, um, sleep study. Didn't the school tell you?"

"Mhmm." She nodded, her blond ponytail bobbing up and down as she pedaled faster. He always found stationary bikes and treadmills to be so weird. You did all that work and literally traveled nowhere. Workout aside, it seemed completely pointless to him.

"Where is everyone?" Lewis asked.

"Your brothers should be home from lacrosse practice soon. And your father's still on his business trip in Oarsville," his mother said, taking a swig of water during a lull between climbs. "And the dog's still at the groomer."

"So, no family dinner?" he asked, a little dejected. He hadn't exactly expected a grand celebration marking his return home, but a home-cooked meal together would've been nice.

"Not tonight, honey. There's leftover spaghetti on the stove. Help yourself. If you'd rather order some takeout, there's money on the counter. Take as much as you need." The music began to pump again and the instructor started shouting something hokey about being your best self.

"Okay, thanks." Lewis left the room and shuffled glumly to the kitchen. He ate the cold spaghetti, then moved on to whatever else he could find in the fridge. He rounded out the meal by eating an entire package of cookies and a half pint of ice cream, because multiple near-death experiences really worked up an appetite. He didn't have any room left in his stomach for takeout, so he pocketed the money and added it to his growing *sorry we're too busy to hang out with you* fund. Lots of kids would probably be psyched to have that sort of cash, but most of the time, Lewis wished his parents would spend less money on him and more time with him.

He left the kitchen and flopped onto the couch in the living room, feeling incredibly full but also sort of empty. As he stretched out, a pillow fell to the floor. He picked it up. It was custom-made, embroidered with their annoying family motto in blue and gold thread: *WYNNERS NEVER LOSE.*

Lewis wondered what it would take for his family to truly notice him. When would any of it ever be good enough? His own mother barely seemed to realize he'd been gone. If only he could tell his family the truth about where he'd been and what he'd done, maybe then they'd see that he was a true Wynner, *and* a winner. Just in a different way than they all expected.

Lewis got up off the couch, grabbed the set of drumsticks he'd brought back from Other-Earth, and took the stairs two at a time, tapping a melancholy rhythm onto the polished oak handrail. Once upstairs, he turned down the hallway toward his bedroom. The door was slightly ajar. He pushed it open.

His room was a total wreck. Shaving cream, feathers, and foam darts covered the walls and floors. *Oh, riiight.* A memory clicked into place. Before he'd left for the field trip, he'd set up an elaborate prank, hoping to get revenge on his older brothers, Winston and Kingston, who constantly picked on him.

Judging from the destruction, the contraption had gone off without a hitch, though Lewis was bummed he'd missed the big crescendo. He wished he could've seen the moment when the pie plates of shaving cream splatted in their faces. It must have been epic! Every string and trap had been tripped, and every overhead bucket was emptied of its contents. He chuckled to himself, visualizing the scene. Then, he heard laughter behind him.

He wheeled around and found himself face-to-face with both Winston and Kingston. Had they grown bigger and more muscular since he'd last seen them? Lewis gulped. They laughed again, seeing the expression on their little brother's face. Their laughter sounded like tumbled rocks, mean and gritty and rough.

"Heyyy! Big bros!" Lewis said, slapping a huge fake smile on his face. "I missed you guys!" For one tiny split second, he actually meant it. They were family after all, and a small part of him *had* missed them. He pointed over his shoulder toward his messy bedroom. "I, uh, see you found my little experiment."

"Experiment, huh?" Winston narrowed his eyes. "We found it all right."

"And you better believe you're gonna pay for it." From behind his back, Kingston produced a lacrosse stick. He smacked it against his palm. Beside him, Winston cracked his knuckles.

"Guys, chill," Lewis said, stepping away from them. "It was just a harmless prank. It was supposed to be funny." Except his brothers didn't look amused. At all. Lewis's pulse began to race. He was fast, but his brothers were bigger and stronger, and they were blocking his only escape route. Plus, King had a lacrosse stick in his hand, whereas Lewis had a pair of scuffed-up drumsticks. Not exactly an even match.

Winston shoved Lewis. He stumbled backward and landed with a *thump*. And a *squish*. And a *splat*. Ugh. He was now the victim of his own prank, sitting in a pile of shaving cream. Fantastic. A little cloud of glitter puffed up into the air, making him cough.

"Not so funny now, is it?" Kingston jeered, wielding his lacrosse stick, ready to give Lewis a whack. Lewis reached for his drumsticks, which he'd dropped when he fell, and defensively raised one up, pointing it at his brothers like a magic wand. "Leave me alone!" he shouted.

Compared to the lacrosse stick, the old drumstick looked like a dinky twig. But something hummed through the wood, sending a vibration from his fingers, into his wrist, and all the way through the length of his arm. It was similar to the sensation he'd felt when they played music in that abandoned band room on Other-Earth. When they'd somehow opened up a portal into another dimension and found a pathway that (thankfully and miraculously) led home.

Lewis's lips quirked into a smile. He wondered with tingling curiosity if he could do it again. But before he could drum a single beat on the overturned garbage can nearby, Winston lunged at him. Reflexively, Lewis thrust the drumstick upward to block the strike.

Heat surged through his hand and an arc of blinding light burst from the tip of the drumstick. The strength of it sent his brothers reeling back, their faces stunned. Winston shook his head, clearly rattled, but charged forward again, mad as a bull.

Lewis took aim with his drumstick again, firing another arc of light at them. It created a field of energy so powerful that it pinned his brothers against the hallway wall. They struggled and kicked their legs but were unable to move.

"Stay!" Lewis commanded, as though his brothers were a duo of rowdy dogs. He rose to his feet and held the drumstick steady, keeping it aimed at Win and King until he was safely down the hall and out of reach. His brothers' mouths gaped open in shock.

As soon as Lewis lowered the drumstick, the force field dissolved and his brothers slumped to the floor.

"Mommy!" Kingston whimpered. He and Winston were uninjured but rattled and a little delirious.

Lewis, on the other hand, was practically vibrating with excitement. He ran down the hall to one of their many guest bedrooms, locking the door behind him. He sat on the bed and tried to catch his breath. Less than an hour ago, he'd felt a cavernous disappointment. His homecoming had been a total bust, and it seemed like their adventures in the multiverse had been for nothing.

He stared at his drumsticks and then over at the clock on the bedside table. Tomorrow morning couldn't come soon enough. He couldn't wait to see his friends and tell them what had occurred. Something told him their adventure was just beginning.

Across town, Isaiah Yoon opened the door to his apartment and found his mother curled up, asleep on the couch.

"Mom?" he said softly.

She awoke with a start. "Isaiah!" She leaped to her feet and rushed over to him. "Are you okay? I was so worried. I had the most awful feeling the entire time you were gone. Why wouldn't you tell me you had agreed to a sleep study?" She hugged him hard.

He hugged her back, then pulled away. "It was a spur-of-the-moment sort of thing."

"I thought guardian approval was required for extra-curriculars? Especially overnight activities." She frowned, studying him. "Are you okay? You don't look like you slept a wink. You've got bags under your eyes, you smell awful, and your clothes are—"

"Mom! Stop," he snapped. "Please. You're fussing over me too much!"

She looked hurt. "That's my job, Isaiah. I'm your mother; I worry because I love you." She crossed her arms over her chest.

"I know," he said, feeling bad. "And I love you, too. But I'm not a little boy anymore. I'm not a baby." Inside, he was thinking, *I even have superpowers!*

"Well, you'll always be my baby, so you'll just have to deal with my fussing." She lowered her eyes. A single tear rolled down her cheek. "You're all I have left, Isaiah."

"Aw, Mom. Please don't cry." He gave her another hug,

hating to see her upset. His heart sank, thinking how different this moment would be if Uncle Ming were with him, what a joyful reunion it would be. There would still be tears, but they'd be happy ones. He wanted to tell his mother that he'd been right all along: Ming wasn't dead, he'd just been lost in another dimension all this time. Lost in several dimensions, to be precise.

Ming had asked Isaiah to tell his mother that he loved her and missed her. That he had tried to return to Earth so that they could be together as a family again. Isaiah wanted to deliver that message so badly, to cheer her up and heal her wounded heart. But now that he was here in front of her, he couldn't bring himself to say anything. He knew it would hurt her too much.

There was also a good chance she wouldn't believe him. She'd call the grief counselor, or his doctor, worried her son was officially losing it. Isaiah didn't want to keep secrets from his mother, but he felt like he didn't have a choice.

"Hey, Mom?" He handed her a tissue. "You know what I really missed while I was gone? Other than you, of course."

"What's that?" she asked, drying her eyes.

"Your famous homemade noodles. The ones in that spicy sesame sauce."

Her face lit up. She marched to their small kitchenette, full of purpose. "Of course. I'll make you a bowl right now. Why don't you take a shower while I cook?"

"Okay. Thanks, Mom."

Outside, the sky grew darker and a fierce wind shook orange and yellow leaves from the trees. For a brief moment, Isaiah worried the smogmonster had followed them through the Rip, but then he glanced at the temperature gauge mounted to the windowsill and realized this must be a shiver. It was only early October, but a flurry of snow began to swirl. He was glad to be inside their cozy apartment with a hot meal cooking on the stove.

"Isaiah, before you go shower, could you hand me the chilis? There's a jar in the fridge," his mother said, pulling a stock pot from the cupboard.

"Sure, no problem." He opened the fridge. The chilis were packed in oil in a glass jar on the top shelf, just out of reach. Without realizing it, his mind sort of took over, moving the jar for him, directing it through the air toward his outstretched fingers. His mother was busy filling the pot with water at the sink, her head turned away from him, but the second Isaiah understood what was happening, he inhaled sharply. His concentration broke and the jar of chilis shattered onto the floor, spicy red oil spilling across the vinyl floor.

His mom snapped her head around. "Isaiah! Are you all right? What happened?"

"I'm fine. It just slipped out of my hands. I'll clean it up. Sorry."

She frowned, a deep crease forming across her brow. "Try to be more careful next time."

"I will," he said, and he meant it.

In his bedroom later that night, out of sight from his mother, Isaiah practiced moving things with his mind. He still wasn't sure how he'd been able to release that sonic boom of energy back on Other-Earth, or move the jar of chilis without touching them, but he suspected that with the right amount of focus, he could probably lift a pencil off his desk using his thoughts alone.

He stared at the pencil. It rolled, then rose upward, hovering a few inches above the desk. He rotated it in the air. Elated, he tried to lower the pencil back down onto the desk. Instead, the pencil took off, whizzing across the room with the speed of an arrow released from a taut bow. Isaiah ducked as it flew past his head, nearly impaling his left ear. It finally came to an abrupt halt when it struck the bulletin board on his wall, lodging itself straight through the cork panel.

He pulled the pencil out of the wall and set it back on the desk, his breath shallow and unsteady. Instead of weakening with each trip across the Threshold, his abilities were definitely growing stronger. It was thrilling but also unsettling. And potentially dangerous. Especially if he couldn't learn to control them.

# CHAPTER IO

THE NEXT MORNING, DEV, LEWIS, MAEVE, ISAIAH, AND BOTH Hawthorne-Scott sisters gathered together on the steps outside the middle school's main entrance.

Lewis was breathless and fidgety. He had called an emergency meeting of the cadets. "I have to show you something!" he told them. "But it's top secret. This way."

"Class starts soon, Lewis. We can't be late," Zoey said, standing beside her sister. Isaiah squinted, regarding the twins, checking to make sure Tessa was Tessa and Zoey was Zoey. They'd pulled a clothes swap before the field trip, but this morning they looked like themselves again, which was a relief. The past few days had been confusing enough; the last thing anyone needed was another incident of mistaken identities.

"It won't take long!" Lewis assured them. "Come on." He led them past the bus loop and around the corner, behind a cluster of shrubs and tall bushes that hid them from view.

He retrieved his drumsticks from his backpack and waved them around mysteriously.

"Okay," Maeve said, yawning. She hadn't slept well the night before, and she was struggling to keep her eyes open. "You have our attention."

"Do I? Because you look like you're ready to participate in another sleep study." Lewis whacked his drumsticks loudly. "Wake up, Greene! I've got important stuff to show you."

"Get on with it already," Maeve grumbled, rubbing her ears. "The bell's gonna ring any minute."

Lewis looked from side to side, checking to make sure they weren't being watched. "Prepare to be amazed!" He aimed one of the drumsticks at a patch of grass and waited for the arc of light to leap out and zap the ground. Except . . . nothing happened.

"Aw, come on," he said, tapping the drumsticks together. He tried the other one. Still, nothing happened.

"What exactly are we supposed to be witnessing?" Tessa asked, checking her new eChron watch. Her mother had replaced her broken one with the latest model last night, and she'd been sending both girls sweet but cringeworthy mom-texts all morning, using slang from the last century, bizarre acronyms, and far too many emojis.

"Grrr," Lewis muttered. "I swear it worked last night. My brothers were trying to beat me up, so I blasted them with my drumstick!"

The others were silent.

"What?" Lewis scowled. "I know I joke around a lot, but I'm telling the truth. These are no ordinary drumsticks."

Dev patted Lewis's shoulder. "I believe you," he said. "I mean, think about what our instruments did back on that Other-Earth, ripping open an entire portal! What you described doesn't sound so farfetched to me."

Zoey looked at them incredulously.

"And sometimes powers are hard to summon on demand. Especially without training," Isaiah added, thinking of last night's flying pencil and levitating chilis.

"What do you mean by training?" Zoey asked. Even though she was their marching bandmate, she couldn't help but feel like the friendship dynamic of the group had shifted since they'd gone on that NASA field trip together. They had all these inside jokes and shared experiences now, and she struggled to relate.

Isaiah described the various incidents on Station Liminus, Other-Earth, and then again last night at his apartment. Telekinesis, premonitions, visions. He'd felled a tree in the Menagerie when the colossadon nearly devoured Maeve. He'd dislodged a piece of fruit in the Station's galley, causing a citrus avalanche and creating the perfect diversion for their escape from Scopes. There'd also been the sonic boom so powerful it had awoken the smogmonster. He'd never been this open with the others about the things he was experiencing, but he was tired of hiding it. Plus, he hoped his friends might be able to help him harness, or at least control, his burgeoning abilities better.

"So, your powers get a boost every time you cross into another dimension?" Zoey asked, still slightly skeptical. How could one of her best friends have changed so drastically in a matter of days? The only transformation she'd experienced over the weekend was the appearance of an unwelcome zit on her forehead.

"It seems like it," Isaiah replied with a shrug. "I also puke my brains out after each trip, which is a lot less fun than getting superpowers."

Dev tapped his chin. "Maybe something similar happened with our instruments? Like an amplification of power."

"Which would explain Lewis's drumstick incident," Maeve said, secretly wondering what her oboe might be capable of now.

"Exactly!" Lewis said, annoyed he couldn't summon the drumsticks' awesome arc of light but glad that his friends believed him. "Maybe it's a sign or something." He slid the drumsticks safely into his bag.

"A sign that you should get a drum solo during regional championships?" Zoey asked with a smirk.

Lewis shook his head. "No. Although I would totally rock a solo." He performed some killer air-drum and head-banging moves. When he stopped, he said, "What I mean is, maybe it's a sign that we need to go back."

"Go back?" Maeve perked up. "Go back . . . where exactly?"

Lewis ran his hands through his sandy-colored hair. His jade-green eyes shone. "I'm not sure. Station Liminus, maybe? It just feels like we have a lot of . . . unfinished business."

"I get it," Tessa replied, touching up her makeup with a small compact mirror.

Zoey's jaw dropped. "Listen, maybe you five don't realize what those of us back on Earth went through trying to get you home. But it was a lot. And now you want to leave again?" She faced Tessa squarely. "You really want to put Mom and Dad through that kind of stress, just so you can have another wild adventure?"

Tessa snapped the compact closed. "It's not just about the adventure," she replied. "There's a lot more to it. The Empyrean One is still out there. The Multiverse Allied Council might've agreed to help our planet with some temporary measures, but we're not in the clear yet. Not by a long shot. Lewis might be right." She turned and looked at him. "Maybe this *is* a sign."

Zoey scoffed. "I believe in science, not signs."

"Me too," Dev said. "At least I used to. The thing is, the multiverse doesn't always work the way we think it will, or the way science tells us it should. It's more complex, more layered, more . . ."

"More weird," Lewis added. "Super-duper-extra weird."

Isaiah nodded. "The weirdest."

"Right," Dev continued. "It's weirder and more wonderful than any of us ever expected."

"And we've only seen a fraction of what's out there." Isaiah was relieved that he wasn't the only one struggling with their return to Earth.

"I know what you mean," Maeve said wistfully. She'd

had a rough time last night. When she and Gramps returned home from dinner at Teeny's, they discovered her mother passed out on the couch, the pungent smell of alcohol on her breath. Maeve and Gramps exchanged concerned looks, but they both knew better than to wake her up in a state like that. Maeve slipped into her bedroom as quietly as possible and sank down onto her bed. Clutching an old teddy bear to her chest, she couldn't help but wish for an escape from her life, even one that might be slightly perilous.

"Think about how much more is left to discover," Isaiah continued. "How much is left to explore." He recounted the Empyrean One's nefarious plans, the darkness and pain she planned to inflict. "Sure, Ignatia and the other council members assured us that the MAC would find Scopes, stop the Empyrean One, and bring them all to justice. But what if they can't? What if they need a little extra help?"

"You're all officially out of your minds!" Zoey practically shouted. "I cannot believe you're talking like this. You've been home for a day, and you want to leave again?"

"Not necessarily. It's just hard, okay?" Lewis sighed. "How can anyone expect me to do pointless stuff like algebra homework when there's a super evil baddie on the loose somewhere out there!" He gestured to the sky, flailing his arms.

The bell rang. The cadets ducked out from behind their hiding spot between the shrubs.

"Lew's right," Dev said, joining the crowds of students heading toward the school's main entrance. "Compared to everything we've been through, homework, quizzes, even bullies like Gage feel small and insignificant right now."

"Hey, band geeks!" a voice boomed. A shadow fell across their path. Dev looked up and found himself face-to-face with Gage Rawley, his lips pulled into a cruel sneer. "Who're you calling small?"

# CHAPTER 11

EM LEFT THE OLD WOMAN'S HUT BEFORE DAWN. SHE FOLDED the blanket, placed it on the pallet, and set a single Empyrean coin on the pillow as a small token of thanks. Of course, the currency had no value here on Earth, but she felt as though she should leave the woman something, even though she knew the woman expected nothing in return.

As she walked back toward the city center, Em realized she'd never asked the woman's name, nor had she shared her own. Maybe that was for the better. Becoming too attached to this dim and its inhabitants wouldn't serve her well.

Em wandered along the road, grateful that the blizzard had passed and the effects of the shiver were long gone; a beautiful autumn day had taken its place. She walked for a while, enjoying the feeling of the sun on her face. It was such a bright, cheerful ball of gas, not a blazing inferno of death, like the suns in so many other dimensions.

She approached a bustling row of stores where she hoped she might locate the cadets. She passed a bakery, and the smells of fresh-from-the-oven pastries wafting out the open windows made her mouth water. A small child exited the shop with his father, clutching a buttery croissant. It would be so deliciously easy for Em to snatch the croissant from the little boy's unsuspecting hands, especially with her pixelator hoodie rendering her invisible. Before yesterday, this would have been a simple choice. Grab the goods and go. Don't think twice, don't act nice. But she couldn't bring herself to steal from the boy.

She carried on, chastising herself for being so weak, so soft. She was glad her aunt wasn't around to witness this failure. She'd need to toughen up a little if she was going to pull off her plan. She had to locate her doppelganger, obtain the special Earthling instruments, then learn to master their portal-cleaving powers.

She searched back roads and alleys, shops and parks. Her feet began to ache and her stomach rumbled. There was no sign of the cadets anywhere, but luckily a delicatessen had a display out front with free samples. She grabbed a few handfuls of cubed meats and cheeses, grateful for the sustenance, then stopped by a public fountain for a quick drink.

The farther she walked, the warmer the day became. By the time she neared the city's central plaza, Em was sweating. Without thinking, she unzipped her hoodie and tied it around her waist. A minute or two later, a gentleman stopped and looked at her curiously.

"Excuse me, young lady, why aren't you in school?" he asked.

Em froze in her tracks, realizing her mistake too late. She couldn't put the hoodie back on now. She'd have to improvise.

"Why aren't you in school?" the man pressed, more concerned than angry.

Em paused. Why wasn't she in school? She'd had an education on her home dim of course—mixed multiverse martial arts, advanced weaponry, strategic deceptions, along with basic language and mathematics lessons taught by private tutors over the years—but she'd never been allowed to go to a community school with her peers. Aside from combat class, she rarely interacted with kids her age. Being the niece of the Empyrean One afforded certain privileges but also came with costs. Aside from her aunt's impossibly high expectations, loneliness was chief among the downsides.

"School?" Em repeated, realizing the man was waiting for her to reply.

He nodded. "Yes, every child your age is required to be in school five days a week."

"Every kid?" Em asked, an idea developing.

"Unless you qualify for a health exemption, or you're homeschooled, in which case there are slightly different requirements." The man wore a tweed blazer and brown slacks and carried a briefcase with the words *Conroy Department of Education* embossed on the front.

"Right, of course. I go to school," Em replied. "I just had an, um, appointment downtown. But I'm headed back now. Except . . . I'm a little lost. Could you help me find my way there?"

The man looked perplexed. "Where is your mother, or your father?"

"Oh, they passed away when I was small," she said with a sad sigh.

"Goodness, how terrible." His expression softened. "And you don't have a guardian who could bring you back to school this morning?"

She shook her head. "No. I'm on my own today," she said, which wasn't a lie, but she made her eyes extra wide and weepy for added impact, a trick she'd learned in her strategic deception class.

He stood upright and inhaled sharply. "Then I will help you. It's a ten-minute walk from here, but I have some time before my next appointment. This way."

"Thank you!" she said, surprised yet again by the kindness of an Earthling stranger. And glad to be one step closer to finding the cadets.

# CHAPTER 12

**"I SAID, WHO'RE YOU CALLING SMALL?" GAGE SNEERED, STARING** down at Dev in the school's main lobby. A crowd gathered, sensing a fight.

"He also called you insignificant," Lewis chimed in.

Dev shot Lewis a look. "Not helping, Wynner."

Lewis made a face, then moonwalked backward. "Sorry, my bad."

Gage snorted with disgust. "You and your corny friends are so pathetic."

"Cut it out, Rawley," Dev replied, puffing his chest a little. He'd never stood up to bullies like Gage before, but he wasn't the same kid he'd been a few days earlier. His trip through the multiverse had changed him.

"Nah, I don't think I will. It's too fun. You band geeks are such easy targets," Gage snickered. Some of the other middle schoolers in the crowd laughed.

"I said, cut it out," Dev replied, his voice growing louder.

Gage shifted his weight back and forth, sizing Dev up, who was several inches shorter. "What're you gonna do about it, freak?" Gage spat. "Freak! FREAK!" he chanted.

"Take it back," Dev shouted.

"Make me."

Dev raised an eyebrow. His pulse was racing, but he refused to back down. He turned to Lewis. "That sound like a challenge to you?"

Lewis nodded, surprised to see his buddy act so boldly.

"That's what I thought." Dev turned and leveled a look at Gage. "Okay. But remember, you asked for it." He pulled his saxophone from its case, lifted it to his lips, and gave a tremendous *BLERK!*

Gage stared, dumbstruck. Then he burst into laughter. He doubled over, slapped his knee, laughing so hard he began to wheeze. "I can't. I can't even take it. You're such a dork!" The crowd around them began to snicker and chuckle. "Who does that?" Gage imitated Dev, playing a pretend sax, making loud farting noises with his mouth.

Everyone was laughing now.

Dev's face flushed with embarrassment. After Lewis's story this morning, he had expected the saxophone to do something a little more impressive than blast a pitchy E-note. This was beyond mortifying.

The second bell rang and the crowd dispersed. Gage was still laughing, joined by his sidekicks, Thaddeus and Lee. "Good luck recovering from that one, loser," he called to Dev as he sauntered away.

Dev hung his head in shame.

Lewis came to his side. "Hey, it's not that bad."

Dev looked up, angry. "Precisely. It's not bad. It's the worst. I'll never live that down. Why did you even tell us that stupid story about your drumsticks? I never should have believed you!"

Lewis's jaw dropped. "Hey man, that was your call. If you want to stick up for yourself, that's great. But you have to deal with the consequences. Don't put that on me." He turned to leave. "And for the record, I was telling the truth."

"Sure, whatever," Dev called after him, power walking to his first period class in the science lab as fast as possible.

"What happened back there?" Maeve asked, hurrying to catch up with Dev.

Dev grumbled. "You witnessed it, didn't you? I don't really want to recap the whole thing."

He steered around a clump of seventh graders from the soccer team. As he passed, they started playing pretend saxophones.

*Bleert! Fronkk! Plarff!*

Even a bunch of eighth graders got in on the action, mocking him.

Dev kept his head down and tried to ignore them, but he couldn't stop his face from turning beet red. He wanted to crawl under a rock and hide. Or slip away into some alternate dimension and escape the incessant teasing. He'd thought Other-Earth was a crummy place to be, but middle school was turning out to be pretty apocalyptic, too.

"I mean, what did you expect to do?" Maeve asked once they were alone in the hallway. "Sonic blast Gage with your sax? In front of the whole school?"

Dev paused. When she put it like that, it did sound pretty stupid. He groaned.

"What about discretion?" Maeve said, repeating the word Mayor Hawthorne had used yesterday. "We're supposed to keep a low profile ... then you go and do that? What if the saxophone *had* worked? What if everyone saw?"

Dev threw his hands up. "I don't know, Maeve. I guess I wasn't really thinking clearly. I was just tired of being bullied. I thought I'd changed. I thought I was stronger. But maybe the rules of the multiverse don't apply to middle school after all. Maybe I was better off being quiet and keeping to myself."

She shook her head. "No. I'm glad you stood up to him. That takes guts. He can't treat you, or any of us, like that. Though maybe ignoring him is the best retaliation. Next time, don't give him the satisfaction of seeing you sweat, you know? At least that's what Gramps always tells me about bullies."

Dev considered this. "Maybe you're right."

Maeve smiled haughtily. "Not maybe. I *am* right." She opened the lab door. "Now come on, before we're officially late for class."

"Here we are," the man from the CDE said, stopping on the sidewalk beside a maple tree.

The Conroy Middle School rose up in front of them. Em looked around, taking in the sights, trying to press the route they'd taken into her memory so she wouldn't get lost again. "Thanks," she said, moving toward the front entrance.

"Happy to help," the man said. He sounded like he truly meant it, too. He waved as he departed, leaving her alone once more.

Em paused beneath the maple tree, surprised to see the tree's leaves ablaze with autumn hues of orange, gold, and crimson. In spite of the holes her aunt's squad had punctured in this dim's ozone and crust, nature proved resilient. Beautiful, even. This place was nothing like she'd been led to believe.

The middle school itself closely resembled the school structure from Other-Earth, though this one was more colorful and vibrant. There were ivy-covered brick walls and bluestone steps. No shattered glass or crumbling concrete to be found. The building was a hive of activity, full of teachers and students. Through the windows, Em could see rows of shiny metal lockers and a large painted mural. A cartoon astronaut—presumably the school's Space Cadet mascot—floated in the center of the mural, with a speech bubble that said, *Welcome!*

Em inhaled deeply and walked up the front steps, fighting off a wave of first-day-of-school jitters. Her toes and fingertips tingled as she recalled her education on Dim8—the grueling physical challenges, the mind games and manipulations her tutor subjected her to—all in the name of sussing out weaknesses or shortcomings. She hesitated on the top step, second-guessing herself and her plan.

*Stop being ridiculous,* she scolded herself. Things here would be different. Based on her previous experiences so far on Dim14, everyone would be kind, warm, and helpful. She carefully zipped up her hoodie, then slipped inside the school unnoticed.

# CHAPTER 13

**AT LUNCH, THE CADETS GATHERED AT A ROUND TABLE IN THE** far corner of the cafeteria, safely away from Gage and all the other kids who seemed intent on making their lives miserable.

Dev approached Lewis. He'd simmered down since their fight in the hallway and he felt bad. "Hey," he said, trying to break the ice.

Lewis scrunched his nose and scowled as he took a bite of his food.

"I'm sorry I snapped at you," Dev went on.

Lewis shook his head. Dev's heart sank a little. For a second, he worried his friend might not forgive him. "Lew, I mean it . . . I . . ."

Lewis held up a hand. Then he gagged. He grabbed a paper napkin and spit a glob of partially chewed hamburger into it.

"Ewww!" Tessa leaned away. "You're disgusting!"

Lewis took a swig of milk. "Correction: *That's* disgusting." He pointed to his lunch tray, where a dubious patty of mystery meat rested between two stale buns. His mom had been too busy to pack him anything that morning, so he was stuck with the lunch lady's version of a UFO—an Unidentifiable Food Object. "And you—" He glanced up at Dev, then down at the paper bag in Dev's hand. "You are forgiven. So long as you agree to share whatever goods you've got in there."

Relieved, Dev plopped down into the seat on Lewis's left. He dumped out the contents of his lunch. "Have at it," he said.

"A homemade samosa! Woohoo! Talk about an upgrade." Lewis did a little happy dance in his seat before grabbing the flaky triangular pastry wrapped in waxed paper. He bit into the flavorful potato and pea filling. "Mmm, this officially earns you BFF status," he mumbled to Dev between satisfied bites.

"Aww," Tessa cooed. "The band is officially back together again!"

Zoey looked up from her chicken Caesar salad. "Technically, Tessa, you're not even in the marching band, remember?" She was surprised that her sister had decided to join them for lunch. Tessa typically held court at the popular table, with Emerson, Blake, and the other cooler kids.

"She's an honorary member," Maeve said, reaching out and patting Tessa's hand.

Isaiah nodded in agreement. "We would've been seriously doomed if not for her voice."

Tessa gave her sister a smug wink. "See?"

Zoey jabbed her fork into her salad, spearing a crouton. "I never thought I'd see the day when you guys were friends."

"Hey, the multiverse is full of surprises," Lewis said. "Just like school lunch." He'd finished his half of Dev's food and now returned his attention to his lunch tray in search of something sweet. He peeled open a plastic cup of cubed fruit floating in a slightly gelatinous syrup. He dipped a spoon in and stirred it skeptically.

Something buzzed, followed by the unmistakable hum-crackle of a lightsaber.

Dev dug around in his pocket and retrieved his phone, quickly silencing the lightsaber alert sound. Students weren't supposed to use devices during school hours, but the cafeteria monitors never seemed to care if kids texted, gamed, or watched videos during lunch period.

Dev scanned the screen, his eyes widening. "Speaking of surprises. Look!" He held up his phone, displaying a message from someone saved in his contacts as *The Fathership*.

"Who's that?" Tessa asked, a smile tugging at her lips. "Your dad?"

"Uh, yeah." Dev blushed.

Tessa took a bite of her apple. "The nerd apple doesn't fall far from the nerd tree, I see."

Zoey jutted out her lower lip. "We're all nerds here, okay? Let's avoid calling each other names. We've already got Gage doing enough of that. Otherwise, you can go back and sit with your cooler friends, Tess."

"Chill out," said Tessa, irked by her sister's tone. "I was just joking around. Besides, when I say nerd, I say it with love."

"Love?" Dev squeaked, his voice rising an entire octave.

Maeve sighed, exasperated. "Can we please focus? We're getting off topic. What is this text all about?"

"Right," Dev said. He studied the phone, rereading the message. "My dad says that the NASA auditory lab just received an incoming message from the universal beta channel."

"The channel we tried to tap into with your potato-radio?" Isaiah asked.

"Exactly. The team is trying to decipher the message now, but he's sending it to us in case we can help make sense of it." He scrolled through the screen. "Huh. All it says is *S21*. Any ideas?"

Isaiah opened up his journal, scanning its pages for a clue. "Maybe it's a code of some sort? Or map coordinates?"

"A date? Or a time stamp?" Zoey offered.

"I've been hoping Ignatia or Duna might reach out. They said they'd be in contact eventually, once things settled down at Station Liminus. Maybe this is their way of communicating with us?" Dev glanced back at the screen.

His shoulders slumped. "Although it doesn't do us any good if we can't understand it."

Just then, the lunch bell rang.

"Let's reconvene after school," Maeve suggested, zipping up her lunchbox. "See if anyone can come up with something between now and then. And don't forget, we have band practice this afternoon. Four o'clock sharp at Baxter Field. Coach Diaz and the rest of our bandmates are counting on us."

"Aye aye, Captain!" Lewis said, doing a goofy version of their signature marching band salute before dumping the contents of his lunch tray into the nearest garbage can.

Zoey wiped her hands on a napkin. "I'll have to talk to Coach and see if he'll lend me a clarinet from the music supply room, at least until my parents can get me a new one." She shot her sister an irritated look. She knew Tessa hadn't *meant* to feed her instrument to some hungry spacebeast, but that didn't make the situation any less annoying. At the very least, she could have grabbed a supposedly superpowered replacement from that alternate Earth.

Maeve paused on her way out the cafeteria double doors, letting the other students stream past her. "That's a good point, actually. I don't think any of us should practice with those other instruments. Especially not in public," she said quietly to the cadets. "I'll see if we can all get some loaners from Coach Diaz. Just in case."

Isaiah nodded in agreement. He'd read enough comics and watched enough movies to know that objects of power could be extremely dangerous, especially if they fell into the wrong hands.

"Wait!" Lewis grinned mischievously. "Maybe *that's* how we can guarantee a win at regionals! We'll play the funky superpowered instruments, bust open a portal, and send our competition tumbling into some other dimension. Ha! Then we'd be declared champions by default. Pretty brilliant, don't ya think?"

Maeve's face was serious. "Victory should be based on merit, not mischief. I would think a Wynner like you would understand that," she replied, emphasizing his last name.

"Loosen up, Greene," he said, flashing his signature smile. "I promise not to blast anyone with my magic drumsticks anytime soon." He waited until his friends filed out of the cafeteria and headed toward their fifth period classes. Then, under his breath, he added, "Unless it's absolutely necessary..."

# CHAPTER 14

WITHIN MINUTES OF ENTERING THE SCHOOL, EM CAME UPON yet another scene of Earthling generosity and kindness. She watched as three girls about her age approached a shy-looking younger kid with a mop of frizzy brown curls and silver braces on her teeth.

"Hi, Beatrice!" they cooed in singsong voices. All three had hair dyed varying shades of honey and gold. They stood in the hallway, teetering in shoes with pointy heels.

Beatrice's face lit up. Clearly, these older girls held higher social positions than their younger counterpart. They radiated cool confidence, whereas the frizzy-haired girl reeked of self-doubt. Or perhaps she hadn't applied an adequate amount of deodorant? Still, without even sifting the girl's mind, it was clear to Em that Beatrice desperately wanted the approval and friendship of the other girls.

"Big news," one of the girls said to Beatrice in a

conspiring tone. "I heard Thaddeus likes you. Like, he like-likes you. Like, a lot."

Em tapped the pale blue translator crystal that hung from a thin silver chain around her neck. The crystal allowed her to speak and understand the myriad languages and dialects of the multiverse, but she wondered if it was perhaps glitching. Surely the girl hadn't meant to use the word *like* quite so many times?

"Really?" Beatrice swooned, giving Em the impression that this Thaddeus character was a highly desirable mate.

"Yaas!" another girl said, her glossy pink lips curling into a smile. "He's going to ask you out. He wants you to be his girlfriend."

"You're soooo lucky, Bea. He's the hottest guy in your grade!"

"And one of the most popular, too," the first girl added.

Beatrice squealed. The sound was painfully high-pitched, rivaling the training whistle Em had used to call off the dragomander. "You're sure? He likes *me*?"

"Totes. One hundred percent."

Beatrice had a faraway look in her eyes. "I always knew he was my soul mate."

The shorter of the three girls snorted, or coughed perhaps, then regained her composure. "He wants you to meet him behind the bleachers after school today."

"Oh-em-gee. Oh-em-gee." Beatrice was nearly hyperventilating now, flapping her hands and repeating some odd phrase that seemed to contain Em's name. Em tapped her translator. She'd have to trade it in for a new one at the nearest interdimensional trading post as soon as she got out of Conroy.

"Cool," the tallest of the three girls said, flipping her golden mane over her shoulder. "I'm so glad we could play matchmaker."

"Thank you! Oh, thank you!" Beatrice gushed.

"Our pleasure, really." The tall girl turned and winked wickedly at her friends.

Em, who had watched the whole scene unfold hidden from view thanks to her hoodie, suddenly understood with a lurch of her stomach that these girls were not being friendly at all. They were not trying to help poor Beatrice unite with Thaddeus. A quick sift of the girls' minds revealed an unkind plan to humiliate innocent Bea. Thaddeus would not be waiting for her behind the bleachers, as they'd promised. Dozens of other kids would be there though, all of them ready to laugh at lovestruck, gullible Bea.

Em's idyllic image of Earthlings popped like a balloon. Compared to her aunt's devious schemes and war-games, this petty plot wasn't *that* terrible. Still, it bothered Em. Especially since she had begun to trust Earthlings, just a little. On Dim8, kids fought each other all the time. Essential Combat was typically the first class of year six training. At least that fighting was fair. Face-to-face. Or, fist-to-face, if you were doing it right. Going behind someone's back to inflict pain? That felt worse somehow. More cowardly, but also crueler. It didn't sit well with Em at all, but it did give her an idea.

Later that afternoon at the end of the eighth-grade lunch period, Em snuck up behind the three mean girls. Just as the tallest one leaned over a garbage can to throw out the remains of her lunch, Em delivered a quick but forceful shove to her back. The girl toppled, headfirst, into the smelly trash. She screamed and kicked her legs wildly.

"Help!" she shrieked hysterically.

One of her friends tried to pull her out, but she slipped on the banana peel that Em had placed strategically on the floor just beneath her pointy heel. She fell to the floor with a loud *smack!*

The third friend hurried to help her up, but she tripped over the chair that Em slid in front of her path. The girl tumbled, tipped over the garbage can (with her friend still inside), and crashed into a nearby table containing plastic utensils and an assortment of condiments. Spoons and forks flew into the air. Glops of ketchup splattered like blood across her face and shirt.

There was a brief moment of total, dumbstruck silence before the cafeteria erupted with raucous laughter. *Good,* Em thought with a satisfied smile on her face, feeling as though some small bit of justice had been restored.

Em was halfway down the hallway, recommencing her search for Maeve, when she noticed the smear of ketchup on the sleeve of her hoodie. She tried to wipe it away, but the stain refused to budge. She slipped into the nearest bathroom, unzipped the hoodie, and attempted to wash the sleeve in the sink. She scrubbed and scrubbed until the pixelated fabric was clean and the rest was (unfortunately) drenched.

She was about to wring out the excess water and dry it beneath the hand dryer mounted on the wall when she heard a toilet flush. A stall door opened and a round-faced, ginger-haired boy appeared. He stared at her. She froze, realizing she was no longer invisible.

"Uhh, what are you doing in here?" he asked, stepping around her to wash his hands. "Don't you know this is the boys' bathroom?"

"It is?" She gave an awkward shrug. "I must have been confused."

The boy eyed her in the mirror. "What are you wearing? Please tell me that's not our new band uniform. I know Zoey was going to talk to her sister about redesigning our look for regionals, but that's..." His lips mashed together. "An interesting choice?"

Em looked down. Beneath her hoodie, she wore a set of standard-issue Empyrean zilks, a form of full-body armor made from arcanium mesh, a lightweight, flexible, and incredibly strong alloy. These particular zilks were onyx and rust-colored, with rows of obsidian buttons along the sides. Neither the old woman nor the man from the CDE had mentioned her unusual attire, but here in middle school, the outfit stuck out like a sore thumb.

"Oh, this old thing?" Em forced a laugh. "This is just a costume. For an, um . . ." She racked her brains. "For a pageant. Yeah, I'm entering a pageant," she said, remembering the spectacle she'd watched the day before where kids wore all sorts of odd ensembles.

The boy raised his eyebrows. "Okay, whatever you say, Maeve." He moved toward the door.

"Wait!" She stepped in front of him. "You know Maeve? I mean, you know me?"

He raised his eyebrows even higher. "Are you feeling okay? Is this some sort of joke? Or a skit, or a prank or something?" Em just stared blankly back. "Of course I know you," he said. "I'm Nolan. I play tuba in band. With you. You're the drum major, remember?"

Em shrugged nonchalantly, trying her best to play along. "Of course I knew that!" She slapped his shoulder playfully. "I'm only teasing you, Nelson!"

His forehead wrinkled. "Nolan."

"Ha!" She fired finger guns at him. "Just keeping you on your toes."

He opened the door, shaking his head. "I gotta get to class," he mumbled, like the whole situation was weirding him out. "And you should probably get out of the boys' bathroom."

She returned to the sink and gathered up her hoodie,

which was still uncomfortably wet. She didn't want to waste any more time in the boys' bathroom, so she ducked down the hall as stealthily as possible. A moment later, she came face-to-face with Beatrice.

"Bea!" she said, as though they were old friends. "I need your help."

Beatrice didn't seem to know who she was, or who Maeve was, rather, but she smiled just the same.

"Where might I find a proper uniform?" Em asked, remembering that Nolan had mentioned band uniforms.

"A uniform?" Bea replied, scratching her head. "The gym, I guess?"

"The gym! Yes." Em bit her lip. "And where might that be?"

Bea gave her an odd look and pointed down the hall.

"Many thanks! I owe you one." Em paused, recalling the scene in the cafeteria, the way the tall girl's legs had looked flailing from the top of the smelly garbage can. Em could barely suppress a laugh. "Actually, you sort of owe me one. Though let's not keep score." Em turned to go, then wheeled back around again. "Oh, and Bea?"

"Yeah?"

"Don't go to the bleachers after school today. I promise you, no good will come of it. Thaddeus is not your soul mate. And those girls are most definitely not your friends."

Beatrice gaped.

"Trust me," Em hollered over her shoulder, with pep in her step, feeling as though she was slowly getting the hang of this Earthling world.

# CHAPTER 15

**ALL AFTERNOON, THE CADETS PUZZLED OVER THE STRANGE** message Dr. Khatri's team at NASA had received. Isaiah could barely pay attention to his history or math lessons, fixating instead on cracking the code. However, no matter how much he wrestled with various ideas, nothing made sense. He'd felt like this before—when Uncle Ming had sent him all those cryptic notes prior to going missing. Everyone dismissed the messages, claiming Ming's mind and spirit were deteriorating, but Isaiah knew better. And he'd been right!

Ming had been onto something big, mapping the drilling sites that were secretly being controlled by the Empyrean One, thanks to double agents like Dr. Scopes. Isaiah slunk lower in his seat as Mrs. Minuzzi droned on and on at the front of the classroom. General Shro had been apprehended on Station Liminus, but Scopes was still at large, shape-shifting into who knew what identity and slipping out of their grasp. He hadn't been able to solve Ming's messages back then because he didn't have the right cipher, and Isaiah couldn't help but wonder if maybe there was some missing key to their current conundrum.

"Isaiah? Ahem, Mr. Yoon?"

He snapped his head up, suddenly aware that someone was calling his name. "Yes?" he asked, his voice garbled.

"Could you read to us from page seven-twenty-one?" Mrs. Minuzzi asked.

Isaiah's heart jumped in his chest. "Did you say S21?"

Across the room, Dev perked up.

Mrs. Minuzzi shook her head and rapped a knuckle against the smartboard. "No. Page seven hundred and twenty-one, please."

"Okay." Isaiah sighed. For a moment, he thought maybe his history textbook contained an important clue. He flipped to the designated page. He was about to begin reading when the final bell of the day rang.

"Saved by the bell, it seems, Mr. Yoon," Mrs. Minuzzi said, straightening her floral cardigan. "We'll pick up where we left off tomorrow. Have a nice afternoon, everyone!" she called out.

Isaiah slammed the thick textbook closed and grabbed his backpack, eager to check in with the others and see if they'd had better luck cracking the NASA code.

Em made her way toward the gymnasium, careful to avoid any other students or teachers. There had been a gymnasium in the other dimension, too, with a warped wooden floor and basketball hoops dangling crookedly from the walls. In contrast, this gym was illuminated with bright lights. The polished floors shone. A cart of cones and orange balls stood in one corner. A large scoreboard hung above the center of the court. Squishy blue mats were folded and stacked in another corner. Adjacent to the gym, Em discovered smaller rooms for changing and showering. This time, she made sure to enter the door marked *Girls' Locker Room*.

Inside, there were wooden benches and rows of small lockers, painted green and yellow. There was a bulletin board on the wall with information about tryouts, game schedules, and equipment swaps. Em searched until she found a bin labeled *Uniforms*.

She rummaged around inside and pulled out a pair of emerald green mesh shorts. Next, she found a tank top with a cartoon astronaut on the front dunking a planet-shaped basketball into a net. The words *Conroy Cadets* were printed across the top in blocky letters. On the back was a large number *8*. Dim8 was her home dimension, so this felt like an auspicious sign. Em yanked off her zilks—including her heavy boots—and stuffed everything into an open locker. She pulled on the shorts and top.

There were a few pairs of sneakers lined up under the bench that seemed available for the taking, so she tried some on until she found a pair that fit. She glanced at herself in the mirror. She realized she was more vulnerable without her spear-proof zilks, but she felt this risk was worth taking, in case anyone else happened to spot her without her hoodie. Speaking of which . . .

She grabbed the damp garment and walked over to the nearest hand dryer. She was about to press the button for hot air when a woman dressed in a striped tracksuit entered the room. Her name, Coach Northside, was embroidered on the pocket.

She looked Em up and down. "Maeve Greene? Going out for basketball?"

Em nodded, unsure what to say.

"Does Coach Diaz know about this?"

Em cleared her throat. "Coach Diaz?"

"Yes, Coach Diaz. He's in charge of the marching band." She searched Em's face. "I thought you had band practice after school most days, but if you can juggle the two activities, we'd love to have you on the team."

"Really?" Em said, feeling something stir in her chest. No one had ever invited her to join a team before. She often suspected that the kids at her training facility on Dim8 hung out with her merely because she was the niece of the Empyrean One. No one would dare bully or exclude her for fear of her aunt's wrath. But this whole be-part-of-our-team thing? That sense of belonging was highly appealing.

Em quickly shook the feeling away. What was she doing? She cursed herself for getting so sidetracked. She needed to execute her plan without any further distractions. Otherwise, *she'd* be on the receiving end of her aunt's wrath.

"Tryouts start in forty-five minutes, Greene," Coach Northside said, grabbing a whistle from the hook on the wall and a clipboard from her desk. "Hope to see you out there!" she added before leaving the locker room.

# CHAPTER 16

"I CAN'T THINK ON AN EMPTY STOMACH," LEWIS SAID TO THE cadets, who'd gathered together after school to swap notes. Unfortunately, no one could make sense of the S21 message, and Dev's father hadn't received any additional information or transmissions from the auditory lab. At this point, the message seemed like an anomaly, or a dead end. "If I'm going to help you guys crack this code, I'm going to need a bag of chips first. Maybe two."

"You'll be late for marching band practice if you go all the way back to the cafeteria now," Maeve scolded.

"I'm not going back to the caf, Miss Punctuality," Lewis snipped back. "There's a vending machine at the end of the hall. Right outside the band room."

Zoey's forehead scrunched up. "There is? I don't remember seeing one there. I'm on the student council, and I'm pretty sure the concessions committee would have let me know about new snack options on campus."

Lewis shrugged. "They just installed it today. I saw a team of burly guys wheel it in this afternoon when I was taking the scenic route to class."

"The scenic route?" Tessa asked, adjusting her messenger bag over her shoulder.

"Fine. I was wandering the halls to kill time and avoid Mr. Phipps's super boring lecture on integers," Lewis replied. "Look. There it is." He jogged over to a vending machine at the end of the hall.

It was the size of a portly refrigerator, made of metal and glass and painted with cheerful primary colors.

"See?" Lewis said, digging in his pockets for money. "Told ya."

"All right, no need to gloat," Maeve said. "You get your snacks, and we'll go pick up the loaner instruments from Coach Diaz. He said he was going to leave them in the music department's storage closet."

"Sure, sounds good," Lewis replied, barely paying attention. His stomach rumbled loudly.

"What a weird place to install a vending machine," Zoey said, looking around. "Hardly anyone passes by this area."

"Except for us band members," Dev said.

"It'll be a struggle to move inventory," Zoey added, making a mental note to bring the issue up at the next student council meeting. They'd recently struck an agreement with Principal Brant that directed all vending machine profits to the student council activity fund. She needed to make sure they were optimizing their fundraising efforts, especially if they wanted to plan a truly epic Winter Snow Ball.

"I wouldn't worry about moving inventory," Tessa said to her sister. "Especially now that Lewis knows about it. I predict he'll empty it out before the end of the week."

Lewis pulled a few bills from his thick wad of *sorry we're too busy to hang out with you* money. He stood in front of the vending machine, weighing his options. Popcorn? Barbeque-flavored chips? Pretzels? Chocolate-dipped granola bar? All of the above?

Then something shiny caught his eye. It was lodged in one of the spiral dispensers, in the upper right corner. It was a little larger than a tin of mints, without any discernable label.

"What kind of snack is that?" he wondered aloud, though no one heard him. The others had moved on down the hall, swapping their Other-Earth instruments for the loaners Coach Diaz had left in the storage closet. Lewis squinted through the glass at the shiny object. Upon closer inspection, it didn't look like it belonged in the vending machine at all. Maybe the delivery guys had left it behind accidentally?

He slid a few dollar bills into the vending machine, then inspected the keypad. "Let's see ... Letter S ... Number 21." He froze, his index finger inches from the keys, a lightbulb suddenly illuminating inside his brain. "Holy hot dogs!" he shouted. "Dudes! Get back here!" He waved his arms frantically and jumped up and down.

Isaiah poked his head out of the storage closet. "Lew looks pretty excited about those potato chips," he said to Dev, who was standing beside him, reaching for his new saxophone.

"Typical," Maeve sighed.

"I cracked the code!" Lewis hollered.

They all stared at one another, grabbed their new instrument cases, and ran toward the vending machine.

"Check it out!" Lewis said breathlessly when they arrived. He pointed to the rows of snacks behind the glass.

Maeve huffed. "Way to get our hopes up! You really think Ignatia sent us the location of highly processed cheesy puffs?" Then she noticed a small sign along the top of the machine that read *Station Snaximus*. Hmm. That *was* an odd coincidence.

"I'm serious," Lewis said. "Look." He punched the keypad. "S21." The spiraled metal wire spun. The silver object dropped into the catch bin. Lewis reached his hand inside and retrieved it. It was cold to the touch. He turned it over in his palms. Embossed on the front was an unmistakable thirteen-sided symbol—the MAC logo.

Isaiah's mouth hung open. "No. Way."

"Told ya so." Lewis grinned. "Can I gloat now, or what?" He shot Maeve a teasing look.

Maeve tried her best not to seem too impressed, but she was pretty astounded. "We still don't know what's inside."

"Exactly. Open it!" Tessa said impatiently.

During their final moments on Station Liminus, prior to departing through the glitchy portal in Gate Hall, Ignatia and Duna had promised to remain in contact once the cadets returned to Earth. The kids had been so preoccupied with getting home that none of them had given much thought to what this communication might look like or how it would operate. The cryptic code from Dr. Khatri's team of scientists seemed like a piece of the puzzle, but it was hard to know for sure. Now they all felt certain this had been sent for them to find. Which meant their work at Station Liminus wasn't over just yet.

"I bet it's a comm device," Isaiah said, his voice uncharacteristically giddy.

Lewis hopped around excitedly, unable to contain his energy. "I hope it's one of those snazzy circular glass lynks that Duna had. My big brothers will be soooo jealous if I get an alien smart phone before they do. Ha ha, suckers!"

"Maybe it's one of those blue translator crystals that delegates wear around their necks. Those were beautiful," Tessa added. "And super functional."

"Dev, you should open it," Lewis said. "Since your dad's the one who forwarded us the S21 message."

"Okay." He swallowed, his hands shaking a little.

The cadets held their breath as Dev opened the case.

Lewis leaned over to get a better view. "Huh?" He scratched his head.

Isaiah frowned. "Is that what I think it is?"

"Seriously?" Tessa muttered, equally mystified.

Dev carefully lifted the object from the case. It was red and yellow and ... plasticky. About four inches long, tapered at one end, with a circular hole on top and a few minuscule buttons along the bottom.

"A kazoo?" Lewis moaned. "You have got to be kidding me! Station Liminus has the best technology in the world—no, in the whole multiverse! They could literally invent anything: hoverdiscs, illumabeams, you name it! But instead of something epically awesome, the MAC sends us a dinky kazoo?" Lewis delivered a swift kick to the vending machine, stubbing his toe and yelping in pain.

"What are we supposed to do with it?" Zoey frowned.

"Isn't it obvious?" Lewis nudged Dev. "Yo, you wanna get in touch with me? No prob. Just hit me up on my kazoo, bro!" he said sarcastically.

The rest of them laughed. It did seem pretty ridiculous.

Maeve tried to hide her own disappointment. "If I learned anything from our recent adventures, it's that the multiverse is full of surprises. Things are rarely what they seem. So maybe there's more to this kazoo than meets the eye?"

"As in?" Zoey asked.

Maeve rocked back on her heels. "Maybe something that meets the ear?"

Dev lifted it to his lips and gave a loud, obnoxious honk.

They waited for something to happen, but nothing did. Dev honked again. The kazoo wheezed, sounding like an asthmatic goose.

"This feels like a bad repeat of this morning," Dev said, depressed. "Why would Ignatia send us a cheesy plastic noisemaker?"

"Maybe it's some sort of joke?" Zoey offered.

"It's a joke all right," Lewis grumbled. "Just not a very funny one. Can I see it?"

Dev shrugged and handed the kazoo over. Lewis tapped it a few times, twisted the nozzle at the top, and gave a little toot. This time, the kazoo sounded less like suffering water fowl and more like a magical flute.

*Do re mi fa sol la ti do!* The tiny plastic instrument played a scale and flared to life. A beam of orange light shot toward the ceiling.

Lewis gasped and nearly dropped the kazoo, but Maeve swooped in and caught it before it hit the floor.

A disjointed holograph appeared a moment later, floating a few inches above the top of the kazoo.

"Whoa! I take back everything I said. This thing is awesome." Lewis watched the holographic pixels stitch together, slowly forming an image. A face came into focus. It was Duna!

Duna had been their first real friend and ally at the Station. A nonbinary humanoid from Mertanya of Dim10, Duna used they/them pronouns and had frilled ears and closely cropped green-tinted hair and proudly served their dim as the youngest member of the Multiverse Allied Council. Duna had advocated for the cadets and their home planet and helped orient them to the strange new world they found themselves suddenly thrust into.

Holo-Duna's mouth moved. A prerecorded message began to play:

*"Greetings, Space Cadets! I hope this message finds you well. As you have now discovered, the Multiverse Allied Council chose to conceal your designated communication device in the form of a small and rather inconspicuous Earthling instrument.*

*"In its current form as a kazoo, this comm device is easily concealable, portable, and quite durable. It operates on a secure channel, linking you directly to Station Liminus's primary triskaidecagon and mainframe. Guard the kazoo well, Cadets. Make certain it does not fall into the wrong hands, for these are tumultuous times.*

*"The Empyrean One and several of her cronies are still at large. In an effort to stop the progression of their nefarious plans, Secretary Ignatia Leapkeene has issued an immediate dimensional lockdown. Aside from a handful of regulated and heavily guarded access points within Station Liminus, interdimensional travel will be halted henceforth. All known portals will be deactivated and will remain closed until further notice.*

*"Our goal is to prevent the Empyrean One*

*from infiltrating any additional dimensions. The lockdown will also prevent her fugitive associates, including Dr. Genevieve Scopes, from fleeing whatever dimensions they might currently be hidden within. To that effect, the council has also deployed an elite search squad responsible for sweeping each primary dimension and its parallels in an attempt to apprehend these miscreants."*

There was a pause, while the second half of the holovid message loaded.

"I guess we're not going on an adventure anytime soon," Isaiah said quietly, thinking of Ming, wherever he might be.

"Nope." Dev shook his head. "Looks like this lockdown will keep us Earth-bound for a while."

*"Prior to closing the portals on your home dimension, our team successfully shut down all of EnerCor's mining and drilling stations and neutralized the Cataclysmosis spores that were incubating beneath your planet's crust. Your planet still has a long way to go before it is fully healthy again, but this is a positive start. As promised, the MAC will assist Earth of Dim14 with the development of regenerative environmental therapies, but the bulk of this work will have to wait until the dimensional borders reopen.*

*"I understand that this might not be the news you had hoped to hear, but I promise that Secretary*

*Leapkeene, myself, and every member of the Multiverse Allied Council have your best interests at heart. In time, we hope to reestablish transit routes between Earth of Dim14 and Station Liminus so that we might see each other in person again. For now, we must all stay on our home dimensions until the Empyrean One is apprehended. The safety of the multiverse is at stake. I know I can trust you to do your part.*

*"Take care of each other, and please, be vigilant. If you observe or encounter anything suspicious, alert us immediately using this device. Its beacon function can be activated by pressing the yellow button. Ignatia or I will periodically contact you with additional updates. Until then . . . stay safe, Cadets!"*

The holograph dissolved and the kazoo's bright orange light faded, then blinked out.

The cadets let out a collective sigh. It was exciting to hear from Duna, and it was a huge relief that the EnerCor sites had been neutralized. But all this talk of the Empyrean One was a bit of a downer.

"No matter what happens, we need to keep this thing hidden," Dev said, placing the kazoo carefully back inside the silver box and closing the lid with a soft click.

"We must protect the kazoo at all costs!" Lewis declared like a total goofball, brightening their moods.

"Protect the kazoo!" the rest of them cheered. Dev held the silver case high over his head triumphantly.

Just then, Gage ambled around the corner, on his way to basketball tryouts. He stopped and studied the bandmates.

"Wow," Gage deadpanned. "Just when I thought you Space Cadets couldn't get any weirder—"

*BAM!*

Gage shot backward through the air, arms pinwheeling. He slammed against a nearby bay of lockers, held in place by a sparkling arc of light.

The cadets turned slowly and looked at Lewis, who held a drumstick aimed at Gage. Unlike the others, Lewis hadn't swapped out his superpowered Other-Earth set for Coach Diaz's loaner drumsticks. With the flick of his wrist, he lowered the drumstick, breaking the arc of light. Gage slumped to the floor, his tongue lolling. He blinked and shook his head from side to side, then scrambled to his feet and hobbled away without looking back.

"Yeah, you better run!" Lewis hollered. "And remember: Nobody messes with the Space Cadets!" Then he blew on the tip of the drumstick as though it were a pistol in an old Western movie. "I sure showed him, huh?"

"Lewis!" Maeve sputtered. "That was awesome, but also, we promised we wouldn't use those instruments, especially not in front of other people! What if Gage tells Thaddeus and Lee? What if he tells Principal Brant?"

Lewis shrugged coolly. "Even if he does run and tattle, no one will believe him, Maeve. We're fine. There's literally nothing to worry about. I'll try not to blast anyone again, okay? But you have to admit, it was pretty satisfying to see the look on his face." Lewis imitated the dumbstruck, or *drumstruck*, expression.

Maeve smiled reluctantly. "Okay, fiiiine. But you need to put those things away before someone gets hurt."

Lewis spun the drumsticks between his fingers, then placed them in his back pockets as though they were holsters. "You got it, Captain! I'll do my best not to blast anyone else . . . so long as they don't tease, provoke, or threaten me or my friends."

"Just to be safe, lock them up, please." Maeve pointed toward the band storage closet.

"If you insist," he said reluctantly. He walked over to the closet and stashed his special, superpowered, Other-Earth drumsticks securely inside, swapping them for Coach Diaz's boring and totally normal loaner set.

"Enough with the drumsticks," Zoey said, looking down at her eChron watch. "We've gotta get going. We're almost ten minutes late for band practice. Coach is definitely going to make us run singing sprints."

"Ugh. Those are the worst," Isaiah groaned, feeling tired already.

"Who's going to take care of the kazoo?" Zoey asked, secretly hoping her fellow bandmates would pick her. She'd missed out on their multiverse adventures, but being the official kazoo keeper might help her shed the lingering FOMO.

"I think Maeve should do it," Tessa said. "As drum major, she's our official leader."

Zoey's eyes grew wide. She couldn't believe her sister was choosing Maeve over her. Tessa wasn't even an official member of the band, at least not in Zoey's eyes!

"I agree," said Dev, offering Maeve the silver case.

Heat rose up Zoey's neck. Instead of causing a scene, she forced herself to shrug, like it was no big deal. "Sure, I guess that's cool."

"Okay." Maeve nodded, her cheeks flushing at the compliment. "I promise to take care of it. I'll only use it when we're all together."

"Unless there's some sort of emergency," Isaiah said.

Maeve slid the kazoo safely into her pocket. "Let's hope we're done with those for a while . . ."

Em had observed the cadets from a distance, slinking as close as possible without being spotted. Her hoodie wasn't dry or functioning yet, so she was forced to go the camouflage route, hiding between a trophy case and a grove of papier-mâché palm trees that were leftover props from the drama department's most recent theatrical performance.

She peeked out between the cardboard palm fronds and fake coconuts. She could see Maeve directing the group as usual. They had retrieved something from the vending machine in the far corner of the hallway, but Em couldn't tell what it was or why it was important. The vending machine made her think of food, and her stomach rumbled. She gripped her belly, willing the hunger pains away and hoping the cadets wouldn't hear the noise. Thankfully, they seemed pretty distracted by the small object in Lewis's hands, which seemed fairly unremarkable until—

*WHOA!*

A beam of vibrant orange light shot out from the top of it. An image materialized. Em squinted. It appeared to be a hologram of some sort. This was certainly intriguing. She strained to hear the message but only got snippets. Portal closures. Her aunt's name. The Multiverse Allied Council. The fragments weren't entirely clear, but they provided important intel.

Em's goal shifted. She no longer cared about obtaining Maeve's oboe or learning how to play music that could tear apart dimensional membranes. She realized with a thrill that this odd new communication device was far more valuable.

The tallest boy held the silver case overhead.

"Protect the kazoo!" they cheered.

*Ah ha,* thought Em, her mind cartwheeling through possibilities. She practiced the word inside her head: *kazoo, kazoo, kazoo.* It sounded funny and looked funny, too. Though clearly this was a powerful and important device. Forged by brilliant inventors and delivered secretly to the cadets, the kazoo provided a direct line to Secretary Leapkeene herself. With the kazoo, the Empyrean One could infiltrate Station Liminus. With the kazoo, her aunt could finally elevate Dim8 to its rightful place within the multiverse, no longer untethered, unwanted, banished to the periphery. *This is the key to everything,* Em thought to herself, energized by the prospect, driven by clarity of purpose. She ducked deeper into the palm-frond forest, pacing and plotting.

A few moments later, she was startled by a loud noise. She peeked back out from between the theater props, surprised to spy a boy sprawled on the floor at the base of some lockers, his expression dazed. He quickly rose to his feet and ran away from the bandmates. It was odd, but she didn't have much time to contemplate the scene.

The cadets began to disperse. Em stared as Maeve slipped the kazoo case into the front pocket of her jeans and headed out the doors, trailed by the others. As soon as the coast was clear, Em squeezed between the fake palm trees and slid beside the vending machine. She reached a hand up inside the machine's catch tray and quickly finagled a few granola bars. These she stashed in the pockets of her shorts, saving them for later. Then she rolled like a ninja across the hallway. She peered through the exterior door's window, tracking the cadets as they made their way toward Baxter Field, where band practice was already underway. She tested the sleeve of her hoodie. Finally, it was dry! She slipped it on, zipped it up, and disappeared, determined to obtain the kazoo by whatever means necessary.

# CHAPTER 17

MAEVE CAME HOME THAT NIGHT AFTER BAND PRACTICE thoroughly exhausted. All she wanted to do was take a hot shower, fall into bed, and sleep for a year. But the second she stepped inside their trailer, she could tell that rest and relaxation weren't on the itinerary for this evening.

Her grandfather sat at the kitchen table across from Maeve's mother, whose eyes were sunken and red. A social worker sat between them. He turned when he heard the screen door squeak open.

"Miss Greene," he said, swiveling in his chair.

Maeve brushed her hair from her eyes. "Yes?"

"Maevy-baby," her mother said, using a nickname Maeve hadn't heard in years. Her voice had a muffled, underwater sound, like she was miles away even though she was only across the room.

"Is everything okay?" Maeve asked, stepping hesitantly toward the table. It was a silly question, stupid even.

Nothing was okay. Everything was a mess, like it had been ever since the farm had gone under and her mother had turned to pills, and sometimes alcohol, to cope with the pain and disappointment.

"Your mother has decided to return to rehab," Gramps said softly, pulling out a chair beside him so Maeve could sit. "She's going on her own accord. It was her idea."

A lump formed in Maeve's throat. They'd been through the back-and-forth, up-and-down roller coaster of substance abuse and rehabilitation programs before. Her mother had never willingly elected to get help. Usually, it was at the urging of Gramps or her doctors and therapists.

"This time'll be different," her mom said.

Maeve couldn't meet her mother's eyes—it was just too hard. She didn't think she could be strong if she did that. And she needed to be strong.

"Maevy-baby," her mom repeated, choking back a sob.

"I'm glad you're going, Ma. But why now?" Maeve asked, tracing a scratch on the kitchen table with her thumb.

"Lotta reasons. Your coach came by when you were gone last weekend. To tell me you were doing something . . . I don't remember exactly. Something about space maybe? It seemed special, important."

"It was." Maeve nodded.

"He said some nice things about you, Maevy-baby. 'Cept I wasn't in a good place. I don't think I was very polite to him."

Maeve swallowed. "Coach Diaz is a nice guy. I'm sure he understands."

"I know you were only gone a few days, but after your coach left, I got to missing you real bad."

Maeve looked up and stole a glance at her mother's face. "You did?"

"Course I did. You're my kid, after all." A tear trickled down her mom's face. She wiped it away with the back of her hand. "When you came home last night, I was in a rough place. Again. I don't want you to see me like that. But you did, and I'm sorry." Gramps offered her a tissue and she blew her nose loudly. "I owe you an apology. For what happened last night. And last week. And the week before that. And heck...the last few years have been hard." She was restless in her chair, never able to sit still. "I want to get better. I want to do better. But I gotta get some help first. So, I'm going away for a little while, to get myself sorted. Get clean. Mr. Reynolds here is going to make sure I keep my word."

The social worker nodded and looked at Maeve. Her mother was looking at her, and her grandfather, too. All that staring was almost too much to bear.

"How's that sound, Maevy-baby?"

Maeve didn't know what to say. She felt too much all at once—relief, hurt, anger, fear. It welled up and spilled over, like water bursting through a dam, with too much force to contain.

"Stop calling me that! I'm not your Maevy-baby! Not anymore!" she screamed. She got up so quickly that her chair tipped over, crashing to the floor. She ran out of the trailer, letting the screen door slam shut behind her.

"Maeve!" her mother shouted.

"Let her go," she heard Gramps say as she fled. "She just needs some space. She'll come back. She always does."

Maeve sprinted away. The evening sky was darkening like a bruise, but she wasn't afraid. She was too upset to be afraid. She ran, her heart hammering her ribs. Her feet pounded against asphalt, then gravel, then grass, until she was far beyond the trailer park and quarry, in the wilder areas past the dairy farm and soy fields, where an orchard once stretched. At one point, it sounded as though her foot-steps echoed, a second pair of feet striking the ground close behind. She wheeled around, teeth clenched, expecting to see her mother chasing after her. But there was no one there.

She was alone with the hills and the stars. Only then did she stop running. She sank into the cool grass, damp with evening dew. She hugged her knees to her chest and cried until there were no tears left.

Em had watched the entire band practice, a feat that she believed merited some sort of medal. She nearly succumbed to death by boredom, and then death by off-key pop medley at the hands of an overzealous horn section. The Earthling pageant had been amusing, but middle school band practice rivaled some of the Empyrean One's most dreaded torture tactics.

Em planned to follow Maeve after practice and swipe the kazoo as soon as the girl fell asleep. But nothing had gone as planned.

Em had been surprised to see the state of her doppelganger's family abode. It was definitely more substantial than the hut of tarp and cardboard where Em had stayed during the night of the intense shiver, yet there was very little warmth in Maeve's home. It was as tense and cold inside that trailer as her aunt's chambers before an execution. Until now, Maeve had struck Em as poised, organized, and assertive. At home, her demeanor shifted completely. She was vulnerable, small, scared.

After the confrontation with her mother, Maeve burst out of the house and Em took off after her, struggling to keep pace. On the hillside in the dark, her doppelganger had revealed a piece of her soul. In that moment of intense grief, Em felt as though the two of them shared more than the same face, hair, and physical form. They shared similar wounds, similar wants. And that realization bound her to the girl in a way she hadn't anticipated.

She knew she should give the girl distance, but Em felt an indescribable pull toward Maeve. She took a step closer, then another, the grass damp beneath her feet, soaking through the fabric of her borrowed tennis shoes. Maeve curled into a ball, knees tucked tight beneath her chin, crying into the sleeve of her sweatshirt. Em didn't need to sift her doppelganger's mind; she felt the girl's pain acutely. She understood the waves of emotion, because she carried the same ocean inside herself. Hurt, anger, and confusion that she'd kept bottled up for so long, afraid to reveal any of it to her peers, tutor, or especially her aunt.

Without thinking, Em took another step forward. A gentle breeze ruffled the pixelated fabric of her invisibility hoodie. Maeve stifled a sob. Em felt an echo of familiar sorrow in her own chest. She stepped closer, and closer, driven by an almost uncontrollable urge to comfort the girl. Without thinking, she reached out and placed her hand on Maeve's shoulder. And then the sky split open and the world tore apart.

# CHAPTER 18

MAEVE WAS ALONE, THE PINPRICKED STARS OVERHEAD HER only company. Or so she thought.

Suddenly, the air crackled with static electricity. The little hairs on Maeve's arms stood on end. She sucked in a ragged, weary breath. For a fleeting moment, she could have sworn she felt the warmth and pressure of a hand—a human hand—upon her shoulder. She gasped and snapped her head to the side, startled. She saw no one, but a second later, the air shimmered and sparked.

The dark sky flared with fluorescent light so bright it burned Maeve's eyes. The gentle autumn breeze became a fierce wind. A tremendous rush of frigid air knocked her over. She screamed and scrambled to her feet, running without looking back. Her lungs burned and her heart pounded as she sprinted away.

Only when she was safely inside with the doors locked did she dare steal a glimpse out her bedroom window at the fields far beyond the trailer park. Nothing menacing lurked or loomed. A lone streetlight flickered on and off, in need of a new bulb. Someone's dog howled at the moon. Across the lane, she spotted their neighbor taking out the trash in her bathrobe, rattling the metal garbage can lids like she did every evening. In the bedroom down the hall, her grandfather snored loudly. Aside from the earlier drama with her mother, it was a normal night—nothing worrisome or out of the ordinary.

Maeve sat on her bed, perplexed, her racing heart slowing to a more reasonable rhythm. Had she imagined the burst of light on the hilltop? The prickle of electricity across her skin? The blast of icy air? Had she been so immersed in her grief that she'd invented the whole scene? Had she longed for comfort so intensely that she'd conjured the feeling of a warm, reassuring hand on her shoulder?

The entire situation left her rattled and more confused than ever. In a sort of half-dazed state, she changed out of her clothes and into pajamas, tossing her jeans and top on the floor in a heap. She climbed into bed, wrapping her blankets around her like a cocoon. She gazed up at the cracks in the ceiling for a few minutes, replaying the events of the night, trying to make sense of everything that had happened. Finally, exhaustion overtook her and she fell into a deep, dreamless sleep.

Maeve woke up before dawn. Her head felt like it was stuffed with cotton. Her eyes were puffy from crying. She was still so shaken by the night's events that she considered taking a sick day. She'd tell Gramps she had a stomach bug or something like that. He'd probably know she was faking, but she suspected he'd give her a pass, considering everything that had happened.

She went back to bed, covering her face with a pillow.

A half hour later, just as the sun was peeking over the horizon, she heard a faint buzzing sound. She got up and searched her bedroom, thinking her phone was making the noise, but its screen was black and its battery dead. The buzzing continued. Finally, after ransacking her desk and upending the hamper of dirty clothes in the corner of her room, she discovered the source: the kazoo.

She retrieved the silver case from the front pocket of the pants she'd been wearing the night before, chiding herself for being so careless. Tossing an extremely valuable alien communication device into the laundry pile was definitely not a good idea. What if it had ended up in the washing machine at the laundromat by accident? That would've been disastrous. Her friends—and the MAC—were relying on her to keep the device safe. She couldn't let them down.

When she opened the case, the kazoo stopped buzzing and lay still. A tiny orange light blinked from the circular opening on top of the instrument. Curiosity clawed at her, but she'd promised her friends she wouldn't use the kazoo without them. She snapped the case closed, her heart quickening. She plugged her phone into the charger beside her desk, waited for the screen to flicker to life. Once it turned on, she messaged all the cadets, telling them to meet her before school behind the old elementary playground, which was being renovated and would be empty this time of day.

Then she got dressed and ready for school. She carefully placed the kazoo case in her rainbow-striped pencil pouch and secured that inside an interior pocket of her canvas backpack. She left a note for Gramps on the kitchen counter so he wouldn't worry, then she tiptoed out of the trailer into the pale morning light.

# CHAPTER 19

"WHAT'S WITH THE SHADES?" LEWIS ASKED WHEN MAEVE, wearing a pair of dark cat-eye sunglasses, joined the cadets behind the playground's defunct twisty slide.

The sky was overcast and the towering play structure provided plenty of shade, but Maeve didn't want the cadets to see her swollen eyes. She tucked her hair behind her ears, getting into character. "You know what they say: The sun never sets on planet cool." She struck her best movie star pose.

"Yas, Queen. Rock those specs," Tessa said, dressed to the nines herself in stonewashed designer jeans, a chunky knit sweater, and vegan leather boots. She waved a hand in front of Maeve's face, assessing the look. "It's all very celebrity-dodging-paparazzi. I'm getting serious incognito-chic vibes."

Zoey shot her sister a skeptical look. Unlike Tessa, Zoey preferred function over fashion, opting for comfortable sneakers, basic black leggings, and oversized sweatshirts.

"Incognito-chic is exactly what I was going for," Maeve replied, striking another pose.

"So?" Isaiah fidgeted. "Why'd you call us here for an emergency meeting?"

"Did something happen with the kazoo?" Dev asked eagerly.

Maeve nodded. She set her backpack down on the ground and removed the kazoo from its hiding place. The orange light blinked. "It started buzzing early this morning. And then this light appeared. I think there might be a message waiting for us." She lifted the kazoo out of the case and gingerly held it out to Dev.

He cradled it in his palms, inspecting the device. He tapped the orange light. Once, twice.

"Connecting . . . connecting . . ." *Ping!* "Commencing messaging sequence," the kazoo announced in a nasally electronic voice.

All of a sudden, a hologram materialized. The cadets gathered round.

This time, the speaker was Secretary Ignatia Leapkeene, leader of the Multiverse Allied Council. Her hair tumbled across her broad shoulders in plaits and whorls. The horns protruding from her temples glowed a deep cerise color. Her eyes were stern and serious.

Zoey, who hadn't met the secretary before, gawked. Tessa elbowed her. "Try to be cool, will you?"

Unlike the first kazoo message, which was prerecorded, this holovid appeared to be streaming live. "Greetings

Earthlings," Ignatia said, the blue translator crystal glowing from its cord around her neck. "By now, Duna has debriefed you about the multiverse-wide lockdown we're imposing until the Empyrean One and her associates are apprehended. Aside from a few council-approved agents and our elite sweeper squad, no one is permitted to travel between dimensions at this time. Station Liminus will remain operational, staffed by a skeleton crew. To ensure that everyone, and *everything*, stays within their home dimensions, we need your help."

"Our help?" Lewis leaned closer, intrigued by the prospect of a new adventure.

"Anything you need, we're here." Maeve lifted her chin, eager for a task to take her mind off her homelife.

"So long as the mission doesn't fall on Saturday, two weeks from now," Zoey said. "We have regional marching band championships that day and . . ." Her voice trailed off as the others turned and stared at her.

"What?" She shrunk back a little. "We've been practicing for a really long time. The rest of the band is counting on us. Coach Diaz had to cancel practice last Friday because you five were off galivanting who-knows-where."

"Seriously, Zo?" Tessa hissed. "I don't think you understand the gravity of this. What Secretary Leapkeene is describing is a big deal." She locked eyes with her sister. A silent battle raged between the twins.

"Listen," said Maeve, eager to break up the tension. "I'm sure we can figure out how to do it all. We'll help the council, and we'll ace regionals. We're skilled multitaskers. Right, Cadets?"

Lewis nodded. "We sure are!" He patted his head, rubbed his stomach, and tapped his feet at the same time, as if that helped prove the point.

"Very well," Ignatia replied, her horns fading to a serene cerulean. "I knew I could depend on you, Earthlings." She paused. "When we first met, I was not very optimistic about the fate of your dimension, but now that I've come to know you better, I have hope."

The cadets beamed, even Zoey.

Ignatia cleared her throat. "Now, to the issue at hand . . ." The image of her face was replaced by a 3D diagram of some mechanical object. "Along with the communication device we are currently using, I have arranged for an additional piece of equipment to be delivered to you. It is called a Membrane Serger, and it can be used to repair unwanted dimensional openings, such as Rifts or Rips."

"Just like in sewing," said Tessa. "Serging is a finishing technique that stops fraying along the seams of fabric."

"Precisely." Ignatia's face reappeared. "A courier has already delivered the Membrane Serger to a secure location within the Station."

"The Station? As in Station Liminus? How are we supposed to get back there?" Dev asked, thinking of the broken quantum collider at NASA. He doubted they could repair it, even with his dad's expertise and help.

"Not Station Liminus. Station Snaximus," Ignatia corrected.

Lewis shook his head in disbelief. "Hold up. You mean the new vending machine at school?"

"Indeed. As you may have deduced, it is more than just a caloric dispensary. Our engineers cleverly disguised it as such, so as not to raise suspicions among other Earthlings. In addition to dispensing snacks, the new vending machine also functions as a juncture box, through which small objects can be transported between Station Liminus and Earth of Dim14 without creating a full-blown interdimensional portal. It is a fairly new invention, and there are still a few bugs to work out. However, it should suffice for our current needs."

"Okay, that is cosmically, sonically cool," Lewis said, grinning.

"Due to engineering and conveyance limitations, the Membrane Serger was delivered in pieces, which you will be required to retrieve and assemble."

The 3D image reappeared. Dev studied the holographic diagram as the parts and pieces came together in slow motion, rotating and attaching, like a live instruction manual.

"As soon as the Serger is operational," Ignatia continued, "you must use it to close up the remaining membrane anomalies."

"Anomalies?" Isaiah scratched his head. "I thought

Duna said there was a specially trained squad responsible for closing up all the openings and portals?"

Ignatia reappeared, her violet eyes steely. "There is, and they completed their work on your planet yesterday. However, shortly after they departed, scans revealed three rogue Rips. Either our team missed these openings during their sweep—which is highly unlikely—or the tears formed late last night, after our team had already left your dimension."

"Hmm, that's weird," Lewis said, scrunching up his eyebrows.

Maeve's stomach somersaulted. Her memory flashed backward to the burst of light on the dark hillside, the electrical charge rippling across her skin. Could she have somehow caused the Rips to form? Sometimes she felt like her world was falling to pieces, but could sadness actually cleave apart the universe? She readjusted her sunglasses, grateful the others couldn't see her eyes.

"Can't the special squad come back to fix the openings?" Tessa asked. "I'm all for a high-tech sewing project, but wouldn't that be easier than having us do it?"

Ignatia stiffened. "Unfortunately, that is not possible. Our team must stick to a rigid schedule. Especially if we are to secure the multiverse and prevent Scopes and the Empyrean One from causing further disaster. Cadets, we need you to close the openings as soon as possible to prevent any cross-dimensional transmissions."

"Like unwanted visitors?" Lewis said, picturing a toothy colossadon lumbering across the Threshold.

Ignatia nodded. "Exactly."

Isaiah regarded the holovid, studying Ignatia's face. "Wait, where are the Rips? What if they're on the other side of the country, or across the ocean? What if we can't get to them soon enough, or at all?"

Ignatia's horns shifted to deep umber. "That shouldn't be a problem. All three openings are located on the outskirts of Conroy."

Isaiah sucked in a breath. "Three? Right here in Conroy?"

"Yes. They appear to be part of a cluster formation, a grouping of tears located within close proximity."

"Is that common?" Dev asked.

"No. It is a very rare occurrence." Her face was stern. "Clusters like this occasionally form when doppelgangers interact, which can destabilize dimensional membranes. Our analysts believe there may have been physical contact between an Earthling and one of their doppelgangers."

The cadets were silent. Maeve bit her lip so hard she tasted blood. Maybe she hadn't imagined the hand on her shoulder after all. But how could that be? The hilltop was dark and empty. She would have seen another person standing beside her. Right?

"This leads me to my next point," Ignatia said. "After departing Station Liminus from Gate Hall, did you travel directly back to your home dimension?"

Dev gulped. "Um, no. We, ah, took a slight detour."

"An accidental detour," Maeve added anxiously. "Totally unintended. Definitely *not* the scenic route." She shuddered, envisioning the parched, desolate landscape.

"I was afraid you might say that." Ignatia sighed. "Please, cadets. I must know exactly what occurred during your journey home."

They took turns recounting the entire ordeal. When they had finished, Ignatia tapped a finger to her angular chin. "This complicates matters. Are you certain you saw no one else during your time on this Other-Earth?"

"Aside from the dragomander, smogmonster, and a small rodent that ran in front of our wiener-mobile, we didn't see anything remotely alive," Maeve told her. "There were signs of life in the distance—lights blinking and smoke puffing from a factory—but the city center appeared to be completely abandoned."

"Still, you may not have been as alone as you believe. There are beings within the multiverse who possess remarkable talent for camouflage, not to mention inventions capable of rendering individuals invisible, allowing them to hide in plain sight."

Maeve was dizzy, her head swirling with ideas and doubts and questions. She pictured the warning scrawled on the locker, the message scribbled in chalk in the band room—all in Maeve's own distinct, slanted handwriting. Yet, she hadn't written any of them.

"Do you believe anyone followed you through the portal created by your music?" Ignatia probed.

The cadets shook their heads.

"Not that we noticed," Dev said, worry creeping into his voice. "We landed on the stage of the city auditorium. As soon as we hit the ground, the portal disappeared completely. We haven't played those instruments since then either, just to be safe."

Ignatia's horns darkened to a deep wine hue. "Good. Do not, under any circumstances, use those instruments. At least not until we can better understand their capabilities. The creation of unsanctioned portals is strictly prohibited under our new edict. There will be serious consequences for those who breach this law."

"We understand," Dev said.

"If one of your doppelgangers did follow you, you must be vigilant. Avoid close encounters with them at all costs."

Goose bumps pricked Maeve's skin. She shivered and glanced over her shoulder, worried someone was watching them. The playground was quiet and empty, the slides and climbing structures cordoned off with construction cones and caution tape. The hologram flickered in and out as the floating pixels began to disperse.

"Ignatia? Ignatia?" Dev said, shaking the kazoo, which buzzed and crackled. "Argh. The connection's breaking up."

He tapped some of the buttons and Ignatia appeared again briefly, a ghostly pale version of herself. Her mouth opened and closed, her voice slightly out of sync, like a movie dubbed in another language. The sound came through in fragmented bursts, interrupted by static.

"Retrieve . . . Serger . . . Mend . . . Rips . . . Protect . . . multiverse . . . Proceed . . . caution . . . Report . . . progress . . . Await . . . message . . . Counting . . . on you."

Em arrived at the playground in time to see the cadets gathered around the kazoo. When she tried to get closer to hear the message more clearly, her presence (or perhaps her proximity to Maeve) disrupted the kazoo's signal, chopping the secretary's parting words into fragments. But Em had heard enough to understand what was happening.

She couldn't deny that she'd felt something deep and important when she'd followed Maeve the night before. But that kinship faded in the daylight, dimming even more as she listened to Secretary Leapkeene speak.

If she didn't act quickly, she would be trapped on Earth of Dim14 indefinitely. Which was not ideal. She had no home here, no kin. Finding food and shelter was a constant struggle, though not as bad as on Other-Earth. She'd spent last night dining on vending machine granola bars and sleeping in an empty backyard treehouse structure with a leaky roof and far too many spiders. While the humans here were surprisingly kind (with the exception of a few middle school snobs), the climate was wildly unstable, and the attire was problematic. She reached behind her and tugged at her green mesh gym shorts, which kept riding up her buttocks in a most unpleasant way. She regretted changing out of her Empryrean zilks and made a mental note to retrieve the armored suit from its hiding place in the girls' locker room as soon as possible.

Shivers and wedgies aside, Em had more important issues to deal with. Like proving her worth to her aunt and returning to her home dimension lauded as a hero. She flexed her fingers and cracked her knuckles. Her purpose and her path were clear. She would steal the kazoo and flee through one of the last remaining Rips today, before the cadets sealed them shut.

She checked the zipper on her hoodie and marched toward Conroy Middle School, pushing aside emotion, girding herself against the complicated tangle of feelings threatening to trip her up and lead her astray. There was no more time to waste.

# CHAPTER 20

**"DID IGNATIA JUST GIVE US PERMISSION TO SKIP SCHOOL?"**
Lewis asked a little too eagerly as Dev carefully placed the
kazoo back in its case.

Zoey shot Lewis a look. "I cannot skip school today. I
have an important algebra quiz fifth period."

Tessa groaned. "Chill out, Zo. You have A's in all your
classes. One missed quiz isn't the end of the world."

Zoey sniffed. "Actually, I have an A+ in math, but who's
keeping track . . ."

"OMG, you're so annoying!" Tessa tossed her long, dark
braids over her shoulder and applied another swipe of gloss
to her lips.

Zoey turned to face her sister and narrowed her eyes.
"If you think I'm soooo annoying, then why don't you go
back and hang out with your popular friends? Leave us real
cadets alone. We were fine before you came along."

"Oh, really?" Tessa glanced at the others. "I'm pretty

sure my singing saved their lives at one point. Besides, I *am* a cadet now, whether you like it or not. And they're my friends, too," she said sincerely. "You said I should try putting myself in your shoes. You even dared me to do it! And I did. Even though you wear hideous shoes."

Zoey's face flushed with anger. "When I said put yourself in my shoes, I didn't think you'd sashay in and runway stomp all over my life!"

"I'm stomping all over your life? Are you kidding me?" Tessa scowled. "You can't stand to share the limelight. That's why you're clinging to your perfect grades so desperately, because it makes you feel better than me. But I bring a lot to this group, too. And not just because I serve the fiercest lewks." She jutted out her chin and pouted her glossed lips. "Honestly, what's more important: your GPA or the fate of the multiverse? Have a little perspective, Zo."

"A little perspective? Are *you* kidding *me?*" Zoey practically shouted.

Isaiah whistled. "So much for the Hawthorne-Scott Twin Truce," he said under his breath. "That peace treaty lasted what? A day?"

"Barely. Should we intervene?" Maeve whispered back.

"Interdimensional diplomacy is one thing. Inter-sister diplomacy on the other hand? I'm not sure I want to tango with that." Isaiah edged away from the warring twins.

"Well, we can't waste any more time listening to them argue." Maeve planted her hands on her hips.

Lewis stepped between Zoey and Tessa, flashing his signature smile, hoping a little charm might help ease the mounting tension. "Hey, I'm no valedictorian, but I'm pretty sure this whole membrane fixer-upper mission is a lot more important than some algebra quiz."

Dev nodded in agreement. "I bet Mr. Phipps would understand, Zoey. He might even let us make up the quiz another day."

Zoey sighed, looking defeated. "Fine. Except we might get in big trouble with Principal Brant if we ditch school," she pointed out. "We can't risk a detention or suspension, not with regionals coming up. Only students in good standing get to compete."

"Are you scared or something?" Tessa asked.

"No," Zoey shot back defensively. She bit her lip. "I'm definitely not scared."

Tessa arched an eyebrow. "Then why does it seem like you're making so many excuses?"

"I'm just being responsible," Zoey snapped. "You should try it sometime, sis."

Maeve held up a hand. "Time out, you two! I'm glad you're concerned about school and the marching band, Zoey. But the leader of the multiverse trumps a middle school principal, too. At least this time."

"Especially since *time* is of the essence," Tessa added, tapping her eChron watch for emphasis.

Zoey gave her twin an irritated look.

"We need to get the Serger and repair the Rips," Dev explained. He wasn't used to seeing the sisters argue and he wanted to make both of them happy. "If we work quickly, we might even make it back to school by fifth period."

"Save the world, ace the quiz! That sounds like a win-win," Lewis mused. "Or a Wyn-Wyn. Get it?"

"Wait!" Isaiah gasped, suddenly realizing a gaping hole in their plan. "Ignatia never told us where in Conroy the Rips are."

"Oh, snap." Lewis's face fell. "That does seem like an important detail."

"Let's try calling her back," Tessa suggested. "The kazoo can send messages directly to the Station, after all."

Dev still had the kazoo case in his left hand. He offered it to Maeve. She waved him away.

"You keep it," she said, her voice brittle, like it was on the verge of breaking. "We don't need to call Ignatia."

"Why not?" Isaiah asked.

Maeve took a deep breath. She removed her dark sunglasses. She squinted into the light. "Because I know where the Rips are," she said, trying to keep her voice as steady as possible.

They all stared at her.

"You do?" Isaiah asked, his gray eyes wide with surprise.

She nodded and exhaled. "They're not far from my home, in the hills between the quarry and the dairy farm."

"Umm, how do you know that?" Zoey asked, frowning.

Maeve swallowed, trying to muster courage and fight off the barrage of unanswered questions growing louder and louder inside her head. "I know because . . . I was there when they formed. I think I may have accidentally created them."

# CHAPTER 21

**A FEW MINUTES BEFORE THE FIRST PERIOD BELL RANG, LEWIS** finished retrieving all of the Serger parts—fifteen bolts, gears, and baubles in all—from the Station Snaximus vending machine while Maeve stood watch. Lewis could often be spotted emptying the cafeteria vending machines of chips and candy bars, so the cadets decided he was best suited for the job and the least likely to raise any sort of suspicion if their classmates or any teachers passed by.

Once the shining silver and copper parts were stowed in his backpack, he and Maeve met up with the other cadets behind the school gymnasium. Dev joined them a few minutes later, his own backpack heavy with an assortment of wrenches, clamps, and screwdrivers that he'd borrowed from the school's STEM lab, in case they needed tools to help assemble the Serger. They waited until the coast was clear, then set off toward the Rips on foot, following Maeve's directions. She opted for a winding route of back roads and footpaths to avoid being seen.

"Do you think we should've told our parents about all this?" Zoey asked Dev while they walked.

"Maybe," he replied, clearly torn. "I know my dad and your mom would want to help. At the same time, I'm worried they'd tell us not to get involved. Or they'd try to stop us." He loosened the straps on his backpack and trudged along the trail. "Honestly, I'm not sure my dad can handle more stress right now. He's still so frazzled and upset about the field trip going wrong. I think it's best if we fix this quickly by ourselves and move on. What they don't know can't hurt them, right?"

Zoey nodded reluctantly. "I guess. According to that Ignatia lady, this should be an easy fix."

Isaiah, who had been walking beside them, mumbled, "Famous last words . . ."

"Hey, that reminds me," Tessa said, slowing her pace. "Maeve, did you call the school office and make up an excuse about us being absent today? The last thing we need is our parents getting a phone call saying we're missing. Again."

"Yup." Maeve cleared her throat, got into character, and performed her best Coach Diaz impression, lowering her voice several octaves. "Hello, Judy? Yes, it's Raul Diaz. Hi, good morning. I'm just calling to let you know that the following students will be out today helping me with some band-related activities." She listed off all their names. "Yes, yes. They have parental permission. Thanks so much.

Buh-bye." She flashed a wide smile and pretended to hang up a telephone.

Lewis clapped. "An Oscar-worthy performance!"

Maeve curtseyed proudly. Her impression had been pretty convincing. She often hoped that acting might eventually lead her to a bigger, brighter life beyond Conroy, but for now, she was grateful her skills could at least get her and her friends out of school for the day.

"I don't see anything unusual here," Tessa remarked, when they finally arrived at the fields beyond the trailer park.

In the distance, they spotted the dusty, gray swathes of the quarry's gravel pits and an old railroad station. Telephone poles and power lines crisscrossed the sky. To the east, they could see the MegaAg soy crops and a small dairy farm, with a tall silo and several black-and-white cows dotting the landscape.

"This way," Maeve said, leading them up and over a set of rolling hills scattered with clumps of thorny shrubs, overgrown weeds, and old apple and plum trees, most of which no longer produced fruit due to the collapsing pollinator population. "Just a little farther."

The grass here was mottled, anemic green and brown. Not the lush, verdant fields Maeve remembered from her childhood. The MAC had promised to help repair Earth's damaged environment, but regeneration would take time, and the citizens of Earth would need to pitch in and take ownership of their actions if they truly wanted to save their ailing planet.

Suddenly, atop the crest of the nearest hill, three portals came into view. From afar, they were hardly visible, unless you knew what to look for. In the daylight, the Rips glowed and hummed faintly. The patches of iridescence were mostly see-through, with a faint sheen of marbleized color. One was about six feet tall and just as wide, while the other two were slightly smaller and more oblong in shape. It was impossible to tell where each portal led; whatever worlds lay beyond were completely obscured. The cadets climbed the hill, their hearts pounding in their chests from exertion and excitement.

Isaiah approached one of the smaller Rips. The air felt charged, electric. Enticing.

"Watch out," Maeve scolded, tugging him back by the sleeve. "You could fall through one of those if you're not careful."

"You're right," he said softly. He moved away, casting a long look over his shoulder.

"Everyone, come over here and help," Dev called. He set up a makeshift camp a safe distance from the openings. He spread his sweatshirt on the grass beneath a crooked tree and laid out each tool. One by one, Lewis emptied his own backpack, removing the parts and pieces from the vending machine.

Unlike the potato radio they'd attempted to construct on Station Liminus, the Membrane Serger came together quickly. The finished object was roughly the length of

Lewis's forearm, curved and tapered like a sleek-looking boomerang, gleaming copper and silver. A fuel cube roughly the size of a gumdrop could be connected to the Serger's center to activate the device.

"How do you suppose we use it?" Isaiah asked, intrigued.

"In the holovid demo, the Serger flew through the air, zigzagging back and forth, stitching up a gaping Rip, before returning to the thrower," Dev said.

"Cool. I say we chuck it toward one of the portals and see what happens." Lewis stood and stretched his body, limbering up. "I'll do it," he offered, reaching for the Serger. He aimed it at one of the glimmering portals. "I bet I could hit it from here. I've got a great arm. Part of my highly athletic Wynner genes, ya know?"

"No way." Maeve leaped up and pried the Serger from Lewis's well-intentioned but seriously clumsy hands. "What if it sails through one of the openings and disappears forever? Then what?"

"Then we're doomed," Isaiah said, matter-of-factly.

Lewis sat back down on the ground, sulking. "No one ever appreciates my talents."

"It's just that your so-called talents often land us in even bigger trouble," Maeve replied, returning the Serger to Dev and giving Lewis's back a pat.

"Hey!" Lewis balked. "Did I blast Gage this morning in your defense? Why, yes I did."

"Fine," she relented. "Sometimes your talents come in very handy."

Lewis folded his arms across his chest and smiled smugly. "Thank you."

"I don't think we should use the Serger until we read the instructions, or at least understand what we're working with," Dev said, tinkering with the controls and tightening a few last screws. "Maeve, could you hand me the kazoo?" he asked, setting his tools down and inspecting the completed contraption. "I want to pull up that 3D diagram Ignatia showed us. Maybe it will tell us how to operate this thing."

Maeve squinted, her forehead wrinkling. "I don't have the kazoo," she said. "I told you to keep it this morning, remember?"

Dev looked up at her, his brown eyes perplexed. "Yes, I remember. But then you came and found me in the STEM lab and asked for it back. So I gave it to you."

"That didn't happen," she said definitively.

The others fell silent, listening.

"It couldn't have been her," Lewis added. "Maeve and I were at Station Snaximus the whole time. She helped me get all the Serger parts."

"Aw, quit joking around you two." Dev laughed nervously.

"We're not joking," Lewis said. He was uncharacteristically serious, no puckish grin or cheek dimple to be found. "That's the truth."

"No, no." Dev shook his head, frustrated. "It was you, Maeve! I'm sure of it. I asked why you'd changed into that basketball uniform and you claimed a bottle of soda from the vending machine had burst and sprayed all over your clothes, so you had to borrow something from the gym. Remember?"

Maeve blinked. "I'm not wearing a basketball uniform now," she pointed out, her heart quickening. "I never was. I swear."

"And you never should." Tessa cringed. "Green-and-yellow polyester mesh shorts are no one's friend."

Dev looked Maeve up and down, as though seeing her with new eyes. She was wearing the same outfit he'd seen her in at the playground earlier that morning—a violet long-sleeved tee, patched jeans, and an olive-green windbreaker. Her hair was pulled into a messy bun. Her clothes weren't stained or dampened with anything that resembled soda. "So, you really don't have the kazoo?" he asked, his mouth dry.

Her lips formed a tight line. She shook her head. Strands of reddish hair came loose from her bun, falling like a curtain across her eyes.

"But . . . how . . . ?"

Maeve brushed her hair from her eyes, trying to see more clearly. And then with a terrible rush, everything became striking clear. "I think . . . I think this is all my fault." Hot tears threatened to spill from her eyes, but she held them back. She'd done enough crying. She needed to focus. There was too much at stake.

"How? You just said *you* didn't take the kazoo back from Dev." Zoey shook her head in confusion.

"I didn't," Maeve replied.

The cadets stared at one another, dumbfounded.

"But someone who looks and sounds and acts like me did. Someone who trailed us through the Other-Earth portal, undetected. Someone who followed me to this exact spot late last night, tearing open those Rips."

A realization crystallized: They'd been duped by a doppelganger. The kazoo was gone. And Maeve's malevolent look-alike had escaped with it.

# CHAPTER 22

"I KNOW I SOUND LIKE A BROKEN RECORD HERE," ISAIAH SAID while the others paced around, wringing their hands, trying to figure out what to do. "But I think we might actually be doomed. For real this time."

"Not helping!" Tessa shot back.

"Seriously," Zoey said, agreeing with her sister for the first time all day.

"After she scammed you out of a highly valuable comm device, where do you think Fake-Maeve went?" Lewis asked like an investigator in some crime show. He meandered around the base of the hill where they'd set up their makeshift workshop, poking between scrubby bushes and drought-parched trees, searching for clues.

Dev finished packing all the tools into his navy-blue nylon backpack, his face distraught. "I don't know. I think she turned left down the hallway after leaving the STEM lab. But I wasn't really paying attention. I wanted to get everything we might need to build the Serger before any-one else came into the lab. It didn't ever occur to me that I might be talking to a Fake-Maeve. She was so convincing!"

"For the record," Maeve interrupted, "I prefer the term Other-Maeve. Or maybe Alt-Maeve. Or Maeve 2.0. Or even Wannabe-Maeve. Fake-Maeve has a really negative vibe."

"Okay, whatever," Dev said, growing increasingly agi-tated. "I'm sorry, but I have no clue where Other-Maeve may have gone."

"Well, you're all in luck," Lewis announced. "Because I figured out exactly where she went."

The others wheeled around.

"Care to share with the group?" Tessa asked.

Lewis pointed toward the three portals, several yards away. The faint iridescent patches hummed and shimmered. "I'm fairly certain she traveled through one of those Rips."

"What makes you think that?" Dev asked, perking up.

Lewis gestured to a trail of footprints pressed into the ground leading directly up the hillside. "My dad and broth-ers like to go deer hunting. Sometimes they make me go with them, even though I've always hated the whole idea of it. Although, I guess learning how to track animals—or, in this case, a runaway doppelganger—finally came in handy." He bent and touched the ground, which was soft and still slightly damp with morning dew. "It's pretty clear someone came up here. And not too long ago either. These footsteps are fresh."

"That's because we made those footprints, genius." Maeve sighed, exasperated. "We literally just climbed that hill, before Dev built the Serger."

Lewis looked crestfallen. His eyes darted back and forth. Then he spotted something behind a nearby tree. He held up a finger, pausing for dramatic effect. "Wait a minute. Aha!" He strode over to the tree. "I present to the jury . . . evidence!" He reached behind the trunk and produced a pair of green polyester shorts with bright yellow stripes running down the sides. He waved them in the air victoriously.

"Eww." Tessa recoiled. "Sweaty gym shorts?"

"Yes!" Dev jumped up triumphantly. "Maeve was wearing those shorts this morning when she swiped the kazoo!"

"Correction: Not me. Other-Maeve." Maeve frowned, then blushed. "Hold on, does this mean my doppelganger is running around the multiverse . . . in her underpants?"

Zoey stifled a laugh.

"Ugh! So embarrassing!" Maeve stomped her feet. "What if someone sees her and thinks she's me?" She moaned miserably, envisioning her look-alike streaking through the streets of Conroy or down the halls at Station Liminus. "I am officially experiencing vicarious mortification."

"Relax," Tessa said, coming to Maeve's side. "I bet she changed into some other outfit. Ditching those butt-ugly wedgie shorts shows that your doppel has good fashion sense. She may be off causing multiverse mayhem, but I bet she's doing it in style."

"As amusing as this is, I think we're all missing the point here," Lewis said.

"Which is?" Maeve asked warily.

"That I was right," Lewis replied haughtily, tossing the green shorts onto a tree branch, where they flapped in the breeze like a flag. "This discarded article of clothing provides clear evidence that your doppelganger came this way today. Given the tree's close vicinity to the hilltop, it's only logical to assume that she escaped through one of the portals."

"But which one?" Zoey asked, eyeing the three Rips from afar.

The cadets climbed back up the hill together. Lewis knelt down to inspect the grass, looking for tracks, but the ground was firmer here and the pattern of footprints impossible to follow.

"So, Sherlock? What now?" Maeve asked.

He stood and looked at her. "She's *your* doppelganger, Greene. Which portal would you have chosen? Door number one?" Lewis wiggled his hips and waved his arm like a gameshow host. "Door number two? Or perhaps door number three?"

"I really have no idea." Maeve huffed. "But if the kazoo falls into the wrong hands, the Empyrean One could infiltrate the Multiverse Allied Council."

"That would be catastrophic. And we'd be the ones to blame," Tessa added.

"Oh, man." Isaiah hung his head. "We are so dead. Beyond dead. The deadest."

"Hold on. Don't go full-doom on us just yet," Dev said. "We can still fix this."

"How exactly do you plan on doing that?" Zoey asked, twisting one of her braids anxiously.

Dev stood tall. "We find the thief and take back the kazoo."

"That would mean breaking one of the MAC's new laws. Interdimensional travel is henceforth banned!" Lewis croaked in his best Secretary Leapkeene impression.

"I'm sure she'll understand," Maeve said, hoping for a chance to redeem herself. "I agree with Dev. The fate of the multiverse is in our hands, after all."

"Our clumsy, kazoo-losing hands," Isaiah mumbled.

"Hey, speak for yourself." Tessa snorted.

"All of you, stop!" Maeve ordered. "This isn't who we are. We're the Conroy Cadets, remember? Hear us roar! Look to the sky, watch us soar!" She gave the marching band's signature salute.

"Fine. Except how do we know where to look?" Isaiah asked. "The thief could be anywhere."

"The MAC has an ace sweeper team, right?" Zoey said. "Shouldn't we just explain what happened to the secretary and let her handle it?"

"How?" Dev replied, pacing the hilltop. "We don't have any way to communicate with her."

"Besides," Isaiah said, "the sweepers are shutting down portals and hunting the Empyrean One herself. They don't have time to deal with some runaway misfit."

"Hey." Maeve glowered. "Who says my doppel is a misfit? Maybe she's fabulous. I mean, she's a talented actress, tricking Dev like that. She's clearly cunning."

"And possibly evil," Isaiah added.

"And potentially pantsless." Lewis chuckled. Maeve gave him a withering glare.

"Enough! Everyone!" Dev said, growing flustered. He couldn't deny that he was a little scattered and anxious, too. But his mother always told him that the enemy of fear is action. "We need to act quickly."

The cadets settled down.

"Here's what I propose," Dev said. "We split into three groups. Each duo enters a different Rip. Once inside the new dimensions, we try to locate someone who looks like Maeve. If you find her, figure out how to retrieve the kazoo. Steal, beg, barter, if you have to."

"Whoa, is that really such a great idea?" Zoey sputtered.

Lewis shoved his hands in his pockets and rocked back on his heels. "Right. What if we go in there and make things worse? What if we break something?"

This made them all pause; Lewis did have a track record of unintended destruction. And they'd collectively caused some pretty big messes on Station Liminus. Accidentally, of course.

Maeve took a breath. She hated the possibility of putting her friends in danger, but the kazoo was missing. In the wrong hands, it could be catastrophic. The cadets had finally managed to get in the council's good graces—a hard-won feat. Now more than ever, Earth needed the MAC's help to repair its badly damaged ecosystems. The cadets couldn't afford to upset their most powerful allies. Even though Ignatia and Duna were on their side, many other delegates still had their doubts about Dim14 and its Earthling inhabitants. As much as Maeve wanted to remain optimistic, she had no doubt that the council would turn against them if this kazoo situation spiraled out of control. She couldn't let that happen.

"We have to make this right. We don't have a choice. Besides, we'll be smart about it. Stick to the buddy system. No solo traveling. No detours, no wiener-mobile rides." She gave Lewis some serious side-eye. "And no unnecessary snack breaks."

He gaped, insulted. "I have an active metabolism, okay? I'm at my peak when I'm well-fed. Snacks equal fuel."

"Speaking of fuel," Dev said, running his hands through his mop of dark, wavy hair. "Unless Other-Maeve has some sort of superpower, or a really speedy getaway car, she can't have gotten too far. If we move quickly, we might still be able to catch her."

Lewis began jogging in place, making a sound like an engine revving. "All right, I'm ready!"

"And whatever you do, avoid your own look-alikes, okay?" Dev added. "Who knows what sort of mischief or havoc they could cause."

"Hey, I bet Other-Lewis is a real stand-up guy."

Maeve chuckled. "Well, you'll find out soon enough, Wynner."

"That's assuming these Rips even lead to Earth-like parallels," Tessa replied. "We could end up somewhere like L'oress, or the moon."

"Good point. Before we go, we need an exit strategy." Dev pulled his phone from his pocket and tapped the screen, checking the time. "If we can't retrieve the kazoo in two hours, we exit the dims and meet back here. Then, if we have to, we'll approach my dad and maybe Tessa and Zoey's mom and ask them to help." He glanced at the cadets as they synched their watches and devices. "If it's okay with all of you, I'll hold on to the Serger. As soon as we all get back—hopefully with the kazoo in hand—we'll use it to close up the three Rips. Like Ignatia instructed."

"Instructed?" Isaiah mumbled. "More like commanded."

Zoey spoke up. "You realize that by crossing into these other dimensions, we're violating the MAC's new lockdown regulations? Skipping school for a few hours is one thing, but breaking interdimensional law sounds like a whole other can of worms."

Isaiah nodded solemnly. "Zoey's right. Remember the judicial hearing on Station Liminus? The MAC ejects rule-breakers into darkspace, sends them to the Praxalian penitentiary, or tosses them into the bile pits. That's a lot harsher than detention with Principal Brant."

"Actually, the smell of Principal Brant's coffee breath might rival the stench of the bile pits," Lewis said, gagging. "Not that I've ever visited a bile pit, but still."

"Okay, so we can all see how high the stakes are, right?"

Maeve said impatiently. "We'll do our best. If the dimensions don't feel safe, abort the mission. Exit through the portal and come back here. Then wait on the hilltop for the rest of us to return. We can't waste any more time. Hup hup!" She tried rallying them with a clap. "Dev, you come with me. We'll take door number one." She pointed to the Rip on the far left. "Lewis and Tessa, you two take the center portal." She would've grouped the twins together, but she doubted the sisters could stop arguing long enough to seek out the missing kazoo. "Zoey and Isaiah, you've got the last portal."

The teams paired off. Dev secured the Serger and fuel cube inside his backpack, tightening the straps across his chest.

"Good luck, cadets," Maeve called out, marching toward the opening. "Atten-hut!"

Dev followed close behind, turning to give a final parting wave to his friends before the surface of the Rip warped, bulged, then swallowed them both.

Lewis and Tessa marched forward next. Zoey watched them carefully. Lewis looked determined. Tessa looked unfairly elegant, swanning her way into some alternate dimension. She was clearly still angry at Zoey, because she didn't even say a proper goodbye.

"See ya on the other side, dudes!" Lewis called out.

The middle Rip swirled and crackled, its edges flaring with quantum lightning, before it sucked them through the opening and into the unknown.

Zoey's chin dropped. Her sister was gone. Again. She suddenly regretted their earlier fight. Why was her relationship with Tessa always such a roller coaster? She turned to Isaiah.

"Do you think we're making a big mistake?"

Isaiah shrugged. "Mrs. Minuzzi says mistakes are part of learning. So, let's just think of this mission as part of an unconventional education."

Zoey's lips twitched, but she couldn't muster a real smile in return, her heart and head too muddled with worries and what-ifs.

"Although, before we go in," Isaiah said, "you should understand that we might get trapped in this other world."

Her face scrunched up.

"Time could fold into itself, erasing our very existence," Isaiah explained. "Or we could get eaten by a carnivorous creature."

Zoey squinted, giving him her most unimpressed glare. "Have I ever told you that you're literally the worst at giving pep talks?"

"I'm just being honest. You're one of my best friends, Zoey. And friends tell each other the truth. You should know what you're getting yourself into. You don't have to come with me, if you're not comfortable. You could stay here and keep watch."

She gritted her teeth. "No way. Maeve insisted on the buddy system, and I agree that we need to stick together. Last time, I was stuck behind on the sidelines while the rest of you had this whole adventure. That's not happening again, okay?"

Isaiah nodded.

She loosened her shoulders. "Am I a little freaked out? Sure. Do I think this is probably not the best idea in the history of bright ideas? Totally. Will my mother blow a gasket if she learns that I not only skipped school, but that I left planet Earth? One thousand percent." She breathed deeply, willing her nerves to settle. "But there is no way I am going to let Tessa have all the fun. Plus, this whole save-the-kazoo mission does sound pretty important. So, I'm going through that portal. And no one is going to stop me!" she declared loudly.

Isaiah looked around. He and Zoey were the only two left on the hilltop. "No one's stopping you, Zo."

"Right." She exhaled. "Here I go." Her feet remained rooted to the ground.

"Any time now would be great. We're sort of in a hurry."

She eyed the portal apprehensively, her knees wobbling just a little.

"Want me to go first?" Isaiah asked.

She turned to him, the veneer of courage dissolving from her face. "Together?" She offered her hand and he took it with a smile.

"Come on, scaredy-cat." Isaiah led her toward the shimmering Rip. "On the count of three, we forward march. Okay? Just like in band practice."

Zoey nodded, gripping his hand tighter. The trio of

portals gave off waves of energy. The pull was magnetic, luring them closer and closer, until the force was too strong to resist.

Isaiah counted, his voice barely audible above the portal's low-frequency rumbles and the crackles of quantum lightning. "One...two..."

As they took their final step, the ground beneath their feet gave out and they fell into unknowable blackness.

# CHAPTER 23

**"HEY, YOU! GET OFF THE SET!" A GRUFF VOICE SHOUTED.**

Em turned around, disoriented from transferring to a new dimension and surprised that anyone could see her. A quick inspection of her attire revealed that her invisibility hoodie was damaged irreparably, the special pixelator fabric torn in a jagged line across the left sleeve.

The damage must have occurred back on Earth when she'd changed clothes quickly behind a tree near the clustered portals. She'd been in such a hurry to escape that dimension and so eager to trade that ghastly tank top and shorts combo for her superior Empyrean zilks. She'd felt a tree branch tug at her hoodie as she ran toward the hilltop, but she hadn't realized until now that it had damaged her only source of camouflage.

"We're shooting here!" a man yelled.

Em instinctively crouched into fight position. Did he

say shooting? Her eyes darted from side to side. Shooting what, exactly?

She scanned her surroundings, which appeared to be a very large mesa in a semiarid climate zone. The ground was sandy and golden, strewn with clumps of pale sage scrub and tall cacti. Tents, trailers, and several other incongruous structures dotted the landscape. Layers of yellow and tan stone formed a deep canyon farther in the distance. A single sun burned high in the azure sky, suggesting she'd traveled to another Earth-variant dimension.

A covered wagon and several wooden barrels lined a dusty street. A lone tumbleweed cartwheeled past Em's feet. A dozen horses, corralled in pens nearby, whinnied and stamped their hooves on the ground, like they wanted to run free, too.

Quite a few people had gathered around as well, most of them wearing black clothes and headsets. To Em, these particular humans seemed very out of place in this location, but at least no one was wielding shockspires, crossbows, or stunclubs of any kind. Em paused. The guy yelling at her was operating a rather large piece of equipment, but it looked more like a camera than a weapon.

"Cut!" he hollered angrily, hopping down out of a folding chair labeled *Director*. He stormed toward Em. "What the heck do you think you're doing barging into the middle of a shot? You're not even in this scene!" He looked her up and down with disdain. "And what's with the wardrobe?

The aliens don't invade the saloon until the third act! What kind of sci-fi Western do you think this is?"

Em blinked. She had no idea what he was talking about. She really wanted to keep moving, to put as much distance between herself and that portal as possible. The sooner she found a way back home to Dim8, the better. The stolen kazoo felt like it was burning a hole in the chest pocket of her armored zilks. Or maybe that was the lingering sense of guilt Em kept swatting away, like the pesky flies buzzing around the piles of horse manure nearby.

"If the talent finds out you're here, she's gonna lose it. And then I'll be out of a job." He mopped sweat from his brow. "Listen, kid. I know we all wanna be stars, but I got a whole crew to deal with, plus the producers breathing down my neck. The costume department is way over budget. I can't afford any more delays."

"Sorry?" Em said, still trying to figure out what was going on.

"Go back to your trailer. Call your agent. They'll find you another gig, okay? You really do look like her." He squinted in the bright sun, studying Em's face. "A spitting image, actually."

Em leaned closer. "I look like who exactly?"

Just then, the crew behind them gasped collectively. "The actress!" someone whispered frantically. "She's coming!"

The crowd parted and a young woman sauntered through, head held high, nose in the air. Her red hair was perfectly coiffed into ringlets. Her makeup was flawless. Her calico dress and thick petticoats swished with each self-satisfied step.

The director's eyes bulged. Sweat poured from his brow. "Maevellina DuVert! Darling!" He left Em and swept hastily toward the starlet. "Your call time isn't for another hour. Go rest in the air-conditioned greenroom a little longer, okay? Drink some sparkling water. Eat some caviar. I made sure craft services stocked all your favorites."

"I want Dom Pérignon. Not Perrier." She pouted.

"Maevellina, you're barely thirteen years old. You know you can't have champagne yet. It's against the law. But I'll have my assistant import more of that gourmet lemonade you like. How's that sound?"

Maevellina didn't reply. She observed the horses and the wagons. "What are you doing?" she asked, her lips pinched into a sour scowl. "This doesn't look like any of the scenes we discussed. This movie must be a hit, Ronald. Otherwise your career will be over. I'll see to it personally."

The director waved his arms toward his crew, who all seemed either petrified or starstruck by the actress's presence. "Not to worry, darling. The movie will be a total smash. We're just getting the set ready for you. Making a few improvements." He gestured to a fake-brick building, which Em realized consisted only of a painted façade with nothing more than scaffolding behind it.

Maevellina lowered her chin and leveled a look at Em, who had been quietly trying to slink away.

The girls locked eyes. Em froze. She swallowed. Oh no. Not another doppelganger.

"What is *she* doing here?" Maevellina sneered. "I told you, I want to do my own stunts from now on! Does no one listen to me?" She pointed her finger at Em, who took several steps backward, putting more distance between herself and the irate starlet.

"She was just leaving. Isn't that right?" The director turned and gave Em a searing look.

"Exactly." Em nodded vigorously. "Leaving. Now. Good luck with the movie!" She turned and ran across the set, ducking into the first unoccupied trailer so she could get her bearings and plan her next move.

# CHAPTER 24

TESSA AND LEWIS EXITED THEIR PORTAL AND FOUND themselves inside a large, futuristic arena filled with hundreds of screaming fans.

"What is this place?" Tessa asked, stepping out of the dark service corridor where their portal had deposited them and into the daylight.

The sky was a pristine shade of blue. The air was crisp and clean, no smog or smoke to be found. Stadium seating rose up in a curved oval shape around a series of four floating fields, each tier punctuated by a single circular net and several vertical wall sections. Sleek, shining trusses arched overhead in an open and ultramodern roof design. From it, a giant solar-powered spherical scoreboard hung suspended by thin cables.

"Looks like some sort of high-tech sports complex," Lewis said. He thought of his jockish brothers and ultra-competitive parents. "My family would lose their minds if they saw this."

"Tournament play recommences in five minutes," a loud AI voice announced, booming through the stadium's speaker system.

Spectators began streaming past Tessa and Lewis, bumping and jostling them on their way to their seats. Some chanted team slogans, others blew on noisemakers. Tessa and Lewis looked and listened carefully, but no one seemed to be playing a kazoo of any kind, and no one resembled Maeve at all.

Nearly everyone was dressed in some variation of bright color combinations: pink and blue, purple and orange, red and white, or yellow and green, signifying their allegiance to one of the tournament's four competing teams. Most carried small circular tokens attached to lanyards around their necks, which seemed to function as tickets, granting access at various checkpoints and turnstiles along the web of aisles leading into the viewing areas.

"How are we ever supposed to find Other-Maeve here?" Tessa asked, scanning the sea of faces filling the stands. Most appeared to be human, although some wore masks, wild wigs, and face paint, which made it hard to tell if alien species were perhaps also in their midst. "There must be a thousand fans in this stadium. Spotting her doppel will be like finding a needle in a haystack!" she lamented.

Lewis pulled out his phone. He tapped the screen and

scrolled until he came to a photograph of Real-Maeve—a candid he'd snapped after band practice a few weeks earlier when the cadets had been goofing around together. It wasn't long ago, but that carefree feeling felt a lifetime away. "We can show this and ask around."

He turned to a woman passing by, carrying a giant foam scepter and wearing a tall hat fringed with orange tassels. "Excuse me? Have you seen this girl? Or someone who looks like her?"

The woman shook her head. "Nope. Sorry." She continued on.

Lewis approached three other people, but everyone was in a hurry to get to their seats before the next game began and no one recognized the girl in the picture.

"Hey," Lewis said, spotting a girl with jet-black hair and a red jersey who looked roughly their age. "Do you know this person?" He held up the small screen displaying Maeve's photo.

The girl grabbed the phone and chuckled, turning it over in her hands. "Where did you get this thing? The stone age?"

Lewis frowned. On their Earth, this phone was top notch. A brand-new model his father had bought for him and his brothers, insisting that Wynners needed the latest and greatest devices. Not even the Jones family down the street had this model yet!

"Where's the CEP?" the girl asked, inspecting the device as though it were some ancient relic. "Where's the porta-sola bar? Does it even have a c-tracker? And why is it so clunky?"

"Clunky? And . . . a what?" Lewis asked, scratching his head.

"A c-tracker monitors your daily carbon footprint. Everyone's supposed to use them. It's part of the president's new environmental policy. We all have to do our part, you know?" She gave Lewis a pointed look. "Clean Energy Packs and solar converters are way more efficient than whatever battery this thing is using, too." She shook the phone. "Do you have any idea how wasteful these old models are? You really shouldn't buy them, not even on the black market. No matter how retro they look."

"Retro?" Lewis scowled and grabbed the phone back. "Okay, well, thanks for the tip. But we're looking for *someone*, not technology advice." He held up Maeve's photo once more.

The girl squinted. "Hmm, sorry. I've never seen that person."

"Play commencing in one minute," the soothing AI voice announced over the loudspeakers.

"Hey, I gotta go. Good luck finding your girlfriend."

Lewis blushed and made a face. "She's not my girlfriend, but thanks." He stuffed the phone back in his pocket.

Tessa shrugged. "That was . . . not super helpful. But we can't give up yet. Come on. Let's go."

# CHAPTER 25

"ALFALFA HERE! GET YOUR CRISP, COLD ALFALFA HERE!" LEWIS and Tessa ducked as a drone whizzed by their heads, a tray of green and white sprouts balanced atop its spinning propellers.

"Rrrrroasted crickets! Protein-packed sustainable snacks heeeere!" another food-vending drone called out, delivering a cup of crunchy crickets to a nearby patron.

Lewis watched, horrified.

"Come on, hungry-boy." Tessa tugged on the sleeve of his sweatshirt. "Don't get distracted. We have to keep looking for Other-Maeve. Follow me."

A third drone zoomed by. "Mealworms! Hot and ready by the dozen! Realllly mealllly mealworms!"

"Blech." Lewis retched. "Whatever happened to roasted peanuts? Ice-cold lemonade? Sausage and peppers? That's true ballpark food. Not bugs and salad."

"Well," Tessa said as they walked, "the worldwide livestock industry accounts for nearly fifteen percent of global greenhouse gas emissions. This dim seems very eco-conscious, and swapping burgers for bugs is actually really smart."

Lewis gave her a dubious glance.

"What? I'm not saying that I personally want to eat a cupful of creepy crawlies, but I read about it in one of my mom's mayoral briefing documents. She wanted to convert some city land into a cricket farm, but the idea never made it far." She gazed out at the gleaming stadium, the clear blue sky, and the lush green landscape beyond. "Maybe if people back on our dimension were a little more open-minded about these sorts of things, our planet wouldn't be in such bad shape."

Lewis nodded. In comparison to their hometown, this version was sleeker, cleaner, and—as much as he hated to admit it—undeniably cooler. A fact only further reinforced when the sporting tournament began. Music blared, the bass so deep and intense that the stadium floor vibrated. The fans stomped their feet to the beat.

"Welcome to the tenth annual FlyAlai junior tournament!" an announcer called out. "Round two of our final match will begin shortly. Let's welcome our players to the field!"

The crowd erupted.

Lewis wasn't an obsessive sports fanatic like the rest of his family, but he still enjoyed a good game now and then, and this match was especially intriguing. The field, the stands, even the equipment looked completely different from anything he'd ever witnessed on their Earth.

"Too bad we don't have one of those token-ticket thingies," he said, standing on his tiptoes in an attempt to get a better view.

Tessa tilted her chin. "You really think we're going to let that stop us? If my mom gave up every time she encountered a barrier, she'd never be mayor. Other-Maeve could be in the stands somewhere, and we have to find her." She looked right, looked left. She waited for a lull in the surging crowd, then hopped over the turnstile in one graceful leap.

"Tessa!" Lewis hissed. "Wait up!"

The corridors were nearly empty now, as the remaining spectators took their seats. Lewis got a running start and jumped the turnstile like a hurdle, just in time to see the players charge onto the lower field.

According to the announcer, each team was comprised of twelve boys and girls ages ten through thirteen. "Let's hear it for the Iverson Innovators! Make some noise for the Elmsley Explorers! Put your hands together for the Dunning Dodos!"

Lewis guffawed. "The Dodos? Why name your team after a dead bird?"

A little girl decked out in pink and blue was standing to his left. She scowled, her pigtails bobbing up and down. "Dodos aren't dead," she informed him in a squeaky but forceful voice.

"They are where we're from," Lewis said. "They're extinct."

"Wherever you're from sounds like a sad place," the girl replied. "Dodos are majestic birds. And the Dunning Dodos are the best team in the league." She looked Lewis up and down. "Who're you rooting for?" she asked, since he wasn't wearing any of the team colors.

"That one!" Lewis said excitedly, pointing to the field as twelve kids jogged onto the grass in formation.

"We're the Cohnroi Cadets!" the team in green and gold chanted. "Hear us roar!"

The crowd roared in response. Lewis did too, extra loud. Tessa shot him a look. "What?" he said with a shrug. "I'm getting into the spirit. This is awesome. When our marching band takes to the field, the crowd usually boos."

"Look to the skies . . . watch us SOAR!"

The team of twelve sprinted over to the sidelines and clipped their feet into shining planks that resembled narrow snowboards. They each secured helmets to their heads, then strapped a scoop-like apparatus to their hands.

A deep rumbling sound echoed through the stadium as the boards lit up and lifted off the ground with the kids balanced on top. The teams began flying through the air, zigzagging and maneuvering with impressive speed and dexterity.

"No way! Are those hoverboards?" Lewis gazed out at the field in astonishment. He turned to another spectator nearby, a teenage boy cheering for Cohnroi, too. "Hey, what is this sport?"

The boy gave him a questioning look. "Really? Where have you been living? Under a rock?"

"Well, more like another dimension."

Tessa elbowed Lewis. "He means we're from out of town."

The boy still seemed surprised. "You really don't know about FlyAlai?"

Lewis and Tessa shook their heads.

The kid's eyes bugged out. "It's only the best sport ever. Like jai alai, but played in lower gravity conditions, by four teams at once. Players move through the air on specially engineered soarboards. And see those scoops they wear on their hands? Those are for catching the ball and whipping it against those walls. Teams have to bounce-pass their ball six times, then throw it through the central net on each tier. But the other teams can intercept, block, or steal the balls, sending their opponents back down to the lower fields."

Upbeat music swelled and the massive spherical scoreboard suspended from the roof began to rotate, displaying all the players' names, numbers, and faces.

"Keep your eyes peeled for Other-Maeve," Tessa whispered under her breath. "Maybe she's on the team, or lurking on the sidelines."

"Look!" the boy beside them shouted. "That's my favorite player." He pointed.

Lewis and Tessa stared up at the screen. "Hold on. That's . . . that's . . . me?" Lewis stammered, surprised to see his own face—nearly two stories tall—staring back down at them.

"No, that's L-Dub!" The boy laughed, pumping his fist to the beat. "He's the Team MVP, and a FlyAlai junior league high-scorer. He's the best!" He turned to Lewis. "I guess you do sorta look like him. But you're a lot . . . scrawnier."

"Excuse me?" Lewis said, thoroughly insulted. "Does this look scrawny to you?" He puffed up his chest and flexed a bicep. Then he spotted his doppelganger, L-Dub, on the field. Lewis's posture deflated as he realized the boy was right. This Other-Lewis was *huge*. Broad-shouldered, muscular, confident, and a lot more coordinated than Real-Lewis.

As the team warmed up, L-Dub whizzed across the tiered fields. He flicked his wrist and sent a FlyAlai ball whistling through the air like a rocket. It slammed into one of the vertical walls and ricocheted backward. He turned his hips, rocked on his soarboard, and snatched the speeding ball out of the sky effortlessly.

The crowd cheered.

"Show-off," Lewis mumbled.

"Oh, he is," the boy replied, grinning. "But he gets the wins, lots and lotsa doubleyous. Which is why he's known as L-Dub. Girls go crazy for him. Guys wanna be him. He's the man."

"Good for him," Lewis huffed.

"Hold on," Tessa said gently, trying not to smile. "Are you jealous . . . of yourself?"

"No. I don't want to be anything like that meathead," Lewis said brusquely. He pushed past the screaming fans and down the aisle. "Let's keep searching."

They spent the remainder of the quarter scanning the crowds for Other-Maeve, to no avail. Every so often, Lewis would sneak a peek at the field, but each time he did, he was filled with an overwhelming sense of envy. Watching L-Dub soar across the field, scoring point after point, made him feel insignificant, small . . . scrawny.

He imagined how proud L-Dub's parents must be, how much attention they probably lavished on him. He doubted L-Dub's older brothers ever picked on him. Lewis wondered what that life would feel like. If he rejoined the lacrosse team or the track team, could he become as good at sports as his doppelganger? He'd probably have to quit the marching band and train 24/7, but maybe it would be worth it? He listened to the fans cheering and chanting. He wondered what it would be like to bask in that kind of adoration. He bet it felt pretty great . . .

Just then, the game paused for halftime. The Cadets were in the lead by seventeen points. The screen cut to a live interview clip of L-Dub sitting on the bench, squirting bright blue juice into his mouth.

"How's it going out there?" a reporter asked.

"It's a tough game, but I'm playing great. My team's not that helpful, to be honest. Sometimes I think they're really only on the field to make me look good. I've scored nearly all our points so far." He shrugged and drank more juice.

"And how has your coach guided you toward victory today?"

L-Dub scratched himself. "Um, I mostly ignore the coach's advice and just play the strategy that suits me best."

The reporter hesitated. "Okay. Is there anyone you'd like to thank? Anyone who's helped you along the way?"

L-Dub coughed. He looked bored by the question. "Not really. The road to greatness was paved by me, myself, and I."

"Wow," Lewis said, shaking his head. "Maybe I don't want to be like this guy after all. I am *such* a jerk in this dimension." He slumped down, his shoulders rolling forward.

"Wait a sec," Tessa said, gazing at the giant projection of L-Dub. "Your giant jerky face just gave me an idea!"

Lewis looked up, his left eyebrow arched curiously.

"At this rate, we'll never be able to find Other-Maeve on our own, but maybe we can enlist the help of all these fans. If two brains are better than one, imagine how great a thousand brains will be! Not to mention two thousand eyeballs!"

"Okay. I'm listening," Lewis said, standing up tall. "But also, thousands of brains and eyeballs sounds sort of gross."

Tessa crossed the aisle and examined a digital map on the wall, indicating the arena's exits, restrooms, concession stalls, and other service areas. She quickly plotted a route in her mind.

"Follow me!" She ran down the aisle and into the inner bowels of the stadium. They wound deeper into the core of the structure. It wasn't anything like Station Liminus, but it was slick and modern with lots of sustainable features, like composting receptacles, wind-powered cooling vents, and walls constructed entirely from recycled materials. "This way!" Tessa said, spotting a door labeled *Media Control Center.*

# CHAPTER 26

**TESSA PUSHED THE MEDIA CENTER'S DOOR OPEN. THE ROOM** was filled with fancy-looking computers and screens. A man wearing headphones sat in a high-backed chair, punching buttons and adjusting various dials. Lewis coughed and the man swiveled around.

"Hey! This area is strictly off-limits to fans."

"Wait. Please," Tessa said, holding up her hands. "Are you the person controlling the images projected onto that huge screen?"

He nodded.

"Then we need your help."

"No way, kid. Can't you see how busy I am?" He gestured to the blinking lights and buttons in front of him.

"I know. But we're here to report a missing person."

"Talk to security," he grunted dismissively.

"Please. It's a friend of ours . . . she's lost, and we need to find her. Soon. In case something bad happens."

"Not my problem. Now get lost." The man tapped the screen in front of him, triggering a series of foghorn blasts over the arena's loudspeakers and making the lights blink in a strobe effect, signifying that one of the teams had scored a point.

"Listen, this is a matter of national, no, international security," Tessa said, inching closer. "Interdimensional security, actually."

At this, the man swiveled back around in his chair. He looked at Lewis and then over at Tessa. He stared, then blinked in shock. He stumbled over his words as he rose to his feet.

"Miss . . . Miss Hawthorne-Scott?" Color drained from his face. "As in President Hawthorne's daughter?"

"Mayor Hawthorne," Tessa corrected, out of habit.

"Real funny," the man said, with a knowing wink. "Trying to fly under the radar, I bet. Avoid the media frenzy. I don't blame you." He wrung his hands nervously. "Your mom's the best president we've had in decades. I voted for her in both elections."

"Oh," Tessa replied, realizing the unexpected advantage this alternate reality presented. "That's so nice to hear. I'll let her know you said that."

"Really?" the man replied, starry-eyed.

"Absolutely. So long as you agree to help us. This is an, um, official diplomatic mission."

The man's eyes grew wider. "In that case, it would be an

honor to assist you. And I didn't mean to be a curmudgeon earlier. You just caught me off guard, that's all."

"I understand," Tessa said, holding her chin high, channeling her best first daughter impression.

The man looked around uncertainly. "Although, if you're Teresa Hawthorne-Scott, where's your secret service detail?"

Without missing a beat, she pointed to Lewis. "He's my bodyguard."

The man assessed Lewis. "Him? Really?" he said, skeptically. "Isn't he a little young? And . . . scrawny?"

Lewis threw his hands into the air and grumbled. "Come on! I'm coming into my height, okay? At first glance, these limbs might appear awkwardly lanky, but I assure you, they are exceedingly strong." He struck a goofy ninja pose and sliced the air with his flattened palms. He kicked his foot in the air. "See? Some say I even resemble L-Dub himself." He flexed again.

The man nodded but seemed unconvinced. He returned his attention to Tessa. "So, how can I be of service?"

"We need you to project this image onto the screen so that everyone can see it. Make an announcement over the loud speaker. Something like, *Missing person alert! If anyone has seen this girl, please escort her to the ticket desk immediately. All tips and leads welcome.*" She grabbed the phone from Lewis and showed the man Maeve's photo.

"Sure, I guess I can do that. But only because you're the president's daughter." He uploaded the image to his computer. Within minutes it would be projected for all to see.

"Thank you! You're doing a great service by helping us." She gave a little salute, then grabbed Lewis's arm and pulled him out into the hallway. "Am I brilliant or what?" she said, practically squealing.

"You're a brilliant liar, and I'm . . . scrawny. What a day. What a dimension." He ran a hand through his sandy-colored hair.

"Aww." Tessa gave him a pat on the arm. "Maybe a snack would help cheer you up? We could grab a bite while we wait and stand watch?"

"Real-Maeve said no unnecessary snack breaks." He sulked.

"Sure, but this is totally necessary. A hangry sidekick would most definitely jeopardize our mission. Besides, there's a concession stand right next to the ticket desk. Consider this multitasking."

"Okay," Lewis said, perking up. "But I am not eating any bugs."

"No bugs," Tessa promised. "Come on."

Tessa and Lewis waited at the ticket desk for over an hour, but no one came forward with any tips or sightings that might lead them closer to Maeve's doppelganger.

"Two vegan corndogs, please," Tessa said, ordering another round of snacks to keep Lewis happy, choosing the closest thing to ballpark food she could find on the menu. "And some fair trade eco-popcorn."

"Hey, wait a minute . . ." The cashier studied Tessa's face. "No way! Are you—"

"Tessa, I mean, Teresa Hawthorne-Scott? The president's daughter?" Tessa fake-laughed. "I wish! I get that all the time. Must be the hair." She casually tossed her long braids over her shoulder.

"Ahh." The cashier nodded knowingly, then lowered her voice. "Truthfully, I'd hate to be confused for that spoiled brat. Especially after her latest debacle."

Tessa's eyebrows bunched together. "What do you mean, debacle?"

"It just hit the news. She got busted for running a cheating ring at her fancy-shmancy prep school. The school board was going to expel her and press charges, but of course her mom intervened to smooth things over. The gossip sites say this could deliver a serious blow to President Hawthorne's reelection campaign." She grabbed two corndogs from the hot coil, wrapped them in waxed paper, then handed them to Tessa. "Do you think Teresa really stole all those test manuals?"

Tessa gawked, her mouth hanging open. Lewis swooped in and grabbed the corndogs, slathering one with mustard and the other with ketchup.

"Honestly, I think the press can be a little harsh on her at times," the cashier continued. "I mean, sure, she messed up. Big-time. But she's still just a kid, and she's been through a lot, what with losing her sister, and her parents' messy divorce. Plus, it's gotta be tough to have a parent who's a public figure. I can't even imagine the pressure." The girl looked at Tessa with sympathetic eyes. Then she leaned in and whispered, "So, what do you think? Was it a power trip? A cry for help? Or is Teresa just going through a rebellious stage?"

Tessa suddenly found it hard to breathe. "Umm, I don't like to gossip about other people. Lewis, let's go." She reached out and grabbed his elbow to steady herself.

"You okay?" he asked as they walked away, struggling to hold all their snacks without dropping anything.

"Yeah. It's awesome to hear that my mom is rocking it as president in this dimension, but all that other stuff? About my sister, and my dad. And me being such a hot mess. It's hard to hear. I know that cashier wasn't describing my *real* life, but still . . ."

"I get it," Lewis said, stuffing his face with salty popcorn kernels.

Across the stadium lobby, a woman in large, dark wraparound sunglasses and a black trench coat watched them.

"Heads up, looks like the secret service is on your tail," Lewis joked.

"Who?"

"That shady lady over there." Lewis finished his popcorn and nodded in the woman's direction. "She's been watching you like a hawk ever since we left the concession stand."

Tessa turned, hoping it might be someone with a tip about Other-Maeve, but the woman was gone.

"That's odd," Lewis said. "She was there a second ago. I'm sure of it."

"Something's not right," Tessa said quietly, the hair on the back of her neck standing on end.

Lewis chewed a bit of his corndog. "You're right. This fake meat substitute is sketchy." He chewed some more. "It tastes like a deep-fried rubber eraser."

A chill ran down Tessa's spine. "No, I'm not talking about the corndogs. I'm talking about something else. Something's just . . . off." She shivered, her skin prickling with goose bumps. She glanced down at her watch. "Our time's almost up, and no one's come forward with a single doppelganger tip. Let's go back to Conroy. I don't think Other-Maeve's here, and I don't want to overstay our welcome."

Lewis shrugged. "Okay. Good riddance." He tossed the remainder of his meal into one of the compacting composters nearby. "Man, I'm so disappointed," he said as they walked back toward the portal, which was concealed within one of the stadium's winding service corridors.

"Why? Because the snacks here stink, or because we couldn't find Other-Maeve?" Tessa asked, quickening her pace and casting a look over her shoulder to make sure they weren't being followed. "Or is this about being called scrawny? Twice."

"No, but thanks for the reminder." He frowned. "I'm disappointed because my doppelganger's a total jock-jerk in this dimension. L-Dub was so cocky and self-centered. Not to mention rude."

"If it makes you feel any better, I'm probably going to juvie! Unless my mom decides to pardon me. What was I thinking?" She caught her reflection in a pane of glass and did a double take. "This version of Earth is super awesome, but you and I are sort of the worst."

"Pretty much, yeah." Lewis chuckled.

"Makes me miss home and our real lives, however complicated and imperfect they might be."

"Same. But before we go, I want to grab one last thing."

"More snacks?" she asked.

"Something else. This way." They jogged up a set of stairs and along a curving hallway. "Hey, do you think the others had any luck in their dims?"

Tessa shrugged. "I hope so. But if I find out my sister's lounging on some tropical beach, I'm going to be so jealous."

# CHAPTER 27

**"ONE...TWO..."**

"MEOW!!!"

"One, two, meow?" Zoey said, tumbling to the ground and landing in a thick drift of white snow. "What happened to three?" she asked, sitting up and looking around. Cold stung her face and hands. She gasped. Her breath made little clouds in the air.

A small, feline creature mewed nearby. "Mrrrooow!"

"Aw, nice kitty. Here kitty-kitty," Zoey cooed, rising to her feet and dusting the sparkling snow from her clothes. "Isaiah, look! This little guy's all alone out here in the—" Zoey gazed at the horizon of the strange new mountainous landscape, her eyes adjusting to the intense brightness. "In the snow...and ice..." She shivered, suddenly wishing she'd worn something warmer. It had been a cool but mild autumn day back in Conroy, but now they were surrounded by a frozen world of blinding white and fierce violet. The cat-like creature huddled a few feet away, its ice-blue fur frosted with snow, its golden eyes bright. The wind howled and the animal mewed again, louder.

"He must be cold," Zoey said, her teeth chattering. "I know I am."

Isaiah retched and threw up into the snow a few feet away.

"Are you okay?" Zoey called out.

"I'm fine. This always happens," Isaiah replied, wiping his lips with the back of his hand. "It'll just take a minute for the nausea to pass." He scooped some snow and used it to wash away the awful taste in his mouth.

"When you're done puking, come look at this little ice-cat. I was expecting creepy crawlies and big scary monsters. But he's so fluffy!" she gushed. "His fur looks like cotton candy. The blueberry flavor you find in big, sweet puffs at the Conroy fair."

"I wouldn't get too close," Isaiah warned as he began trudging through the snow. He squinted at the horizon. "Things in the multiverse are never quite what they seem."

Jagged mountains rose up all around them, glinting in the harsh light. The sky was a piercing shade of amethyst. Three faint white moons hung above the ice-capped range like massive pearls. Aside from the small, feline creature, there were no signs of life. No buildings. No roads. Any vegetation was concealed by a thick blanket of white snow.

"I don't think Other-Maeve came this way," Isaiah declared, rubbing his arms with his hands to stay warm. He had held on to a small shred of hope that maybe—impossibly, improbably—they'd discover Uncle Ming in their travels. But looking around now, that didn't seem likely. No one could survive long in this icy, inhospitable place. "I don't see any tracks in the snow. Aside from that creature's pawprints. Which, I'd really stay away from, if I were you."

"But he's soooo cute," Zoey cooed, taking a step closer to the animal. "Yes, you are. You're a cutie pie, you're—"

"MMMRROOOWW!" The tiny ice-cat hissed, then bared its teeth—displaying two surprisingly large rows of razor-sharp fangs. It reared back on its haunches, preparing to pounce.

"Oh! You're not cute, you're vicious!" she scolded, tumbling backward in the heavy snow drifts, her limbs numb with cold. "Isaiah!" Zoey cried out as the ice-cat sunk its teeth into the rubber sole of her sneaker. She kicked furiously, but the cat wouldn't let go. It snarled and scraped at Zoey's shin with its claws, slashing the thin material of her leggings. She yelped in pain and kicked harder, sending the cat and her shoe flying through the air.

Isaiah came to her side just as the small but fierce ice-cat tossed the inedible sneaker aside. It licked its lips and prepared to attack again. It reared back, its long blue tail twitching. Its hungry golden eyes regarded the two cadets like prey.

The cat leaped, claws extended, teeth glinting.

Zoey ducked and tried to roll out of the way, but the heavy snow made it hard to maneuver quickly.

"Mmmeeoooww!"

Right before the ice-cat landed on Zoey's back, Isaiah opened his palms and released a burst of power, forming a force field of colored light around them. It looked as delicate as a soap bubble, but the protective dome was powerful. The cat struck the barrier and shot backward, its fur standing on end. It landed in the snow several feet away. It climbed out of the deep drift, hissed angrily, then shook snow from its blue fur and bounded off in the other direction.

"I told you to stay away from strange creatures!" Isaiah shouted, slowly lowering the force field and turning to Zoey. "What were you thinking?"

Zoey's mouth hung open. "I . . . I . . ."

"Sorry, Zo," Isaiah said, more gently. "I didn't mean to yell. You just scared me, that's all."

Zoey didn't say a word, probably because she was still rattled from the near-death experience, or perhaps because she was in awe of his powers. She scrambled to retrieve her partially chewed sneaker and tugged it onto her foot. She lifted her eyes and gasped.

"Zo?" Isaiah asked. "Are you okay?"

He followed her gaze, swiveling on his heels. That's when he spotted something even larger and stranger than the ice-cat loping toward them on impossibly long mechanical legs. Thick snow and bitter wind were no match for this part-yeti, part-robot creature. Its jaws gnashed together, sending sparks flying from its metal mouth. Shaggy fur hung in matted clumps from its midsection. As it drew nearer,

Isaiah could see that the white fur was stained red in places. It looked like blood.

"Quick!" Isaiah shouted. "Back through the Rip! I'll hold him off as long as possible."

He clenched and unclenched his hands, willing the flare of power to return. But his hands were too numb with cold. No matter how hard he tried, he could only summon the smallest orb of light in his palm. It fizzled and faded before he could channel it into something more powerful. "Go, go, go!" Isaiah cried, nearly shoving Zoey toward the Rip.

Zoey didn't waste a single second. Thankfully, they hadn't traveled too far from their original entry point. Still, the creature was moving terrifyingly fast. Zoey ran as quickly as her frozen feet and legs would take her.

Isaiah sped up, tripping through the snow toward the portal. Its outline shimmered so faintly in the blinding arctic light that he worried the opening had disappeared. Then he spotted a familiar flash of quantum lightning.

"There!" Zoey shouted, seeing the burst of color. She reached out for Isaiah's hand and the two of them dove through the Rip right as the robo-yeti's mechanical claw slashed through the frigid air.

# CHAPTER 28

MAEVE AND DEV STEPPED THROUGH THEIR PORTAL AND stumbled directly into a patch of prickling cacti.

"Ouch!" Dev yelped instinctively. But then he realized the cactus he'd landed on wasn't sharp at all. The saguaro was spongey, made of painted foam, its thorns no more menacing than the bristles on a toothbrush.

He and Maeve stood up, but lingering dizziness from the Transfer process made them disoriented and clumsy. They took a few unsteady steps, then bumped into each other and knocked over a large wooden barrel. It rolled away, crashing into another row of fake plastic cacti, which toppled like big, green dominoes.

"Cut!" someone shouted.

"Not you again!" a gruff voice yelled from somewhere behind them.

Hot midafternoon sun beat down. Maeve and Dev

shaded their eyes with their hands, trying to see who was speaking to them.

A heavyset man sidestepped the fallen cactus and plodded toward them, sweating profusely. "How many times do I have to tell you? Get lost! No body doubles. No stunt doubles. If I see you skulking around here again, I'll call security myself and get those roughnecks to personally escort you outta here!"

"Sorry!" Maeve replied apologetically. "We don't mean any harm. We'll leave right now."

"You'd better. She's in rare form today!" the man hollered, a vein in his neck bulging.

"Who's in rare form?" Dev asked in a hushed voice. "Do you have any idea what he's talking about?"

Maeve shook her head, hurrying away.

Dev followed close behind. "Well, that wasn't exactly a warm welcome, but it beats being attacked by a dragomander or some other hungry beast."

Maeve nodded. She was half listening to Dev. Mostly she was trying to figure out where they were. She pivoted on her heels, taking in the sights, sounds, and smells of their surroundings. She spotted a director's chair, lights, and cameras. There was a massive prop table with lassos, straw bonnets, and pretend pistols. People in old-timey Western clothing mingled around coolers of cold drinks and nibbled food from a buffet table beneath a makeshift tent. "I can't believe this," she breathed.

"What?" Dev asked. "Do you see Other-Maeve? Did you spot the kazoo?"

She shook her head, a smile tugging her lips. "The portal led us from Conroy to a movie set!" She fought back a flutter of excitement.

She'd always dreamed of visiting a real Hollywood movie set. She'd starred in a commercial when she was eight years old. It was for a local used car dealer called Dud's. The owner, a balding guy named Dudley, wanted a kid in the ad to make the sleazy dealership seem more family friendly. Maeve landed the gig shortly after they lost the farm, when her mother and grandfather were desperate for income to keep them afloat.

Maeve hadn't minded working. In fact, she loved it. Memorizing lines came easily, as did cheesing for the camera. And she quickly learned that acting was the perfect way to channel complicated emotions. To disappear and become someone else temporarily. To reinvent herself, or imagine a happier life than the one she actually lived.

"Maevellina!" a woman's voice trilled. "What on Earth are you doing out here in the sweltering heat!"

*Maevellina?* Dev mouthed. Maeve shrugged, then turned to see a woman who looked very much like her own mother hurrying toward her in a chic white linen suit and impossibly high heels. Multiple strands of luminous freshwater pearls hung from her neck, and large gemstone rings glittered from her manicured fingers. This clearly wasn't Maeve's real mother; her mom never wore anything like that. Plus, this lady's ensemble probably cost more than Gramps's pickup truck.

The woman gasped. "Why aren't you in hair and makeup?" She looked Maeve up and down. "What happened to your dress? It takes wardrobe ages to lace that corset!" Her brow furrowed with concern. "Your next scene starts in twenty minutes, Maevy-baby. We must hurry!"

"Maevy-baby?" Maeve repeated, the nickname sticking in her throat like a glob of peanut butter. She coughed.

She gazed at Maeve adoringly. "You may have chosen a glamorous stage name, but you'll always be my Maevy-baby."

Maeve coughed again. The woman quickly produced an ice-cold bottle of mineral water from her handbag. She handed it to Maeve.

"Thanks," Maeve said, gulping the water down gratefully.

"Of course, darling. Can't have you ruining your precious vocal cords. Aw, my shining star! Light of my life!" The woman took the empty bottle from Maeve's hand and pressed a coral-pink lipstick kiss onto her cheek.

Dev stared, mouth agape. Maeve froze, shocked by the unexpected display of affection.

"Umm, what's happening?" she asked, rubbing the lipstick away.

"What's happening is that you're late. Again. But don't you worry. Mommy will fix everything. Hurry! Hurry!" She shooed Maeve forward, then paused and eyed Dev, who was hanging back, hoping she wouldn't try to kiss him, too.

"You must be the kid from Maevellina's fan club who won the backstage pass in that charity lottery. Correct?"

Dev had no idea what the woman was talking about, but he played along. "Yeah, that's me. I'm her biggest fan."

Maeve beamed and winked at Dev, starting to enjoy this starlet mix-up a little too much.

The woman nodded curtly. "Fine. You can come along as well." She led them toward a trailer with a maroon awning marked *Hair & Makeup*. As they walked, the woman craned her neck and whispered so only Dev could hear. The tone of her voice shifted from bubbly to gritty.

"Keep in mind, kid, autographs are an extra fifty bucks, and absolutely no unauthorized photography. You signed an NDA, so I better not hear a peep about her bad attitude or lousy work ethic. No leaks to the press. Got it?"

Dev stared back, surprised. He nodded.

"Good." She flung open the door and swept them inside. The tone of her voice shifted again. "Here we are! I'll run and tell Ron to shoot a filler scene with the extras while you get ready. Why don't you run your lines a few more times while Sebastian curls your hair? This is such a crucial scene, one that will really show your range." She thrust a script into Maeve's hands, planted another bright-pink kiss on her cheek, then fluttered away frantically, kicking up a plume of dust in her sky-high heels. "See you soon, my shining star! I can't wait to watch you soar!"

# CHAPTER 29

MAEVE LOWERED HERSELF INTO ONE OF THE SALON-STYLE chairs. The hair and makeup trailer was empty except for her and Dev. She stared at her reflection in the mirror, her face illuminated by a row of glowing bulbs. The counter in front of her was covered with curling irons, blow driers, hair clips, brushes, makeup palettes, and cosmetics of all sorts. Bouquets of fresh flowers—all containing tiny cards addressed to Maevellina—helped mask the lingering chemical scent of hairspray and self-tanner. Maeve leaned back in her chair, clutched the script to her chest, and breathed in deeply. She exhaled and closed her eyes.

"Maeve?" Dev asked hesitantly. "What are you doing?"

She flicked open one eye. "I'm savoring the moment."

"Oh. Cool. Okay." He shuffled his feet. "But, um, we're sort of on an important mission."

Maeve sighed and opened both eyes, sitting up straight.

"I'm pretty sure this Maevellina person is the doppel-ganger we're looking for." Dev pointed to the wall, adorned with newspaper clippings, Polaroid pictures, and a signed headshot of a girl who looked nearly identical to Maeve, just with more makeup and a fancier hairdo.

"Look at me!" Maeve said, hopping up and inspecting the photograph. She read one of the newspaper clippings—a front page piece about the incomparable talent of Hollywood's rising star, Maevellina DuVert. A black-and-white photograph showed the girl lounging by a pool, a sprawling mansion in the background. "Gosh, I'm so famous!" Maeve gushed.

"Not to burst your bubble, but *she's* famous. She's your doppelganger, Maeve. And she's here. Somewhere on set. And chances are, she has the kazoo. We have to find her."

"Right," Maeve said, leaning in to read a review of her doppel's most recent escapades on Broadway. "A sold-out show. Wow!"

"Um, Earth to Maeve? Did you hear me? We need to find this girl now, before it's too late." He tapped his foot anxiously. "Our friends are depending on us. Not to mention, the fate of the multiverse could be in jeopardy if we fail."

"We're not going to fail," Maeve assured him, sitting back down in the salon chair and flipping through the script. Her lips moved as she mouthed the lines. She stopped and looked up, her eyes sparkling in the glowing lights. "This is my time to shine!"

"Ah, good. I'm glad you're finally coming around. You had me worried there for a minute," Dev laughed nervously, wondering why Maeve was still sitting in the chair, bent over the script. He stepped toward the door and held it open. "Coming?"

She shook her head. "No, Dev. Not yet."

"Not yet?" he balked.

"We have time, okay? We're not meeting the others for two hours." She held up the script. "I am going to shoot this scene. I have a whole monologue!"

His mouth hung open. "What? You can't shoot any scenes! We have to find this girl—now. What if she gets away?" He clenched his jaw, trying to look as stern as possible to convey the seriousness of their predicament. "You're getting too lost in this other dimension. This isn't your life, Maeve."

She set the script on her lap. "Listen, Dev. This may not be my real life, but this is my dream." She gazed around at the trailer. Through the open door, she watched the bustling set with a wistful look in her eyes. She turned back to Dev. "This is literally everything I've always wanted, ever since I was a little girl. An opportunity to act, to share my artistic talents with the world. To be surrounded by people who believe in me."

"I believe in you, too," he said through gritted teeth. "And so do the other cadets. Don't let us down by losing sight of what's really important. Don't get caught up in this illusion of fame and fortune."

"It's about more than that, Dev. Please. Just let me have this one moment. This one scene." She glanced at the clock on the wall. "It won't take long, promise. But it matters to me, okay? More than you know." Tears sprang to her eyes. She wiped them away. "I've had a really tough time lately. My family situation is a mess. No matter how hard I work, or how big I dream, I'll probably never get to do something like this in my real life." A heavy tear rolled down her cheek and splattered onto the open script. "I need this, Dev."

Before Dev could respond, a bevy of hairstylists and makeup artists burst inside the trailer, fluttering and flapping like a flock of colorful birds.

"*Oh, mon dieu!*" a man with a platinum-blond Mohawk cried upon seeing Maeve in the chair, bare-faced, with her frizzed hair pulled into a messy bun. He clapped three times, and an entire glam team descended upon Maeve, transforming her into the star she longed to be.

Dev stormed out of the trailer, furious. He scanned the groups clustered around the set and outbuildings, hoping to catch a glimpse of Maeve's doppelganger. Nearly all of the people were adults, either actors in costume or behind-the-scenes technicians. Dev kicked a loose rock and sent it skittering across the film lot. The rock came to rest at a fence post, behind which several mahogany-colored horses were corralled. He walked over to them, stopping to pet one on the snout. The horse snuffled his hand, searching for a sugar cube or an apple slice.

"Sorry, boy," he said to the horse. "I don't have what you're looking for." He sighed. "Any chance you have what I'm looking for?" The horse whinnied. "No? I didn't think so." Dev leaned back against the fence. "Geez. I'm talking to a horse. This is officially a new low."

"I come here when I need to clear my head, too."

Dev jolted back. Had the horse just spoken to him? This dimension had seemed like a close parallel version of Earth, but maybe there were some critical differences, like linguistically advanced livestock.

"What did you say, boy?" Dev asked the horse, giving him a scratch behind the ears.

"I'm not a boy." A figure emerged from the shadows behind a wall of saddles and tack gear. Dev jumped.

"But I come here, too, when I need to escape for a bit. Cool off a little, you know?" A girl strode into view, her face obscured by a wide-brimmed ten-gallon hat. "They say I have a temper. The horses help me calm down."

Dev was equal parts relieved and disappointed that the horse couldn't speak. He turned to the girl, who was roughly his height. Aside from the big hat and a pair of purple cowgirl boots, she was wearing fairly normal-looking clothes—denim cutoff shorts and a tank top—not the old-timey costumes most of the extras were dressed in.

"Do your parents work on set?" Dev asked.

The girl laughed. "I suppose you could say that. My

mother works for me. And I work on set." She reached into a pouch hanging on a peg nearby and scooped up a handful of oats. She fed them to the horses.

"You help take care of the horses?" Dev asked, wondering why the girl was being so cagey with her answers.

"You really don't know who I am?" the girl said.

Dev shook his head. "I'm, um, new here. Just getting the lay of the land. I don't really know anyone. Although, I am looking for someone, and *something*, very important. Maybe you could help me find it?"

The girl slowly lifted the brim of her hat. A slash of sunlight illuminated her face and set a strand of red hair aflame. Her blue eyes glinted. Dev gasped—it was Maevellina, Maeve's doppelganger.

"Ugh. Don't get all starstruck on me," the girl muttered, rolling her eyes as she stepped out of the shadows. "I can't stand the whole adoring fan charade."

Dev's heart was racing. He needed to play this right. "Charade?" he asked. She'd fooled him before, tricking him into giving up the kazoo. She wouldn't outsmart him again. He wasn't leaving until he got the kazoo back.

"Please. Everyone wants something—money, fame, attention. The crew, journalists, even the director! They tell me whatever they think I want to hear. Except most of them don't truly believe I can act. I'm just another 'talentless social media sensation' to them." She rolled her eyes. "Yet they hitch themselves to me, because my star's on the rise and they want to come along for the ride."

Maevellina fed a horse another handful of oats, her eyes downcast. "I've heard my own mother call me lazy and entitled behind my back. Though she'd never dare say it to my face. Not while she's on *my* payroll!" She turned to Dev, her eyes softer now, less intense. "She's the one who pushed me into acting. Most kids get a childhood. Me? I got a career."

She nuzzled the horse. "These fellas are different, though. They love unconditionally. Horses don't care how many followers you have or how often you get invited to walk the red carpet. They're not concerned with sponsors or production schedules. They don't push you to work longer and longer days on set so they can afford bigger and bigger diamonds." She reached into her pocket and pulled out a small, white cube. She offered it to the horse, who gobbled it up and whinnied contently. "All they need is love . . . and the occasional sugar cube."

Dev had been working up the nerve to confront her. "Actually, I did come here for something."

Maevellina sighed. "Let me guess . . . an autograph? A selfie?"

"No. You took something from me. And I want it back. Now," Dev demanded, trying to make himself seem as tall as possible.

"Chill. You're starting to creep me out." She took a step back. She slid a phone from her back pocket and held it up for him to see. "One tap on this screen and my bodyguards will come running. Believe me, you do not want to mess with them."

"I don't want to mess with anyone," Dev said. "I just want the kazoo. Give it to me. Please," he added.

She looked at Dev like he was completely insane. "Did you just say . . . kazoo?"

"Yes." Dev clenched his hands into tight fists. "The fate of the multiverse depends on me bringing that kazoo safely back to Earth!"

Maevellina stared at him. She burst out laughing.

"It's not funny!" His face reddened. "I promised I would protect the kazoo at all costs."

She was giggling uncontrollably now. "You're hysterical! Is this like some sort of method-acting exercise? A new addition to the script? Improv? Wait—did my mother send you here to help me practice my lines?"

"No, this is real. You know what you did!" Dev yelled. A few people across the film lot glanced his way, but he didn't care if he made a scene. With Maeve off playing make believe, he was on his own. And he was not going to mess this up. "You tricked me," he sputtered angrily.

"I did no such thing." Maevellina sniffed, dismissing him with a wave of her hand. "I'm bored of this conversation. You can leave now."

Dev planted his hands on his hips. "I'm not going anywhere. Not until you give me what you took. You're a liar and a thief!"

Maevellina's nostrils flared, her temper awakening. "Excuse me? I am movie star! How dare you speak to me like that? I am not a liar, I am an actress. The only thing I steal is the limelight." She turned toward the stable.

"Admit it!" Dev said, stepping in front of her, desperation creeping into his voice. "You pretended to be my friend so I would give you the kazoo. You look identical! How was I supposed to know who was who?"

Maevellina paused. "Hold on." Her eyes narrowed. "Is that wannabe stunt double still hanging around here?"

Dev blinked. "Who?"

"That look-alike girl in the stupid space suit who showed up today. The one Ron must have hired for the chase and combat scenes, even though I told him I could handle it. Grrrr!" She stomped her foot. "No one thinks I can do anything on my own. It's infuriating! I don't want or need a body double. I swear, if she's still on set, I am going to completely lose it!"

Dev's mind spun. Could there really be *three* Maeves in one place? This dimensional hop was going from bad to worse.

"She seemed pretty shifty, too," Maevellina said to Dev as she pushed past him toward the set, looking ready for a fight. "I bet she's the one who took your kazoo."

# CHAPTER 30

**"IF YA DON'T LIKE IT, YER GONNA HAVE TO ANSWER TO ME!"**
Maeve declared dramatically while standing atop a rocky outcropping, the wind whipping her hair and ruffling the tattered hem of her long calico skirt. "Because I'm the sheriff now!"

She raised her arm high and fired a fake pistol into the air. The shot echoed across the canyon.

A metal crane hinged overhead and the camera zoomed in for a final close-up, capturing the look on Maeve's face, her dark blue eyes brimming with ferocity, determination, and hope. She held the pose for a beat, her chest rising and falling and then—

"Cut! We got it! That's a wrap, people!" the director shouted, stepping out from behind the video monitor.

The set erupted into thunderous applause. The sound of clapping brought Maeve back to herself. She lowered her arm and shook herself free from the character she'd been playing. Someone reached up and helped her off the rock, setting her gently on solid ground.

Maevellina's mother pushed through the crowd of extras and production assistants. She ran toward Maeve, embraced her tightly, and peppered her forehead and cheeks with kisses.

"Maevy-baby, you were sensational! I mean it. That was the best performance I have ever witnessed!" the woman gushed. "I am so proud of you!"

Maeve leaned into the woman's embrace. She even hugged her back, letting herself believe for a brief but perfect moment that this was her real mother, her real life.

"Brava!" the director said, looking elated but also a little shocked. "This is bound to be a blockbuster. That scene took us to a whole new level. Your performance today was award-worthy!"

"Really?" Maeve replied, buzzing with the rush of post-performance adrenaline.

"You thieving little rat! You no-good, nasty imposter!"

Someone gasped. The real Maevellina stomped toward them in her purple cowgirl boots. Dev hurried behind her, madly searching the crowds for Maeve's other doppelganger. "You stole my role! And you stole his kazoo!"

The crowd parted and Dev finally got a view of the girl Maevellina was so mad at. He squinted. He felt like his eyes were playing tricks on him. Was it Real-Maeve in a costume? Was it Other-Maeve? Was it just a stunt double? Ack! This was so confusing.

The girl waved at Dev, then gave the signature Conroy Cadets salute, something only Real-Maeve would do. He felt relieved knowing her true identity, but that still didn't help with whole missing-kazoo issue.

"No one steals my roles!" Maevellina shouted, her temper flaring with each step. As she passed one of the prop tables, she grabbed a large wooden mallet. She swung it angrily, shattering a ceramic jug to smithereens. The mallet was definitely not fake or made of foam like those dummy cacti they'd seen earlier; this was a real weapon. And as Maevellina headed straight for Maeve, the furious starlet looked ready to use it.

After her run-in with the director, Em had infiltrated the wardrobe closet and changed into a costume labeled *Outlaw*. Which, she supposed, was pretty appropriate given her current status. She'd shed her zilks and tossed aside the torn invisibility hoodie, then dressed in the chaps, button-down shirt, boots, and leather vest—all in shades of brown and tan. She pulled her hair into two braids to keep it out of her face. Then she grabbed the biggest cowboy hat she could find on the rack.

She planned to saunter out of the trailer and across the set, disguised as a member of the cast. From there, she'd search for signs of another portal. She didn't want to linger too long on this dim in case the cadets figured out where she'd gone. Although that seemed highly unlikely.

Then she'd heard the commotion. First, a pistol shot. Next, loud cheering. Later, pottery smashing, followed by lots of yelling. She peered out the trailer window. Two girls who looked exactly like her were duking it out, yelling and running. Could one of them be Maeve from Dim14? If so, it meant the Earthling cadets *had* followed her here. She needed an escape plan, fast.

She exited the trailer and hid from view behind a large cart of rocks, some of them flecked with fake gold. The chasing and fighting raged on inside a tent stocked with food and beverages. Everyone on set was busy trying to defuse the doppelganger drama. Perfect. This was the diversion Em needed.

# CHAPTER 31

**"MAEVE! RUN!" DEV SHOUTED AS MAEVELLINA TORE THROUGH** the crowd, swinging the mallet.

Maevellina's mother looked back and forth between the two girls, utterly perplexed. "I'm seeing double," she said, woozily, pressing a hand to her forehead. "Ooh, must be this desert heat."

"Get back here, you imposter!" Maevellina bellowed, slamming into a sound technician.

"Heck hath no fury like a child star scorned," someone muttered, jumping out of the way.

"Don't let her touch you!" Dev shouted, struggling to keep up. "You have to stay away from your doppelganger! She doesn't have the kazoo! There's another one!"

"Another what?" Maeve yelled back, hitching up her skirts and sprinting between a group of extras.

"Another you!" Dev hollered.

"Arghhhhhh!" Maevellina screamed, smashing the

mallet into a barrel, splintering it into pieces and spilling a brown, oily liquid all over the ground.

The girl seemed like a complete lunatic, but Maeve was relieved to see that her starlet doppelganger was at least wearing pants. Well, shorts, to be precise.

"Hurry! She's gaining on you!" Dev cried out.

Maeve turned left and slipped in the slick mud. She skidded, nearly twisting her ankle in her old-fashioned boots. She scrambled to her feet and took off running, casting a worried look over her shoulder. Maevellina was gaining on her, swinging that mallet, madder than a hornet. No one else on set seemed to know how to stop her or which girl was at fault. The other cast members looked around, bemused.

"Is this some sort of publicity stunt?" someone asked.

Dev knew he had to do something before the dueling Maeves tore open even more Rips in the multiverse. He looked around at the movie set. There was a miners' village, a trading post, and a tavern. He didn't exactly consider himself an actor, but he would need to channel the grit, gumption, and guts of a real hero. He dashed through a swinging set of saloon doors and out into the sound stage beyond. That's when he spotted a covered wagon with two chestnut-brown horses hitched to the front. Behind that, a girl with braided red hair and shifty eyes threw a saddle over a dappled gray pony. He gasped.

"Hey! You!" Dev yelled. A third mirror image of Maeve—this one dressed like an outlaw—turned a sharp gaze in his direction.

Without hesitating, he ran toward her. She mounted the pony in a flash and took off riding west, away from the sprawling film set and toward the canyon edge, presumably taking the kazoo with her.

"Get away from me!" Maeve shouted, sprinting toward the craft services tent, trying to keep a safe distance between herself and the enraged starlet. She grabbed a folding chair and threw it behind her to block Maevellina's path.

"Girls! That is quite enough!" the director shouted, flapping his arms, trying to regain some sense of order. "Put down the weapon! Put down my chairs! There are enough parts for both of you! You're both stars!"

"No!" shouted Maevellina, bringing the mallet down hard on a table and sending a platter of sandwiches flying into the air. "I'm the only star here!" she hollered. "This town ain't big enough for the two of us!"

Maeve ducked and rolled under a table. Maevellina jumped on top, tipping over a basket of muffins and bagels. "Where do you think you're going?" she yelled before somersaulting off the table's edge, landing nimbly on two feet a few yards in front of Maeve.

The girls stared at each other. It was like looking in a mirror. "See?" Maevellina called to the director, who was cowering by the water cooler. "I told you I could do my own stunts. Now watch this!" She took a series of fast lunging steps, then delivered a roundhouse kick.

Maeve felt as though she were living in slow motion. She reflexively twisted her body, arching backward, feeling the whoosh of air as her doppelganger's purple cowgirl boot swept mere inches from her head. Her flight instinct triggered and she darted for the tent's exit, making a beeline for the abandoned mining village set.

Exhausted, she risked a look over her shoulder. To her dismay, mallet-swinging Maevellina wasn't far behind, gaining on her. Marching band practice could be grueling, but even Coach Diaz's singing sprints and cardio choreography hadn't prepared her for a chase like this. Her lungs burned and her muscles ached, but she couldn't stop. She had to get away from her doppelganger.

A stampede of hooves pummeled the ground, pulling a covered wagon at breakneck speed.

"Oh, fantastic," Maeve muttered. Outrunning a girl on foot was one thing, but there was no way she could outrun a duo of powerful stallions. Up ahead, a fence separated the film set from the wilds of the mesa beyond. A steep bluff rose up behind the fence. The wagon wouldn't be able to follow her there if she attempted the vertical climb. Even though her legs burned and her heels were raw with blisters, she knew this was her best shot. Her only shot. She turned and ran toward the fence as fast as she could.

The wagon swerved, nearly mowing her down. Her legs pumped hard, but she couldn't keep it up much longer. Suddenly the wagon pulled beside her, its wheels churning up a cloud of dust. Maeve coughed; her eyes burned.

"Give me your hand!" someone hollered. Maeve recognized that voice. It was Dev! He was driving the wagon, trying to help, not hurt her. He gripped the reins with one hand and reached out to Maeve with the other. She stretched her arm. Their fingers touched, but then the horses pulled away.

Dev yanked the reins and tried to slow the horses, but Maeve was exhausted and couldn't keep up the pace. Maevellina, on the other hand, continued to sprint and shout, gaining on Maeve with each second.

A coil of rope lay on the wagon floor by Dev's feet. He reached down and threw one end over the side of the wagon. "Grab on!" he shouted to Maeve.

She caught the rope and held tight. Dev secured the reins onto a hook near the driver's bench. Then he used both hands to heave the rope—with Maeve attached—closer to the speeding wagon.

She used all her remaining strength to climb upward, clutching the rope, throwing one leg over the side of the wagon, then the other. Dev helped her aboard, and she fell into a tired but relieved heap. As soon as he knew she was okay, Dev grabbed the reins again and urged the horses onward.

"You won't get away with this!" Maevellina called after them, nearly out of breath. "Remember, I'm the star around here! I'm the best actress in the whole, wide—" Before she could finish, Maevellina tripped and fell face-first onto the ground.

"Yeehaw!" Maeve cried out, watching from the back of the wagon. "Direct hit!"

"We've been hit?" Dev asked, taking his eyes off the path ahead for a split second. "By what? A flying mallet?"

"Nope. Not us. Maevellina. She finally got her close-up . . . with a fresh, steamy pile of manure." Maeve couldn't help but chuckle. She moved toward the front of the wagon and took a seat next to Dev. She exhaled and stared out at the amber-colored sky. "Can you even believe it?" she asked, leaning back and stretching her tired limbs.

"Believe what? That your evil twin just got a horse poop facial?" He cackled. "I mean, I guess you could call it karma. Except, she wasn't entirely awful when I talked to her, until her temper got the best of her and she completely bugged out. I mean, that mallet was totally unnecessary. And the whole name-calling thing wasn't too nice either."

"No, not that," Maeve said, sitting up. "Can you believe that I just gave the performance of a lifetime, lived through an actual high-speed chase, and now we're riding off into the sunset? Literally, in a wagon, with horses and everything." She sighed and ran her hands through her hair. "Could this be any more perfect?"

Dev considered this, his gaze focused on the horizon. "A kazoo would help."

Maeve bit her lip, her perfect moment fizzling. "Oh, right. That."

"Yeah, that," Dev replied, giving her a look. "Lucky for us, I'm on the trail."

Maeve scanned the mesa. "What trail would that be?" she asked. Now that the film set was far behind them, there didn't seem to be a whole lot of anything for miles in any direction.

"Over there." Dev pointed to the west, where a fiery orange sun slowly ambled toward the horizon.

Maeve squinted, and then she saw it: a lone rider on horseback. A girl, graceful and athletic, with a shock of red hair that caught the sunlight like flames. "Is that . . . ?"

"Yup." Dev nodded. "That's you. Er, her. Your other doppel."

The scene was downright cinematic, but there were no cameras or crew members for miles. Then, in a terrible twist, a massive shadow descended, momentarily tamping out the golden light and darkening their path.

"CRAWWW! Cah-craaaw!" A bone-chilling screech echoed across the mesa, followed by the whump of vast wings.

Maeve and Dev looked skyward. A bird descended—part vulture, part hawk, and pure terror. Practically prehistoric in size, it swooped downward, its greasy black feathers carrying the stench of rotted carrion. Its beak was dagger-sharp, curved like a scythe. The wrinkled skin around its head and gullet was a grisly shade of pinkish gray.

"What. Is. That?" Dev breathed, gripping the reins

tighter, hoping the horses wouldn't spook and tip their wagon over with a crash.

The giant bird soared closer and closer. "Get down!" Maeve cried. But the bird passed by them, beating its wings and rising upward on a thermal draft, coasting with missile-like speed toward the lone rider in the distance. It screeched again, a deafening hunting call. In the wide-open mesa, there was nowhere to hide. The bird dove, its enormous talons extended, and plucked Other-Maeve from the back of her horse.

"That thing snatched my doppelganger!" Maeve cried, horrified. "Follow that raptor!"

"Are you nuts?" Dev yelled back as their wagon bumped along. "I am not messing with big bird. That thing looks like a killer."

Maeve was on the brink of hysterics. "We have to help her, er, me. My doppelganger, I mean."

"No way. This ends here." Dev yanked on the reins and slowed the horses to a trot. "We have to turn back. Return to the portal and our friends. We gave this our best shot."

Tears sprang to Maeve's eyes. "We have to go after her! Her life is in danger, Dev."

He clenched his jaw. "By stealing that kazoo, she put *our* lives in danger."

"Maybe she had good reason."

"What?" He gaped at her. "What happened to you back on that movie set? How are you on her side all of a sudden?"

The bird screeched again and ascended high into the air, with Maeve's look-alike kicking and fighting in its claws. She punched, thrashed, and appeared to even bite the bird in an attempt to escape. The bird squawked angrily and released the girl. She plummeted toward the earth, limbs flailing. Right before she struck the ground, the giant bird swooped down and snatched her out of the sky, clenching her tightly in its talons. The girl's body hung limply, like a rag doll.

"She's hurt!" Maeve said, pointing. The bird flapped its wings and flew toward a rocky plateau, landing just out of view.

"Yeah, that's probably a clear indication that we should stay away, too. That creature is dangerous, Maeve. It's not some special effect like in the movies. It's lethal."

"Stop the wagon!" Maeve demanded. "Let me off. I'll go on foot. Alone." She shot him a livid look.

"Up to the top of that bluff? Where a giant raptor is probably feasting on a girl that looks exactly like you? Great idea," he muttered sarcastically. "She'll be the appetizer and we'll end up the main course."

The wagon came to a halt and Maeve hopped out. Her legs were stiff and tired from running, but she forced herself to continue onward.

"You're serious, aren't you?" he called to her.

Maeve didn't reply. She didn't even look back. She began to scale the winding vertical trail.

Dev exhaled loudly. "I cannot believe you're making

me do this." He climbed out of the wagon and reluctantly tied the horses to a dead cottonwood tree. Beside it, a trail led upward along a steep escarpment toward a craggy bluff overlooking the sprawling canyon. "In the history of bad ideas, this might be one of the worst," he grumbled. "Could you be any more stubborn?"

"Could you be any more noisy?" Maeve scowled, wiping beads of sweat from her brow. She tugged at her dress, annoyed by the corset's thick boning that kept jabbing at her ribs. "We have the element of surprise on our side. Though not for long, if you keep whining."

"I'm about to be eaten alive. I think I'm entitled to whine a little, okay?" He hurried to keep up. "Of all the ways to die . . . death by big bird while in pursuit of a lost kazoo is just not how I pictured this going down."

Maeve gritted her teeth, scrabbling for purchase along a crumbly slope of rock and sand. "No one's going to die today," she said, pulling herself up and over the ledge. "Not if I can help it."

# CHAPTER 32

FOR A MOMENT, EM FELT OUTSIDE HERSELF, LIKE SHE WAS suspended in the air, looking down at someone else. A poor, broken girl lay below amidst a pile of sticks and dried grasses, her body bloodied and curled into a ball like a help-less grub. *Get up,* Em thought, instinct kicking in. *Get up and fight. Defend yourself.*

A terrible shrieking sound brought her back with sud-den force. Em inhaled sharply and sat up, causing her head to swim. She squinted into the glaring light. Her bones ached, and her outlaw outfit was in tatters. Several fresh lacerations slashed her stomach and legs—not deep enough to be mortal wounds, but still raw and stinging. How had she gotten them?

"You're a tricky girl to track down," a voice croaked. Em turned her head slowly, still disoriented. A monstrous feath-ered creature stood before her, its beak clacking. It stretched its wings wide and blocked out the sun, casting Em in ominous shadow. The putrid stench of decay wafted her way, making Em gag. The bird's talons—sharp as knives—scraped the parched earth. Suddenly, Em understood where her lacerations had come from.

The bird squawked again, an ear-splitting, toe-curling trill. "CRAWWW! Cah-craaaw!"

Suddenly, the creature began to shake violently, molting. A flurry of greasy black feathers fell to the ground. The bird's neck extended outward, then wrenched backward. Its beak morphed into a mouth, its bones reconfiguring. Em recoiled, turning away from the ghastly transformation. When she opened her eyes again, she was face-to-face with the Empyrean One's trusted advisor, and Em's longtime tutor.

"Gen! You came back for me!" Em said forcing herself to stand, even though her legs felt weak and unsteady. She was flooded with emotions: exhaustion, relief, hope. But something about Gen's expression made Em pause. As a shape-shifter, her tutor could assume the form of countless creatures, yet she'd never been particularly effusive when it came to revealing emotion. In her current human form, her face was stern and rigid. Em couldn't help but wish that Gen would show some glimmer of tenderness.

Gen brushed a rogue feather from her suit. She wore a set of charcoal-gray Empyrean zilks, armored and shining, with flat-soled boots that reached her knees. Her dark hair was twisted into a severe knot atop her head. "With all these irritating lockdown orders, I had to take quite a detour to find you."

"I'm so glad you did," Em said. She winced and touched one of the scrapes across her thigh. "I just wish you'd been a bit gentler."

"Avian extractions are always challenging. Talons are less dexterous than you might imagine. Plus, you put up quite a fight."

"As you trained me to do," Em replied, bowing to her tutor.

"Indeed. Here." Gen produced a vial from the sash slung diagonally across her chest.

Em took the salve—a blend of herbs from Dim8 like bitterstalk and morrowroot—and smeared the medicine over her lacerations, numbing the pain. Within seconds, the skin began to heal. She nodded thanks, but Gen's face remained stoic. "So . . . how did you find me?"

"Silly child. You really think we'd let the last known blood relative of the Empyrean One out of our sights without installing a tracker?" As Gen spoke, Em noticed that something was amiss with her face. Her skin had a smudged effect, as though her features had lost definition over time. Cellular degradation happened occasionally, especially to those who traveled between dimensions too frequently. Beneath Gen's human flesh, greenish reptilian scales showed through in places. The effect was startling, even for Em, who'd grown up surrounded by a varied assortment of Empyrii shape-shifters and other life-forms.

"You've been tracking me? This whole time?"

Gen strolled along the plateau's edge, taking in the

scenery. They were high up, hundreds of feet above a roaring river that snaked along the canyon's sandstone floor. "Yes. We had a chip installed when you were a baby."

"Installed? When I was a baby?" Em was horrified to hear Gen talk about her body like a piece of machinery that could be meddled with so intrusively, especially since no one had ever asked for her consent. "Where is it?" she asked, rolling up her sleeves, scratching at every mole and freckle suspiciously.

"It's a burrowing mite chip. By now, it's so deeply embedded that it can only be removed surgically. Consider yourself hardwired."

Em hated the idea of the mite chip. She wanted to claw it out from beneath her skin, but she knew that was impossible. "If you knew where I was all along, why didn't you come sooner? I was in danger. I went without food for days. I nearly froze to death. Not to mention the inhospitable locals I encountered."

"Oh, the Earthlings? Despicable things, I know. I applaud you for tolerating them as long as you did. Not an easy species to get along with."

Em shook her head. "No, not them. They actually weren't that bad. I'm talking about the dragomanders, the smog-monsters, and all the other creatures that seemed intent on devouring me!"

Gen waved her hand dismissively. "Stop being so dramatic. Your emotions have always been your downfall."

Em struggled to keep her tone calm and her face neutral, but her heart battered her ribs. This was not the happy reunion she'd imagined.

"Why did you leave me alone for so long? I could have died."

Gen pursed her lips. There was little warmth in her expression, no remorse or worry. Not even an inkling of affection. "Your banishment was not only a punishment for overstepping your station. As you might recall, it was also meant to be a learning experience. A time of growth and reflection, if you will."

"So, this was all a test?"

Gen stepped away from the cliff's edge. Her eyes bored deeply into Em's. "Everything in life is a test."

Em had heard this a million times before, during their training sessions and academic lessons. "And did I pass?" she asked, her voice raw.

Gen blinked. Her human eyes were normally brown, but now they seemed to glow a faint amber. "That is yet to be determined. Which is why I'm here."

"She wants me to come home?" Em asked hopefully, the word *home* hitching in her throat. "She sent you to retrieve me, right? To lift my banishment and escort me back to Dim8?"

Gen frowned, her lips drooping. "Not exactly." She walked in a circle around Em, regarding her from new angles. "As you know, your aunt is not a forgiving person. She may never agree to let you return."

"What? That wasn't part of the deal."

"There is no deal. You are in no position to negotiate with the Empyrean One. The supreme leader of the multiverse does not bow to the wishes of self-entitled tweens."

Em thrust her shoulders back defiantly. "I'm not just some stranger. She can't abandon me forever. I'm her blood!"

"Which is why your betrayal is that much more serious."

"I never betrayed the Empyrean One. I merely asked a question." Em's posture wilted. She shuffled her feet in her leather boots. "Okay, maybe a *few* questions."

Gen's eyes glowed. Her pupils morphed from circular to slitted. "Questioning the Empyrean One, doubting her decisions, undermining her authority, speaking out of rank. All of those are treasonous acts, punishable by death. You are lucky she spared your life. You should be grateful that you were only banished. Many have met far worse fates for far lesser transgressions."

"I merely asked why she wanted to release the Cataclysmosis spores. I could never understand why she was so intent on creating chaos and destruction. I asked her if fear was truly the only way to lead." Em gestured to the valley and canyon below. "Why would she want to ruin all this?" She gazed at the apricot-colored sky, the tumbling river, the sage-green mesa grasses. "Sure, these worlds are flawed. The life-forms imperfect. But that's also what makes them so beautiful."

Gen clucked. "You are naïve, young one. Where you see beauty, we see pain. Those of us who endured the

Untethering understand that history is a dark and complex web. There is no right or wrong, no black and white. Who wins and who loses is always up for debate, depending on who is telling the story." She strode across the rocky ground. "Your aunt and I sought to shield you and the rest of Empyria from the suffering we were forced to endure." She glared down her nose at Em. "You've been on Earth and its variants for a few days. We've been unwanted and unwelcome for millennia."

Maeve and Dev reached the top of the escarpment, which opened up into a broad, flat plateau overlooking the mesa on one side and a deep, sprawling canyon below. They were about to peek over the edge when Dev grabbed Maeve by the arm and yanked her back down. "Wait, what's our plan?" he whispered.

Maeve looked over her shoulder. "I don't really have one. I was sort of going to wing it."

"Wing it? First of all, that's a terrible bird pun. Second, this isn't an improv exercise in drama class, Maeve. This is a serious life-or-death situation!" he hissed.

She tucked her hair behind her ears, then reached down and picked up a couple loose rocks, clutching them in her palm. "Fine. Grab a few of these."

Dev's eyes were wide with concern. "We're about to confront a carnivorous bird that's ten times our size, and your plan is to throw a couple of pebbles at it?" He smacked his palm to his forehead. "In the words of Isaiah, we are so totally doomed."

"You still have the Serger in your backpack, right? It's basically a boomerang. Use that if you have to."

Dev clenched his hands into frustrated fists. "That is not its intended purpose!"

"Just stay calm and be quiet, okay?" She climbed the last few feet upward. The wind was stronger there, and she clung to the rock face so she wouldn't fall. She peered over the edge of the escarpment. Hundreds of black feathers lay scattered on the ground, but the bird itself was gone. In its place stood something—*someone*—even more unexpected.

Maeve ducked back down, breathing rapidly.

"What? What is it?" Dev asked.

"See for yourself," she replied, wondering if the desert heat was creating a mirage. Perhaps her eyes were playing tricks on her?

Dev peeked over the ridge and sucked in a breath. He was about to duck back down when a gust of wind threw him off balance. The rocks and sand beneath his hands gave way and he slipped, tumbling forward onto the open plateau.

"Well, well. We meet again, Earthling."

# CHAPTER 33

"DR. SCOPES?" DEV SAID, BRUSHING SAND FROM HIS EYES. SHE looked the same as he remembered from their field trip at NASA, but also different. Instead of a white lab coat, she wore armored suiting. And something was very wrong with her face. "What are you doing here?"

"I could ask you the very same question," she snarled, regarding him like a hungry predator stalking its prey.

"Scopes?" Em asked, confused by the name.

Gen turned and gave an exasperated shrug. "Dr. Genevieve Scopes was my alias during my last stint on Earth of Dim14. I worked at NASA with this young man's father. Such a gullible fool."

"Don't talk about my dad like that!" Dev shouted, anger welling up.

"Calm down, boy. Your bravado won't do you any good here. You are clearly outnumbered, and my protégé and I are skilled combat warriors." Her eyes glowed like embers.

"She's your protégé?" he asked, turning to Other-Maeve. The girl was still dressed in the outlaw costume from the movie set, but the fabric had been badly torn and was stained with something that looked like blood. Her face was smudged with dirt and her red hair blew wildly in the breeze.

"Em? Ah, yes. I've been her tutor for years. I taught her everything she knows." Without warning, Gen spun around, delivering a powerful palm strike in Em's direction. Instinct and training kicked in, and Em ducked just in time. Gen struck again. Em lunged, deflecting the blow. She flipped backward with an agile handspring, then thrust a defensive punch toward the center of Gen's armored chest plate. Fast as lightning, Gen caught Em's fist, twisted her wrist, wrenched her arm, and slammed her onto the ground. She landed hard, yet within seconds, she was back on her feet in fighting stance, dusty but undeterred.

"That's enough for now," Gen said, brushing off the shoulders of her gleaming gray zilks.

Dev gulped. There was no doubt these two could kick his butt all the way into the next dimension. He glanced around anxiously. Maeve was still hidden behind the rocky outcropping at the edge of the plateau. Great. He was on his own with no plan and no defenses.

"I deceived them all," Gen continued, recounting her time on Earth. "Building a collider with direct access to Station Liminus, coordinating a group of fake emissaries, infiltrating the EnerCor drilling operations, disseminating the Cataclysmosis spores beneath the failed planet's crust, orchestrating a rigged vote for compactification." She rubbed her palms together, her long fingernails filed to sharp points. "It was a deliciously devious mission—one of the Empyrean One's most brilliant schemes—and it nearly succeeded." She turned to Dev, her eyes ablaze. "Until these meddling little Earthling pests arrived and ruined everything."

He was frozen, unsure what to do next. There were a million things he wanted to shout at this Scopes-like person, but he held his tongue. He wanted to fight, to strike her down, but even his marching band moves were no match for her cosmic combat skills.

Gen strode closer to Dev. "I planned to hunt down the so-called Space Cadets eventually. Though I never imagined you'd come directly to me, and so soon." She sneered, her lips curling into a cruel smirk. "It's almost too easy." Gen cocked her head to the side. "Tell me, Earthling boy, what brought you here, of all places?"

He pointed to Em.

Gen's slitted pupils dilated. She turned, slowly, and regarded Maeve's doppelganger anew. "This was your idea? A trap so that we could finally exact revenge on the Earthling cadets? How clever. How cunning." Her demeanor shifted. For the first time in a very long time, Gen appeared proud of Em. "Perhaps you are worthy after all."

Em swallowed, but a lump remained in her throat. The praise she had longed for didn't feel right. The words made her itch.

With almost liquid agility, Gen struck Dev in the stomach. He doubled over in pain. She grabbed him by his backpack and lifted him effortlessly into the air, as though he weighed no more than a feather. Em held her breath, preparing for the worst.

"Put him down!" Maeve screamed, jumping up from her hiding spot and hurling at rock at Gen. It stuck her armor with a sad, ineffectual *plunk*.

"With pleasure." Gen dropped Dev to the ground. He coughed and rubbed his neck, gasping for air. Gen stepped over him and wiped her hands, as though she had touched something filthy. She turned to Maeve. "Look who we have here."

Em stared at her doppelganger. Maeve stared back. She was wearing heavy stage makeup and an old-fashioned calico dress, but it was definitely the same girl she'd comforted on the dark hillside. Like before, Em felt as if an invisible thread connected them. It pulled and tugged her toward the girl, even though she knew she should stay far away.

"Tell me, exactly how did my protégé lure you here?" Gen asked, placing herself between the nearly identical girls.

"We're here because she took something that belongs to us," Maeve replied. "And we want it back."

"We also thought you were going to eat your protégé, and Maeve had this ridiculous idea that she might somehow stop you," Dev added, coming to Maeve's side.

Em couldn't hide her surprise at this last bit. The Earthlings had wanted to help her?

"Is that so?" Gen's eyes darted back and forth, assessing the situation. "And what might be so precious that you would willingly risk your lives to retrieve it?"

"This," Em said, slowly pulling the kazoo from her breast pocket. She showed Gen the silver case embossed with the Multiverse Allied Council's thirteen-pointed symbol. "It's a communication device. A direct link to Station Liminus's primary triskaidecagon and Ignatia herself."

Gen inhaled a sharp, greedy breath. "How did you acquire such a valuable item?"

"I may not be able to shape-shift like you, but I obtained an invisibility garment. Later, I impersonated my doppelganger." She pointed to Maeve and then Dev. "I pretended to be her, then I stole it from him." She had imagined this moment feeling so . . . different. Instead of elation or pride, Em was saddled with regret.

Gen flicked her forked tongue between her teeth. "Yesss, very good. We will use this to our advantage. Intercept classified messaging, infiltrate the council, regain our stronghold across the multiverse. This is even better than I expected. Well done."

Em nodded reluctantly.

"Give it to me, girl," Gen demanded. She opened her palm, waving Em forward with her claw-like nails.

"No." Em shook her head defiantly.

"No!" Maeve echoed.

"No?" Gen spat. "You deny me, child?"

Em took a deep breath, fortifying herself. "I will deliver the kazoo to the Empyrean One myself. To prove my loyalty."

Gen considered this. "Very well. Nevertheless, in order to earn your way back home, you must complete one additional task."

Em nodded, wrapping her fingers tightly around the kazoo. "Anything."

Gen gestured to Maeve and Dev, who were cowering several feet from the canyon's edge. "Dispose of them." She snapped her fingers. "And do it quickly. We don't have all day. Our exit portal will close at sundown."

Em's mouth hung open. She desperately wanted to return home, and she craved her aunt's attention and approval. But not if it meant harming the cadets. They were innocent in all this.

"Won't the kazoo be enough?" Em asked, trying to remain calm. If she showed any sign of weakness or emotion, Gen would seize upon it and dig her claws deep into whatever fears or feelings Em might be stupid enough to reveal.

"No. Eradicating the Earthling cadets is a matter of pride. They are responsible for the ruination of our plans. You aunt is very, very angry at them. And you know how the Empyrean One gets when she's angry."

Em bristled. Maevellina's meltdown had been one thing, but a tyrant's tantrum was frightening on a whole other level.

"Kill them," Gen commanded. "Now."

"I won't," Em said between gritted teeth.

"Excuse me?" Gen leered, her tongue flicking inches from Em's face.

"This is not who I am."

"You are whoever we tell you to be. You follow orders. You do as you're told." Her face hardened. "Not all of us have a choice in the paths our lives take."

"That's not true," Em replied earnestly. "Look around the multiverse and you can clearly see the myriad ways a life can change, for good or bad. Every choice we make has a lasting effect on our futures and the futures of those around us. During my banishment, I witnessed it firsthand."

"You're enlightened now, are you?" Gen said condescendingly.

"The Empyrean One teaches us that others should be feared. Trust no one. Hunt or be hunted. But *she's* the one I should have been afraid of."

"Stop! I will not hear it!" Gen shouted, her face reddening with rage.

"She feeds us lies, Gen. She stokes hatred in our hearts. Then she harnesses those feelings and makes us do unthinkable things."

"Blasphemy!" Gen recoiled, as though the words had a caustic effect.

"It doesn't have to be like this." Em lowered her voice. She cast a long look at Maeve and Dev, huddled together. "Let them go home to their families."

"Enough!" Gen screamed. Em fell quiet. "I had such high hopes," Gen lamented. "I thought I saw potential in you. Now I realize how mistaken I was. Your aunt and I both envisioned your ascension through the ranks. A seat beside her at the head of the multiverse. But time away from home has only made you more brazen. Where is your gratitude? Your respect?" She stamped her foot on the ground. "You should bow down and give thanks!"

Gen rose up, suddenly growing several inches taller. Her face became more angular, her eyes dark as coal. Hardened scales protruded from her temples. "You ally yourself with them?" With a single swipe of her arm, she struck the cadets, knocking them to the ground. "You defy your own dimension? Your own blood?"

Maeve helped Dev to his feet. They scrambled a safe distance away from the canyon's jagged precipice.

"You tried to destroy their planet!" Em shouted back, fury rising.

"Insolent child," Gen purred cruelly, shaking her head. "The Earthlings did *that* all on their own. Burning fossil fuels, clear-cutting their forests, constantly consuming more, more, more. We may have expedited the degradation process, but their planet was in shambles long before we arrived. Compactification would have made everything so much simpler." She whipped her head around, halting Maeve and Dev in their tracks as they tried to sneak away, back toward the trail. "But no! These two and their rag-tag band of misfits had to intervene and ruin everything."

"They were only trying to protect themselves and the people they love," Em said sullenly. "Not that I'd expect you to know anything about love."

"Love, you say?" Gen quirked a scaly eyebrow. "Is that what this is all about?" She began to laugh maniacally. "The multiverse is a heartless place. There is no room for love here." Her eyes narrowed. "You sound like your mother when you talk like that," she growled spitefully.

"My mother?" Em said, gutted by the thought of the woman she had never known but whom she thought of frequently.

"Didn't you know?" Gen's voice curdled. "Your mother wanted to raise you in a less hostile world. She eschewed the Empyrean One's brutal rule, she betrayed her own sister, and she escaped with you when you were only three weeks old."

The words struck Em harder than any physical blow. "No." She shook her head. "That's impossible. She died in childbirth. That's why my aunt has always carried such disdain for me, because I am a constant reminder of her loss. I caused my mother's death."

Gen met Em's eyes. "Believe what you wish, though I speak the truth. Your mother made it a few months on the run before we found her, clutching you to her breast in a cave on Zervoya. Sniveling, pathetic, weakened by love. Softened and irrational."

Em blanched, blood draining from her face. "What did you do to her?"

"The Empyrean One had her permanently exiled for treason, of course."

"Where?" Em asked, tears stinging her eyes.

"Some abominable dim on the outer reaches of the multiverse." Gen shrugged, unperturbed. "I doubt she survived a day, not with her heart shattered to pieces like that."

"She was brokenhearted?"

"When we snatched you from her arms, yes." Gen's back stiffened. "We did what we had to do." She traversed the plateau. "With no heirs of her own, sparing your life was a strategic move on the Empyrean One's part. Your aunt took pity on you then, but I guarantee she won't be so kind again."

Something in Em's face changed, a nearly imperceptible shift. No one but Maeve caught it, and the only reason she did was because Em's face was also *her* face. A slight adjustment of the brow, a tightening around the corners of the lips, a steeliness in the eyes. It was the face Maeve made whenever she was about to get in character. It was the face of a performer, which, in an odd way, was also the face of a liar. Even though she'd noticed the slight change in Em, Maeve didn't understand what it meant.

"Put an end to these Earthlings now. Prove your loyalty. Or I will do it myself." Gen pushed past Em, heading directly for Maeve and Dev.

Maeve tried to escape, but she and Dev were cornered. The sandy ground crumbled underfoot. Dislodged rocks crashed into the canyon below.

"Stop!" Em cried. "I'll do it!"

Gen paused, pivoting slowly on her heels. "This is your last chance."

Em thrust her shoulders back. Maeve and Dev clung together. Backed against the sheer-faced precipice, there was nowhere to run or hide.

"Please," Maeve pleaded as Em stepped closer. Closer. The air between the two girls became electrified. The wind began to blow more forcefully. Goose bumps prickled their skin. Their toes tingled curiously.

Em lowered her chin. Just when Maeve thought she had changed her mind, Em charged. As fast and as powerful as a bull, she plowed into Maeve with both palms, pushing her dangerously close to the cliff's edge. The second her hands touched Maeve, a jolt of energy surged through them.

A burning sensation scorched through their nerve endings. Their hair blew back. Their spines arched. Dev jumped between them, frantically trying to tear the girls apart, but it wasn't enough. Em was a trained fighter. She lunged and rolled impossibly fast, her body a blur of strength and agility. With one last powerful shove, she heaved both Maeve and Dev over the edge of the cliff.

"Nooooooo!"

Arms pinwheeling, the cadets fell down, down, down. They reached for each other and screamed, their terrified cries echoing for miles.

Far below, the raging river rapids churned, fierce and frothy white. Even if they survived the fall from several hundred feet up (not likely), the river would surely finish the job.

Maeve pressed her eyes shut. The movie reel of her life flashed before her, too quickly. Her body spun and tumbled out of control. The wind roared and whooshed as she plunged down into the cavernous canyon. And she knew with total certainty that this was the end.

# CHAPTER 34

**THE CADETS LANDED—NOT WITH A BONE-CRUNCHING CRASH OR** a dramatic splash but with a squishy, muddy *plop!*

Just as the canyon floor rushed up to meet them and they braced for impact, a Rip tore open. The air thickened, slowing their fall. As they passed through the dense field of energized particles, the cadets' limbs pulled and stretched like taffy. The skin on their hands and faces dissolved into pixels, floating and shimmering in a rainbow of colors before reassembling. There was a flash of fluorescent light, a crackling noise, and then, somehow, Maeve and Dev found themselves lying on the banks of a shallow creek.

Maeve sat up and rubbed her temples. Her entire body vibrated like a plucked guitar string.

"I expected that to hurt a whole lot more," Dev said, dazed.

"I expected to be a whole lot more dead," Maeve replied,

standing slowly and wiping mud from her dress. She wriggled inside the uncomfortably tight bodice.

Dev surveyed their surroundings. "We never hit the bottom of the canyon," he observed. "But how?"

Maeve looked upward. Hovering a few feet above their heads was a gaping, jagged-edged Rip. It shimmered with iridescence. "Looks like we were sucked through that portal in the nick of time." She remembered the night on the hillside when she'd felt Em's invisible touch in the darkness. "Do you think my doppelganger knew a portal would open when she touched me?"

"If that were the case, couldn't she just high-five you, instead of pushing us off a cliff?" Dev shuddered. "She seemed pretty intent on 'eradicating' us."

Maeve nodded, but she wasn't sure what to think or believe. Her head was spinning, and her heart ached in a way that she didn't fully understand.

The dimensional tear above them warped, its surface undulating and rippling. Quantum lightning flared. Bright blue sparks fizzed along its edges.

"That looks highly unstable," Dev said, concerned.

A terrible realization dawned on the cadets at the same moment.

"Get the Serger! Hurry!" Maeve said frantically. "Close the portal before Gen follows us here!"

"I don't know where it is!" Dev sputtered, searching the muddy banks for his backpack, which had fallen off on impact.

"There!" Maeve said, spotting the bag lodged between a clump of mossy rocks on the far side of the creek.

Dev waded through the knee-high water as fast as possible, praying that the Serger hadn't been damaged. He unzipped his pack and pulled out the contraption, which appeared intact.

"Phew." He breathed a sigh of relief.

"Uhh, Dev?" Maeve pointed to the portal. The pale iridescent membrane darkened. A shape appeared in the wide opening. It was small and blurry at first, then rapidly grew in size as the object moved closer and closer.

Maeve screamed. "It's her! It's Scopes! She shape-shifted again!" She splashed through the water toward Dev, the soaked ruffles of her old-timey skirt weighing her down, making it hard to move. "Big bad big bird is back!"

As if on cue, the creature screeched. The sonic vibrations of the high-pitched hunting call were so powerful that they crossed the dimensional threshold, chilling Maeve and Dev to the core.

Beak aimed downward, glossy black wings pinned skyward, the bird sliced and spiraled through the air, aiming straight for the portal.

"Load the power cartridge! Activate the Serger!" Maeve cried.

Dev's hands shook and he nearly dropped the small fuel

cube into the mud. He caught it, then clicked it into place. The Serger whirred to life.

The massive bird screeched again, dive-bombing, picking up speed.

"Close the portal! She's getting closer! Don't let her through."

Dev gripped the Serger. He aimed for the Rip. He pulled his arm back, then released the boomerang-shaped device, hurling it upward with all the strength he could muster.

It shot out of his hands, buzzing and humming. The portal bulged and sparked. For a fleeting moment, it looked as though the Serger had been completely swallowed by the Rip. But then the portal made a popping noise and the Serger reemerged, wheeling through the air. It turned sharply and began zooming back and forth across the perimeter of the opening, stitching it closed like some sort of alien sewing machine.

"It's working," Dev breathed, relaxing his shoulders. Sure enough, the portal began to shrink, from the size of a round dining table to the size of a Frisbee. The volatile quantum lightning around its edges calmed and faded.

Perhaps realizing that her exit point was rapidly disappearing and that she was traveling too fast to stop, Scopes screeched one last time before the Rip closed entirely and she crashed with a sickening crunch.

With a final puff of bluish smoke, the portal disappeared completely. The Serger's lights blinked off and the device boomeranged back into Dev's open palms.

"Whoa. That was kind of intense. But also seriously cool." He clutched the Serger gratefully and gave Maeve a broad, relieved smile. "We did it. We're safe now."

"Not so fast," Maeve said, worried they'd landed on yet another remote dimension. "Where are we exactly?"

"I don't have a clue," Dev said warily. "Duna told us the kazoo has a beacon function. If only we had it, we could send the council a signal."

Maeve took in their surroundings. She held up a finger. "That might not be necessary." She stepped cautiously along the muddy creek bank and toward a densely wooded forest. "I feel like I know this place. It looks like the area behind our old farm. But that creek's been dry since the drought. And the fields are brown, not green like this." She bent down to look at the grass.

"Well," Dev said, following Maeve into the woods "Ignatia said the MAC shut down the EnerCor drilling sites on Earth, and they started assisting with some regenerative therapies. Maybe this is a sign that nature is healing." Dev inspected the Serger, turning it over in his hands. "I wonder if this thing could be modified a little. Do you think it could help repair the holes in the ozone?"

Maeve shrugged. "It's possible. The technology is pretty impressive. It reminds me a little of your dad's invention. That reverse dynamite thingy."

"The Syntropitron?"

"Yeah. Could you somehow combine elements of the Serger with parts of the Syntropitron to make something extra epic?"

"That's an awesome idea," Dev said, the engineering wheels in his mind beginning to turn.

They traversed the woods for a few minutes, exploring. Maeve's eyes lit up as she walked over to an old willow tree. She ducked beneath the curtain of swaying branches and yellow-green leaves. There, carved into the bark were the initials *GG*, for Gil Greene. Below that were the letters *MG*.

She gasped. She knew those letters. She knew this place. She reached out and touched the tree bark, memories flooding back. Her grandfather had lived on this property as a boy, and he'd taken Maeve to this very spot when she was small, carving her own initials right below his. She traced the letters with her fingertips and breathed in the crisp October air. She wasn't on a glamorous movie set, or poolside at some glitzy mansion in the Hollywood hills, but she was home. She felt happy, thankful, grounded.

"Maeve? You okay?" Dev asked, walking beside her.

"I'm good. Great actually. We're not lost," she told him. "We made it back to Earth. Our Earth."

# CHAPTER 35

**MAEVE AND DEV EXITED THE WOODS. FAR IN THE DISTANCE,** they spotted the hillside where their adventure into the multiverse had begun earlier that day. Beyond that, the Conroy skyline rose up, a glittering silver silhouette against a golden autumn sky.

"It's so beautiful," Maeve said. "I never realized until now."

"Uh-oh." Dev stopped in his tracks.

"What is it? What's wrong?" Maeve asked, her brief moment of peace dissolving.

"The other portals," he said. "They're still open. I'm pretty sure Scopes crashed in the canyon. But your doppelganger is still on the loose. She might try to escape back through the Rip she initially emerged from. Let's go!"

They hurried along the valley, past the old quarry, and across the rolling hills behind the trailer park. Sure enough, the three portals were still there, with the other cadets waiting nearby. Tessa, Zoey, and Isaiah were chatting together while Lewis napped in the grass.

"Yoohoo! Sleeping Beauty!" Maeve called out, nudging Lewis with the tip of her boot.

He jolted upright and rubbed his eyes. "Aw, why'd you have to wake me up? I was having the best dream. I dreamed I could fly, and I had big muscles, and . . ."

"We're so happy you're back!" Tessa and Zoey cried out in unison, embracing Maeve and Dev in a group hug. Dev blushed a deep shade of crimson. No matter how many dragomanders or evil shape-shifters he might encounter, none could make him weak in the knees quite like the Hawthorne-Scott sisters.

"Wait? Why are you coming from that direction?" Isaiah asked, perplexed. "We thought you'd exit the same way you went in . . ."

Dev bit his lip and shot a look at Maeve. "There was a slight change of plans."

Lewis smirked. "Let me guess, you took a detour again?"

"Something like that. We'll fill you in later. Right now, we've got to close these pesky Rips and make sure Em stays trapped in that other dimension."

"Who's Em?" Zoey asked, wrinkling her nose.

"My doppelganger," Maeve replied.

Isaiah gasped. "You found her?"

"Was she wearing pants?" Lewis asked.

Maeve rolled her eyes. "Yes, she was wearing pants. Leather chaps, to be specific."

Tessa made a face. "Bold choice."

"And cowboy boots. It was a whole look."

"Speaking of looks, what in the world are you wearing?" Tessa gave Maeve a full up-and-down. Her movie set makeup was smudged. Her hairdo had transformed from flawless ringlets to windswept frizz-fest. The calico dress was wrinkled and splattered with mud. The puff sleeves drooped, and the ruffled hem unraveled at her feet.

"It's a long story," Maeve said, tugging at her corseted bodice. "Like I said, we'll tell you everything later, okay?"

"You'd better," Tessa replied, eager for every juicy detail. "These two had a bit of an adventure, too." She pointed at her twin sister, whose right sneaker was torn to pieces. And were those . . . bite marks on the sole?

Zoey gave her foot a wiggle and nodded in agreement. "Safe to say, my FOMO has officially been cured."

Dev activated the Serger and offered it to Maeve. "Would you like to do the honors this time?"

She looked down at the invention in Dev's outstretched hands. She knew what had to be done, but a twinge of uncertainly lingered. If they closed the last remaining portals, they'd be cut off from the multiverse for the foreseeable future. Who knew when or if they'd be able to travel from dimension to dimension again?

As much as the thought scared her, it was thrilling, too. There was an entire world—no, *worlds*—out there, and part of Maeve desperately wanted to explore them. To learn more about who she was meant to be and what she was truly capable of. And though it felt strange and almost wrong to admit, she worried about Em. As soon as they sealed the portals, Em would be trapped and alone in a foreign dimension. Maeve didn't know whether Scopes had survived the canyon fall, but either way, the Empyrean One was still out there.

"Not to rush you or anything, but we sorta kinda need to do this soon." Dev placed the Serger in her hands and nudged her forward. "I don't want to leave these things open too long. You never know who, or what, might stumble through."

"Right." Zoey nodded. "I'm not sure about you guys, but I've had my fill of excitement for one day."

Maeve gave a faint smile. She turned to Lewis. "You should do it," she said, offering him the Serger.

"Me? Seriously?" He blinked. "Is Maeve Greene actually letting me—no, *encouraging* me to push some buttons on a super-special device?" He sighed dramatically and placed a hand over his heart. "I thought I'd never see the day."

"Do it, or lose your chance," she replied, giving his shoulder a playful shove.

He took the Serger and aimed it at the first portal. It shrank and closed. He did the same for the second portal. He paused before sealing up the third and final portal. "We sure about this?" he asked, turning to the other cadets.

"Yup," they replied in unison, although there was a note of regret in each of their voices.

Lewis took aim one last time, released the Serger into the air, and sealed up the final Rip. With a puff of acrid bluish smoke and a bright pulse of light, the portal was gone.

# CHAPTER 36

**"HEY, DON'T LOOK SO GLUM," LEWIS SAID, HANDING THE SERGER** back to Maeve. She passed it to Dev, who placed it carefully inside his backpack. "This doesn't mean the end of our adventures together."

"You're right," she said, looking up at him.

"Don't forget," Zoey chimed in, "we still have marching band regional championships. Approximately two weeks from today, in fact."

"Yeaah! That's gonna be a blast!" Lewis jogged over to a grassy area where he'd left his backpack and jacket. He reached down and pulled a shiny, skinny skateboard with no wheels out of the tall grass. "Think we can incorporate some aerial moves into the choreography?" He hopped onto the board and rose into the air.

Dev's jaw dropped. "Where on Earth did you get that?"

"That's just it—I didn't get it on Earth, or at least not our version of Earth. It's a souvenir from the dim Tessa and

I visited. It's called a soarboard. Pretty sweet, right?" He whizzed over their heads, wiggling his hips and practicing the cadets' signature salute.

"Speaking of souvenirs, did you guys have any luck with the kazoo?" Isaiah asked.

Dev shook his head forlornly. "We tried, but it was too difficult."

"Speaking of difficult," Maeve grumbled, adjusting the bodice of her rumpled dress. "How the heck did women wear these torture devices in the olden days?"

"That's the price of fashion, honey." Tessa laughed. "Looks like the corset might have boning in it, to keep the structure." She eyed the garment closer. "Where did you even get this thing? It looks legit."

"It's a costume from a movie set. Although I don't think it was designed for high-speed chases, canyon climbing, or cliff diving." She yanked on the laces in the back, trying to loosen the archaic contraption that was digging into her chest painfully.

"Cliff diving?" Lewis said, landing his soarboard a few feet away. "That sounds epic."

"Yeah," Dev scoffed. "Epically terrifying."

Maeve squirmed, tugging harder on the dress fabric. With a loud *rrriiiippp* one of the seams tore open. An object fell to the ground.

Zoey gasped. "The kazoo!"

Maeve knelt and picked up the silver case, her hands shaking. She found it hard to breathe, perhaps because the corset had been constricting her ribs, or perhaps because she suddenly understood with striking clarity that Em must have intentionally slipped the kazoo into the lining of her dress. There was no other explanation that made sense in her mind.

"Wait, you said you never got the kazoo?" Isaiah asked, his brow furrowed.

"We didn't. Not that we knew of, at least." She turned to Dev. "My doppelganger had the kazoo in her hand before she pushed us over the canyon edge, right?"

"Yeah, I think so. You two fought for a minute," Dev said. "I tried to break you apart, but Em was so fast and so strong. Her movements were a total blur."

"Exactly. I never saw or felt her slip the kazoo into my dress, but she did. And I think she did it on purpose."

"Real nice parting gift," Dev said angrily.

"I know it seems weird, but I actually think she was trying to help."

Dev balked. "Help? We nearly died!" He shook his head, appalled. "I think that last trip across the Threshold really did a number on your brain."

"No, no. Just listen," Maeve pleaded. "The last time Em was close to me, we disrupted the space-time continuum, tearing open a series of Rips, right here on this hilltop."

"Okay, so?" Zoey asked, trying to follow.

"So, Em had to know, or at least assume with a pretty high degree of confidence, that if she touched me again, another Rip would form. To Scopes, it probably looked like Em was finally coming around to her sinister scheme, hurling us off that cliff. But really, Em was helping us escape. She created a diversion by fighting with me, and in the midst of that whirlwind scuffle, she somehow concealed the kazoo in my dress. Then she pushed us, knowing a portal would open nearby."

"And what if it hadn't?" Dev said, still angry. "Or what if the portal had formed above us? Or across the canyon?"

Maeve bit her lip. "Then we'd be very, very dead."

"Well, I'm very, very glad you're still alive," Tessa said.

"And I'm very, very glad the kazoo of doom didn't fall into the hands of a super galactic baddie," Isaiah added.

"Same," Lewis said, hovering a foot off the ground. "But I'm also very, very hungry. So could we please wrap this up and go get something to eat?"

"Only if you let me ride that soarboard," Dev said, smiling.

"And only if you buy me a hot dog with a side of tater tots," Maeve said. "There's a Teeny's not too far from here."

"Hold on," Isaiah said as they turned to leave the hillside. "If Maeve's doppelganger wasn't evil after all, should we have left the portal open for her?"

Dev tightened the straps of his backpack, the Serger nestled safely inside. "Too late for that now. Besides, we were following Ignatia's orders. We were given a multiverse mission, and we completed the task. End of story."

The others nodded and turned their attention to what toppings they were going to order at Teeny's. As they departed the hillside, Maeve couldn't help but wonder if they really had done the right thing.

# CHAPTER 37

for the ultimate test of teamwork, coordination, and musical ability: Central Ohio's middle school marching band regional championships.

"Are we ready?" Coach Diaz hollered, raising his arms, pumping everyone up.

"Yeah!"

He cupped his hand beside his ear. "I can't hear you! I said: Are. We. Ready?"

"YEAH!" the kids cheered loudly.

Coach Diaz smiled broadly at the band members gathered outside the middle school, awaiting the buses that would take them to the big competition, an hour drive from Conroy.

"You've really stepped up your game lately, cadets. I'm proud of you all." He gazed out at the sea of faces. "We've worked hard these past few months, and I think we're poised to win this thing. I know this is our biggest competition yet, but don't let nerves get the best of you. Stay focused, watch and listen to each other, and remember what we practiced." Everyone nodded enthusiastically. "You've got this."

"Coach? Could I say a few words?" Maeve asked, coming to the front of the pack.

"Of course. The stage is yours. At least until the buses arrive." He stepped to the side.

Maeve cleared her throat. "I just want to echo what Coach said. You guys are the best. This band has been a bright spot in a challenging year for me personally. Being a band member has always been a sort of escape, a way to forget some of the harder things happening at home or at school. But today I don't want to escape. I want to embrace every moment, every note. There is literally no other place I'd rather be right now than with all of you." She smiled. A single, happy tear streaked down her face. "Sorry," she said wiping it away. "I don't know why I'm so emotional today."

"It's all right," Coach Diaz said kindly. "It's a big day. We busted our behinds to get here, and we should reflect on the moment. It's good to recognize something special."

Maeve nodded and turned back to her fellow cadets. "You're all one-of-a-kind. No one else in the world—or the multiverse—is quite like you. Every one of you adds something unique and valuable to this ensemble." She gave props to each cadet individually—Nolan, Jamila, Raylene, Alba, Markus, and all the others—briefly highlighting their strengths and growth over the past season.

"Lewis, your drum rhythms are the heartbeat of this band, and your sense of humor keeps us all laughing."

Lewis blushed. "Aw, shucks, Greene."

"He also makes sure the refreshment cooler is fully stocked at all times," Coach Diaz added.

Lewis held up a huge bag of candy and snacks for the bus ride. "You know I got you, Coach."

Maeve peered out over the crowd. "Dev, you were new to our team and our school this year, but I feel like we've known each other forever. No matter what happens—be it high-speed wagon chases or complicated alien electronics—I know I can rely on you."

"Huh?" Nolan asked, scratching his head.

"Must be an inside joke," Jamila whispered back.

"Plus," Maeve added, looking at Dev. "Your sax solo was off the charts at practice yesterday. I can't wait to hear you play today at regionals. You're gonna blow the judges' socks off!"

"Yeah, buddy." Lewis hooted and gave Dev a fist bump.

"Isaiah, not only do you wail on that trumpet, but you've got all sorts of hidden talents, and you're often the voice of reason in our group."

"More like the voice of doom," Zoey hollered playfully.

The crowd laughed and Isaiah shrugged. "Hey, I call it like I see it. But today is looking the opposite of doomy. I have a really good feeling about what's to come."

"That's the optimism we need!" Coach Diaz said, giving his whistle a peppy toot.

Maeve turned to Zoey. "Zo, you're a born leader and a gifted musician. You're smart and organized and thoughtful. Like your mom, I know you're bound for big things."

Zoey beamed. Tessa, standing beside her, wrapped her arm around her sister's shoulders and squeezed tightly.

"And Tessa, the most recent addition to our marching band crew as our guest vocalist and head of wardrobe. You're the piece of this puzzle we didn't even know we were missing. Without you, we wouldn't look nearly this good." Maeve did a twirl in her recently redesigned band uniform, then struck a fierce pose. Instead of the white, green, and gold polyester monstrosities of the past, the new band attire was chic and streamlined, with a little NASA-inspired flair.

Just then, a big yellow school bus rounded the bend and slowed to a stop at the curb.

"Wait!" Lewis said before the crowd dispersed. "We all got shout-outs, but what about you?"

"Me?" Maeve replied.

"Of course!" Coach Diaz said, clapping his hands. "We wouldn't be here without you, Maeve Greene."

"Absolutely." Zoey nodded in agreement, their rivalry a thing of the past and their friendship restored. "You're a true star performer."

"And a fearless leader," Tessa added.

"You keep us on our toes," Dev said.

Isaiah nodded. "And you push us to be better."

"You have a seriously dazzling mind wrapped up in an occasionally annoying personality," Lewis said.

The others turned and stared at him.

"What?" he said with a shrug. "It's the truth. And I mean it in the nicest way possible."

Maeve rolled her eyes, but a smile tugged at her lips. "Thanks, Wynner. I can always count on you to keep me humble."

It wasn't a Golden Globe award or an Oscar, but hearing praise and encouragement from her friends and fellow band members felt really good. "It's been my privilege to serve as your drum major." The bus door opened and she climbed up onto the first step. "And now, let's kick some serious band butt!" she shouted, raising her oboe case high over her head. "Atten-hut!"

The cadets cheered and chanted in unison, "We're the Conroy Cadets, hear us ROAR! Look to the sky, watch us SOAR!"

Coach Diaz blew his whistle in a peppy rhythm as the band members loaded their instruments into the lower storage area and boarded the bus.

Isaiah was about to stow his trumpet when the bus driver held up a hand. "Sorry. No more room. A second bus is coming in a few minutes to take the rest of you to the competition."

"Oh, okay. Thanks." Isaiah stepped back and looked around. The Hawthorne-Scott twins, Nolan, Jamila, and a few others mingled on the sidewalk in their uniforms, instruments in hand. Dev, Lewis, and Maeve were already in their seats on the yellow bus.

"You coming?" Lewis called out the open window, the big feather on his band hat sticking up at a funny angle.

"We're going to meet you there. Another bus is coming in a few minutes."

"Cool. See ya on the flip side, dudes!" Lewis said waving one of his drumsticks as the first bus pulled out of the parking lot.

# CHAPTER 38

**THE REMAINING KIDS WAITED FOR THE NEXT BUS TO ARRIVE.** Markus took out a hacky sack and began passing it back and forth, kicking the mesh ball to Jamila and Nolan. Isaiah sat by himself, scribbling notes in his Journal of Strange Occurrences, which Zoey had returned to him two weeks earlier. He was trying to document everything they'd seen and experienced during their recent adventures into the multiverse, but none of his words or charts seemed to do justice to the real thing.

He flipped the page. The cipher Ming had given him fluttered to the ground. He felt a pang in his chest, missing his uncle deeply, wondering if maybe he was still out there somewhere. If so, Isaiah hoped he was happy and safe.

He reached over to pick up the cardstock cipher, turning his head just in time to spot a strange creature with purple-and-white checkerboard fur scamper across the parking lot. His sucked in a breath.

"Psst," he hissed to Zoey and Tessa, who were sitting nearby, shoulder-to-shoulder, sharing sister secrets and giggling about something. "Did you two see that?" Isaiah whispered, quickly stashing the cipher and notebook inside his backpack.

"No." Tessa shook her head "What was it?"

Isaiah nibbled a hangnail. "Probably nothing. Never mind."

Then, a few seconds later, another rat-sized animal with purple fur and huge eyes dashed across the concrete sidewalk, mere inches from the new sneakers on Zoey's feet.

"Yikes!" she squealed, jumping up.

A third creature scurried by so fast it was merely a purple blur before disappearing down a nearby storm drain.

Luckily, the hacky-sack kids were too involved in their game to notice.

"Okay, what's going on?" Tessa said, smoothing the front of her snazzy new uniform.

"Whatever you do, do not get close to those things. No matter how cute they might look," Zoey said sincerely. "Believe me, I made that mistake once before and it did not go well."

Tessa scanned the parking lot, looking for more of the speedy purple fluffballs. "Do you think those things followed us through one of the Rips?" she whispered, making sure Markus and the others didn't hear.

"It's possible," Isaiah said, his stomach twisting in an

anxious knot. "Except I don't remember seeing anything like that on the frozen dimension we visited."

"Me neither," Zoey replied. "So...where did they come from?"

Isaiah glanced around. "Another portal?" he ventured. "Has anyone been using the superpowered instruments?" They'd all agreed that no one would play the instruments from Other-Earth or use the kazoo unless absolutely necessary. And Dev vowed to keep the Serger safely stashed in his closet at home until Ignatia contacted them with further instructions.

"Not that I know of," Zoey said, biting her lip.

"We've gotta talk to the others." Isaiah looked down the road, tapping his foot impatiently. "Where is that bus?"

A few minutes later, a big blue bus rumbled around the bend, slowing to a stop in front of the middle school. "Finally!" Isaiah muttered.

The bus door folded open. "You kids need a lift?"

"Benni?" said Isaiah incredulously. "You're back!"

"You're late!" Zoey said, pushing past Isaiah and climbing aboard.

"I encountered a few, um, roadblocks along the way," Benni replied.

The band members began to board.

Benni stopped them in their tracks. "Tickets?" he asked, pointing to the machine at the front of the bus. "We can't go anywhere without a ticket."

Nolan frowned, lugging his heavy tuba case up the steps. "We don't have tickets."

"He's right," Zoey replied. "This is an extracurricular activity organized by the school. As a member of the student council, I'm positive that all transportation costs are included in our yearly student activity fees. There should be no out-of-pocket costs for this ride."

"Hold on," Isaiah said, reaching into the back pocket of his uniform. "I still have this." He held up the last remaining pink square that Kor had entrusted them with back on Station Liminus. He still didn't know what exactly it was, but he'd kept it with him ever since their last trip aboard Benni's bus. "Will this work?" he asked inquisitively.

The pink square glowed faintly. Benni nodded, a glint in his eye. Isaiah inserted the square into the machine near the dash and the bus lurched into gear.

Jamila took a seat. "You're going to take us to regionals, right?" she asked, setting her trombone case on the floor, then adjusting her headscarf. "The rest of the band is counting on us."

"I'll get you there." Benni checked his mirrors and hit a few buttons on the dashboard. "Eventually."

"Eventually?" Tessa asked, shooting her sister a look.

Benni nodded, his eyes keenly focused on the road. "First, we need to make a quick pit stop."

Nolan gawked. "A pit stop? No way! Maeve is going to freak out if we're late."

"Yeah, does Coach Diaz know about this?" Markus asked.

"They'll understand," Benni said, rapidly pressing buttons and adjusting dials. He mopped sweat from his brow, then fastened his seat belt across his barrel-chest. "Take a seat and buckle up," he called over his shoulder.

Right as he hit the accelerator, another fuzzball—this one lime green with white spots—ran in front of the bus. Benni swerved just in time, barely missing the creature. He spun the steering wheel and jammed his foot against the pedals. "Hold on! Something tells me this is going to be a bumpy ride!"

Isaiah's heart beat wildly in his chest. He gazed out the window at the wide world beyond. "Here we go again . . ."

# ACKNOWLEDGMENTS

I wrote the first *Mission Multiverse* book and this sequel in the midst of the COVID-19 pandemic. Most days, I worked from home while my children made a spectacular amount of noise and terrific messes all around me. In many ways, these books were born out of that creative chaos. One day, my daughters spent hours building a rocket ship using carboard boxes and materials scrounged from the recycling bin. When I inquired about their destination, they told me they would be traveling to outer space to find a cure for what my five-year-old referred to as the "stinkarona" virus. Then, finally, they would be able to return to school, play with their friends, and hug their great-grandmother again.

"Don't worry, Mama," my seven-year-old assured me. "We'll save the world."

And here's the thing: I believed her. In fact, I was in the process of writing a book about children doing just that. Thrust into uncertainty and peril, the Space Cadets rise to the occasion as only kids can. Sure, they make some mistakes along the way, but in spite of these challenges, they remain resilient, resourceful, compassionate, and clever. Watching my daughters play and grow, I didn't need to look far for inspiration.

During our quarantine days, reading offered my family a much-needed escape. As the world slowly returns to some semblance of normal, I hope the *Mission Multiverse* books continue to open portals into dazzling new dimensions, where readers can laugh, explore, and wonder alongside a set of lovable, brave, unforgettable friends. Most of all, I hope the Cadets' adventures empower you to undertake some world-saving actions of your own—whether it's merely wearing a face mask, delivering groceries to a neighbor in need, or building a cardboard rocket ship in your living room.

Publishing is never a solo expedition, and I'm so appreciative of everyone who has helped make this series a reality. Marching band salutes to the fantastic team at Abrams/Amulet, especially Anne Heltzel, Margo Winton Parodi, Katherine Furman, and Jessica Gotz. Additional thanks to Laura Berman, Christa Heschke, Daniele Hunter, and Allison Hellegers. My trusty critique partners, Erin Cashman, Diana Renn, and Sandra Waugh, helped me amp up the action and hone a messy draft into a shiny, book-shaped story. The middle grade writing community, booksellers, educators, and young readers inspire me and keep me motivated. Thanks to my friends for cheering me on, no matter how bumpy the ride.

When I'm deep in drafting or revision mode, my evil doppel-ganger is known to make appearances. She is usually cranky, full of self-doubt, and in need of chocolate. Luckily, my husband and children know how to vanquish this "deadline doppel" and coax the real me back to life. I am forever grateful to my sweet family for your love, patience, and support.